THE HEART OF SMOKE

K WEBSTER

DEDICATION

To Holly, my sister and bestie for life.
I love you more than Jude loves pie.

From USA Today Bestselling Author K Webster comes a new enemies-to-lovers MM bi-awakening, hurt/comfort romance!

**He's a mysterious recluse with an unhealthy obsession with his therapist.
He doesn't want help... He just wants him.**

Love is for those who deserve it. I certainly don't. The person I loved most in this world died in my arms decades ago and I am to blame. I'll forever be tormented by what-ifs where I was Mom's hero instead of this repulsive, mask-wearing beast I've ultimately become.

All that's left of my heart is black smoke—suffocating and toxic. I'm nothing but a shadow of a man, locked in my dark fortress of a home, away from people and hidden in my carefully walled-up world.

My family is all I have to live for. Somehow, they look past the fact I survived when Mom didn't. Like it's not my fault. It's also why I'll protect them with every single fiber of my being.

Even from *him*.
Tate Prince has been paid by my father to infiltrate our family. Invited not just into our homes, but into our past, our heartaches, and even our minds. Dad thinks this young man—a therapist with a captivating grin—is the key to repairing all the damage we've sustained over the years.

But I know better.
I can see through Tate's friendly disposition and
easygoing nature.
In his eyes are dark secrets that haunt him like ghosts from
another life. He's not as perfect as he seems. Underneath his
mask of smiles are ugly truths I'm desperate to uncover.

And I *will* uncover them.
If that means keeping him under lock and key where I can watch
his every move, I will.
It's not captivity if he's being paid, right?

However, when I start unraveling his life, I learn there's a lot
more to Tate than meets the eye. The more I discover, the more
obsessed I become. My heart, the dusty, charred, still-smoking,
useless organ sparks to life, making me come to a startling
realization. I want him.

I'm not the only one who feels this way, though. Tate's biggest
secret is he already has a monster in his life. A terrible, spiteful
monster—one who'll stop at nothing to get what he wants.

But I'm uglier, nastier, and a hell of a lot more vicious. I may have
failed to save my mother, but I will *not* fail this time.
Tate is mine.

***This is a complete MM standalone novel with a happily
ever after. Tropes for this book include: forced proximity, size
difference, pie loving hero, hurt/comfort, bi-awakening.***

Shameful Secrets Series

1 – The Teacher of Nothing (Callum's Book)
2 – The Tangle of Awful (Hugo's Book)
3 – The Heart of Smoke (Jude's Book)

TRIGGER WARNING

This book has triggering scenes for some readers including stalking, previous sexual assault and domestic violence, discussions of past self-harm, and other potentially upsetting subject matter. Please read with caution.

THE HEART OF SMOKE

PROLOGUE

Jude
Sixteen Years Old

COACH IS GOING TO KILL ME WHEN HE FINDS OUT I skipped out the rest of the school day just so I could avoid practice. Will that get me benched for Friday night's game? Nope. Coach wants me to go pro after high school—to skip right over college. With all the scouts that have been sniffing around to watch me play, he's confident I'll get drafted into the NFL just as soon as they can snag me. Benching me would impact his dreams.

What about *my* dreams?

He never asked me if I wanted to play for the NFL. Maybe I *do* want to go to college, fuck my way through all the sororities, drink like a fish with my buddy Baker, get a degree in computer science, and enjoy the whole experience rather than being thrust into a position that requires so much attention and is weighed down by outlandish expectations.

I should just quit football.

He'd have a coronary.

As much as I used to love the game, I find it harder and harder to focus on that now that Mom and Dad are separated. All she does is sit in the house, pissed at Dad. Literally, she never stops complaining about him. While Dad continues to go to the games each week, Mom holes up in our house all alone. It feels like a betrayal to her. Like we've all moved on with our lives and left her behind.

I can't do that to her.

I refuse to.

If I go to PMU here in town instead of following Coach's dreams, though, I could continue to live at home and look after her. I may be the baby of our family, *until Jamie gives birth,* but with Dad out of the house, Hugo already gone off to college, and Callum severely fucked in the head over losing his girlfriend to our father, it's my responsibility to protect Mom and ensure her happiness.

Dad's a major dick for what he did. I don't know how it happened, but one day Jamie was Callum's long-time girlfriend whom he planned to marry after high school and then the next day our family blew up over the news of Dad leaving Mom because he'd professed his love for Jamie. They'd been sleeping together behind Mom's and Callum's backs. Shit really hit the fan not long after when Jamie learned she was pregnant, too.

Definitely a dick move. Mom and Callum will never forgive Dad. It fucking sucks because Mom was still raw over losing their "oops" baby not even a year ago. The baby might've fixed their marriage had she carried it to term.

She unfortunately didn't, though, and their fighting not only continued but got worse with each passing day.

"Dude, are you gonna hit it or not?"

I blink away my daze to glance over at my friend Chip. He's dressed in his Park Mountain Lodge uniform, gesturing for me to pass him the blunt. Chip—your typical stoner— is the total opposite of my best friends Baker and Dennison and Langley, who are also football players.

Nodding, I bring it to my lips and pull in a drag. The pungent air fills my lungs, causing me to cough. Chip sniggers as I hand the blunt back to him. With my eyes now watering and the weed hitting my system, I relax against the rooftop door.

At one time, I'd have been worried about not just getting benched, but kicked off the school team for failing a drug test. Now, I actually hope it happens.

"Sandy said your dad's not getting in trouble for what he did," Chip says casually as he studies the blunt.

His words cause me to stiffen. "So?"

"Jamie's not eighteen yet," he says slowly as though I'm dense as fuck. "Jailbait."

Irritation chases away my high and I step away from the door, crossing my muscular arms over my chest. "Who's going to turn him in? You?"

Chip scoffs. "Your mom?"

Before I can stop myself, I swing a fist, clobbering Chip in the jaw and sending him sprawling to the rooftop gravel. "Don't talk about my family," I spit out. "Stay out of our business."

He scrambles to his knees and scowls at me. "Fuck off, bro. You don't have to be a dick. It was just a question."

"Tell Sandy to stop gossiping," I snap. "We have enough problems without getting the police involved too. My dad's not going to jail over this."

As he stands, he holds his hands up. "Whatever, man. I was just making fucking conversation. Next time you want to get fucked up, don't call me."

I wait for the guilt to swarm over me, but it remains at bay. My family isn't perfect, but they're mine. We Parks sort our shit out together. As a family. The last thing we need are strangers poking their noses in our business. Even Mom, as hurt as she is, wouldn't do that to our family.

Chip's angry expression morphs into one of confusion as he squints past me. "Is that smoke? That's down by where you live, right?"

I whirl around unsteadily and fixate on where Chip's pointing. Sure enough, black smoke billows up past the trees at the base of Park Mountain. Is Grandpa burning trash?

In the distance, I hear sirens.

Holy shit.

I take off in a sprint toward the rooftop door and burst through it. The race all the way down three floors feels like it's taking forever. When I pass by Uncle Theo, who owns the lodge, I manage to bark out that there's a fire, rushing by him without waiting for his response.

My heart thrums rapidly in my chest and the world around me spins. Stupid weed. I'm an idiot for smoking it. Especially now, when my family could be in danger.

Grandpa's house is ancient. What if he accidentally set it on fire burning limbs or trash? He's been flighty ever since Grandma died.

What if it's *my* house?

Bile creeps up my throat. It can't be my house. I refuse to believe it. Launching myself into my black Jeep, I fumble for my keys and then stab the correct one into the ignition. Then I peel out of the parking lot and barrel down the mountainside, taking the private road that'll pass right by my house.

As I come around the bend, the smoke is much thicker. It takes me a second to realize the house burning is indeed mine. Flames billow out the windows on the second floor from both my room and Callum's.

No.

I floor it, racing across the road until I'm in our driveway. I barely get the Jeep into park before I'm out of it, charging toward the house. The first thing I notice is the heat.

Fuck, it's so hot.

But Mom could be in there.

I storm up the porch steps and grab the door handle. White-hot pain sears across my palm and fingers, making me howl in response. I jerk my hand back and shake it as I curse. The sirens in the distance are growing louder as they approach.

Maybe I should wait for the fire department.

Someone screams inside.

No!

With inhuman strength, I kick the front door with all my might. It flings open, the doorframe splintering with the explosion. A burst of heat and black smoke blasts out of the home, causing me to cough and wave off the thick cloud.

Another scream.

I can't leave her there to die.

Sucking in a huge breath of tainted air, I rush straight into the burning house. On a mission to find Mom, I no longer care about burning my hands or inhaling smoke or fucking dying.

I just have to save her.

Parts of the ceiling crash and fall, burying the living room sofas in fiery debris. I stumble away from the scene, hoarsely calling out for my mother.

"J-Jude?"

Her voice is so small. So far away. Hidden beyond the flames and sparkling embers. It's too hot—too fucking terrifying—to go that way. But she's my mom. I have to.

Choking on the smoke and with tears flooding down my

cheeks, I stumble toward the sound of her croaking voice. I find her pinned beneath a burning beam of wood. She reaches a hand for me, eyes wide with horror.

"W-What are you doing here?" she hisses. "You're supposed to b-be in school!"

Though I'm struck by her confusing words, I don't let them scare me off. I grab onto her arm and pull. She screams but doesn't budge an inch. Panic pulses through every nerve ending in my body.

We're going to die.

Another black cloud of smoke washes over me, sending me into a fit of coughs. I don't wait to recover and instead launch myself at the fiery beam, grabbing onto it and lifting.

Into the dark recesses of my mind, I bury away the sickening pain, instead focusing on using my foot to shove Mom away. She rolls several times from the force of my kick, but it's enough to get her out of here.

I stumble, landing on my palms. My skin sticks to the wood and sizzles. With a roar, I pull them off and grab hold of my mother, hauling her to her feet. She's limp and heavy, unable to stand on her own. A sob of frustration rips through me, but I push through, scooping her into my arms.

I can't think or speak or fucking see.

All I know and feel is fire and pain.

We have to escape.

More debris crashes down around us. I trip over parts of it, sending both me and Mom slamming to the floor. Before I can pick her back up, the rest of the ceiling starts dropping hellfire on us. All I can manage is to cover her body with mine, hoping it'll be enough to keep her alive until the fire department arrives. Mom doesn't make a sound while I cough and cough and cough.

Fiery heat engulfs us from all sides and I'm helpless to do anything.

Blackness blankets over me and frees me from hell.

"I've got you, son," a deep voice rumbles. "We're going to get you out of here."

The pain slams into me and I start coughing again. Wait, is someone carrying me? It's not until the cool air outside allows me to take a smoke-free breath that clarity seizes my mind.

"Mom!" I croak out, my voice barely a whisper. "Mom!"

"We've got the other one," another man yells. "Let's go!"

Several men rush past us, toward the fire, while we run away. I strain in the man's hold, whimpering against the pain, searching for my mother.

"Where is she?" I rasp. "Where's my mom?"

I'm once again ignored as I'm passed off to a couple of EMTs. Overwhelming pain blots out the commotion around me, once more sending me into peaceful darkness.

I wake to a faint beeping sound. I'm no longer hurting like I was. In fact, I feel as though I'm floating on a cloud. Worry niggles at me, desperately trying to remind me of something.

What is it?

Slowly, I crack open my eyes, needing to get off this cloud as soon as possible. Everything around me is bright and sterile.

I'm in a bed. A hospital bed.

I drag my stare over my arms, which are wrapped heavily in gauze. Memories sting the back of my mind like tiny pinpricks.

Fire.

Smoke.

Mom.

Voices rumble from nearby, earning my attention. I follow the sound to where Dad and Uncle Theo stand, speaking lowly to one another. Hugo and Callum must be with Mom. A relieved sound escapes me. I remember the firefighters getting her out of the fire too.

Dad pauses and jerks his head my way. With tears in his eyes, he rushes over to me. I watch as he bats at his cheeks to swipe them away before the sadness in his expression permeates the fog I'm in.

"Jude, Son, I'm sorry."

I'm barely able to shake my head. Whatever he's about to say, I don't want to hear it. I can't. I can't handle what he's about to say.

He sniffles and closes his eyes. Then, with a ragged huff, he says, "Your mom didn't make it. I'm so fucking sorry."

Mom didn't make it.

Mom didn't make it.

Staring down at my bandaged hands with tears steadily streaming down my cheeks, I shudder as his words fully sink in.

I was there and managed to save myself, but I couldn't save her.

I'm a monster.

A useless failure of a monster.

I should have died too.

CHAPTER ONE

Tate
Present Day

FIRED. *AGAIN.*

It's not that I'm not good at my job. In fact, I'm great at my job. I worked my ass off in school to climb out of the cesspool I came from. To be something better than what I was expected to be.

To become *someone.*

Only problem is, with a last name like Prince, you're bound to attract a bunch of frogs. In my case, my most recent frog has made it his mission in life to destroy me.

I shudder at remembering the look of disgust on my last employer's face. She called me a delinquent. A damn heathen. I wish I could say I was surprised, but since this crap kept happening on repeat, I calmly gathered my things, not at all shocked, went back to my lonely apartment, and then cried all of my woes to my cat, Funky.

But things are changing.

Well, one particular phone call was the catalyst of change.

A wealthy man named Nathan Park wanted to hire me—*me!*—to be the private therapist for his entire family on some huge compound they all live on. Apparently, they've all got issues and I'm their magical solution.

Me.

Tatum Oliver Prince.

Dread consumes me as I follow my GPS, making the turn down the road that will take me to my destination.

How long until I'm fired from this job too?

Nathan promised to be discreet and to pay me under the table. Not to mention, I'll be given free room and board. My apartment will sit empty like a tomb, cold and welcoming for frogs, but free of me.

God.

Freedom is so close I can taste it.

So why the underlying panic?

Why the dread that's consuming me?

Anytime something felt easy in my life, I was immediately proved wrong. And yet, I still keep believing my life will take a turn for the better. That I can be free of the chains of my past and actually find happiness.

I pass by three really nice houses, wondering which one I'm supposed to be living at. But none of them boast of the address I'm looking for. I continue down the road until a monstrous, dilapidated home comes into view, sitting at the bottom of Park Mountain like some grumpy gargoyle.

My heart rate picks up.

Of course I'd have to live in the one that looks haunted.

"Funky, we're home," I say, voice tight. "I promise we'll be safe here."

Lies.

Poor Funky.

He's used to my lies.

I put my car in park and then step out, taking in the massive home. Dark paint is peeling from the wood and it appears that half the porch is leaning slightly to one side. With my luck, it'll probably collapse the moment I step on it.

Not that I'm anywhere remotely big.

Shrimp. Baby. Little Pussy.

For someone who helps people get past their traumas, I have a heck of a time getting past mine.

Funky meows loudly and I fetch his carrier from the back seat. His golden eyes are wide, assessing our new home with suspicion.

"It's fine," I chirp, voice high and not at all reassuring to either of us. "Everything's fine."

Meow.

Funky is apprehensive. Understandably so. It's not the first time I've said this phrase seconds before my life blew up.

"This time is different," I hiss.

Meow.

In kitty-speak, he means to say, "No, it won't be, Tate."

I have to believe this is the turning point, though.

Ever so gracefully, I climb the steps, leery of weak boards, and make my way over to the front door. I swallow down my unease and then force myself to take a few steadying breaths.

Breathe, Tate.

You got this, man.

Knock. Knock. Knock.

Heavy footsteps thud through the house. Nathan mentioned I'd be helping the whole family but that I'd be staying with his son, who needs me the most. He didn't elaborate, but he said his son lost his mother tragically and hasn't taken it well. That was nearly two decades ago. There's going to be a lot of trauma to unpack.

Thunk.

The sound of a deadbolt unengaging echoes loudly and then the door opens. I'm not sure what I expect, but it certainly isn't the Boogieman.

Funky hisses in terror.

I freeze, mouth agape.

The man—no, the monster—who towers above me is straight from nightmare territory. He wears a white latex mask, sporting all black.

"I, uh, I'm Tate Prince. Your dad hired me. I'm the therapist who—"

"No."

I blink at him, shocked at him cutting me off so rudely. The muffled word barely constituted a word and was more of an animalistic grunt.

A shudder runs down my spine and I visibly shiver.

Don't get me wrong, I've had my fair share of patients who've gotten nasty with me, but I've always handled those situations with professional ease.

This feels different.

They were in my office seeking help.

But now, I'm in *his* territory. I'm on *his* doorstep with my cat. I'm an intruder. A trespasser. I clearly don't belong here.

He starts to close the door in my face, but my foot kicks out, stopping it with my shoe. Funky hisses again.

I should leave.

I really should.

But I can't. I can't go back to that apartment. I can't keep hunting for job after job, only to have it taken away the second I get comfortable. This job was supposed to be my way out. And I'll be damned if I let some Halloween freakshow send me packing.

I lift my chin, giving the beast before me as much attitude as I can muster. "Your dad hired me. I'm not going anywhere."

He's silent for a beat and then he leans down, bringing his masked face close to mine. I'm forced to stare into his icy blue eyes that peer out beyond the eyeholes. His eyes are cracking open my head and raping my thoughts against my will.

I feel exposed.

Seen.

Fileted and molested.

"You're fired," he snarls through his mask. "Now go before I break your foot."

I squeak in horror, jerking my foot back. As promised, he slams the door hard in my face. If I'd left my foot there, I'd probably be missing a few toes by now.

"What now, Funky?" I ask, voice shaking and heart beating a million miles a minute. "What do we do now?"

Funky meows.

It's kitty-speak for, "Whatever it takes, Tate, because we're quickly running out of options."

The walk back to my vehicle—a severely scarred Ford Explorer—feels like a walk of shame. Like I did something wrong despite being completely faultless. It's so reminiscent of each shameful walk out of my places of employment after getting canned each time.

Is this my life now?

Will it always be like this?

I slide Funky's carrier into the back seat once more, trying to ignore the way my hand trembles. Sometimes my fear and anger are so perfectly woven together, it's hard to discern which one is getting the best of me. Maybe, moments ago, it was fear, but it's quickly transforming into anger.

Maybe it's for the best if I quit now, pack up my meager belongings that weren't a casualty of my never-ending war, and disappear into another state.

He'd find you there too, dummy. He always does.

Ignoring those thoughts, I back the vehicle out of the driveway and slowly creep toward the other homes on the otherwise empty street. I should turn my phone on and call Nathan, but I don't want to risk it. The longer I can remain hidden, the better.

Figuring I have to start somewhere, I pull into the first driveway I come up to. I'm not sure if this is Nathan's house, but it likely belongs to someone in this family. Apparently, they all need my help.

"I'll be right back," I tell Funky. "Be a good kitty."

Steeling my spine, I climb out and stride toward the house. This home, unlike the last, is modern, clean, and perfect. Despite it being mid-November, the grass is still green and trimmed neatly. I walk up the porch and knock on the door, hoping this encounter goes better than the last.

When the door opens, my breath catches. The man standing before me is a god. Tall, muscular, donning an expensive three-piece navy suit. His tousled hair gives him a slightly boyish look, but his stern features are all business. Sharp blue eyes—much like the ones that split me in two moments ago—burn into me.

"No soliciting," the man says icily. "This is a private drive."

Is everyone in this family cold and rude?

I clear my throat, ready to answer, when a deep voice chuckles behind me. The fact someone easily snuck up on me doesn't bode well, sending a fierce shiver down my spine.

Whipping around, I'm met by another god-like man who resembles this one.

"Nathan Park," the older of the two greets, smiling at me. "We spoke on the phone. Mr. Prince, right?"

The chill running through me warms several degrees and I smile back, offering my hand to my new employer. "Call me Tate. I, er, wasn't sure where you lived." I rub at the back of my neck, hating how my cheeks burn hot. "I ran into a snag at the address you gave me."

The man behind me snorts. "Jude's address?"

Nathan frowns, turning to look back at the monstrous house that should have been condemned decades ago. "He didn't let you in." Not a question. A statement. He expected this. Lovely.

"And he fired me," I grumble.

The other man laughs, deep and clearly amused by this thought. Nathan pins him with a sharp glare that could cut through someone like me, so I'm glad it's not aimed my way.

"Callum," Nathan says, "talk to your brother. He actually listens to you."

Callum—hottie in a suit—steps out of the house to stand beside me. His scent is expensive and spicy. My mouth waters and I quickly banish any salacious thoughts because I'm supposed to be a professional here—not foaming at the mouth when surrounded by hot guys.

"Jude does what he wants," Callum replies, shrugging. "Who's the kid?"

Kid?

I bristle at the condescension dripping from his words. I'm twenty-seven, not seventeen, despite my youthful features.

"Family therapist," Nathan cuts in, saving me from having

to explain myself to this prick. "And he needs a place to stay now apparently."

Shifting on my feet, I mutter, "I can stay at my apartment and commute—"

"Nonsense," Nathan huffs. "We need you here full time. You'll stay with my other son."

"Hugo?" Callum asks, voice tight.

"You," Nathan says with a smirk.

"You hired him," Callum growls. "You take him in."

Wow. This job is going to be super-fun. Not.

"Look at him." Nathan flicks his fingers my way. "Gemma won't leave him alone. I won't have my teenage daughter pregnant by Christmas."

What?

"I, uh, I'm not going to—"

Callum cuts me off, stepping closer to his father, shoulders tense. "I'm supposed to let some stranger live in my house? Willa *is* pregnant, for fuck's sake."

Who do these people think I am?

Some psychotic rapist?

"Callum, this isn't up for discussion. Either you convince Jude to take Tate in or he stays with you."

It's like I'm not even here.

These two have some serious beef if the thick tension in the air is anything to go by. Makes me wonder if I'll get to dig into that soon in a session.

"I'm gay," I reveal with a sigh. "Your daughters and wives are safe."

Callum's head jerks my way and he smirks. It's not a cruel, teasing kind of smirk—at least, not toward me. I realize my words will soon become ammunition based on the evil glint in his gaze.

"He could room with Dempsey," Callum taunts, his eyes cutting back over to his father. "Since Gemma would be safe and all."

Nathan, thankfully, doesn't take the bait. "It's settled. He stays with you."

Callum shrugs, no longer interested in arguing now that my sexuality isn't a threat to him. The dynamic between these two is brittle and flammable.

"How, uh, do you want to do this?" I ask Nathan. "The sessions, I mean."

"Settle in," Nathan says, gesturing for Callum's house. "Tomorrow, at family dinner, I'll properly introduce you to everyone. Jude, Spencer, Audrey, and Dempsey will need to be put on the schedule immediately. My home is two doors down. You may use my office for your sessions."

With those final words, Nathan turns on his heel and strides away without so much as a thank you.

This job is going to be a challenge.

"I'm doubling our agreed-upon rate," Nathan calls out over his shoulder. "There's a twenty-thousand-dollar bonus if you can make headway with Jude."

Holy shit.

Twenty thousand dollars to get the freakshow to talk to me?

"Damn, man, he's desperate," Callum says, shaking his head and shooting me a look of pity. "I wouldn't get too excited about the twenty k, though. Jude's not going to go for it."

Maybe not yet…

Twenty thousand could make a huge dent in the debt

I've managed to accumulate in the past two years. It costs a lot to have my slashed tires replaced three times, windshield smashed more times than I can count, and all the times I've had to get the keyed words buffed out of my paint. And that's just the debt I've gotten buried in over my car.

"We'll see," I reply, flashing him a challenging smile. "Let me just grab my stuff and my cat. Be right back."

His eyes widen at the mention of my cat, but I don't wait for permission, hurrying back to my car. I fling open the door and peer into the carrier.

"Funky, we're going to be rich. Mark my words. All we have to do is tame the beast and draw out his demons so we can slay them. Easy-peasy."

My intelligent cat doesn't reward me with an answer because he knows better.

Nothing about this job will be easy.

CHAPTER TWO

Jude

CAN'T AVOID DAD FOREVER.

He'll inevitably show up, bitching at me relentlessly until one of us gives in. He should know better. It won't be me.

I'm not going to see a therapist because my past is a Pandora's box I have no intent on opening anytime soon, if ever.

The past fucking hurts.

At least, by me showing up for family dinner, I can leave when I've had enough of Dad's guilt trips. Not to mention, there'll be the buffer of all the other usual Sunday drama. I can always count on Dempsey or Callum to cause a little chaos at mealtime.

Now that fall is upon us, it's dark early as I prowl through my brothers' front yards toward Dad's house. I love this time of year when I can stick to the shadows, slipping in and out of view whenever I feel like it. Winter is even better because when it snows, I'm not forced to do this bullshit dinner each week.

Voices can be heard, laughing and cutting up as I step onto Dad's porch. I hesitate before opening the door, adjusting my mask to make sure it covers me properly. The wood creaks to my right and I snap my head in that direction.

"We've all seen you without it," Callum says from the shadowed corner. "Still not sure why you insist on wearing that shit twenty-four seven."

He and Spencer give me the most grief about the masks I wear. Fuckers.

I lift my hand, flipping him off, knowing good and damn well he can see it perfectly in the glow of light from the window.

He chuckles and approaches, coming into view when he's just a few feet from me. "You dodged a bullet, man. Dude has a cat."

Tension claws at my muscles, hooking them and pulling them taut. A familiar ache burns along my rhomboids on both sides.

"The therapist is staying with you?"

Callum nods, crossing his arms over his chest. "Thanks for that, by the way."

"Better you than me." I lift one shoulder, ignoring the ache there.

"If it makes you feel any better, Tate's not just yours."

Tate.

Therapist *Tate.*

"What's that supposed to mean?"

"Dad wants him to fix everyone apparently, starting with you, Dempsey, Spencer, and Aubrey." Callum shakes his head. "He's paying this guy *really* well."

Dad's paying some stranger to learn every goddamn secret of this family? Is he going senile? Seriously, what the fuck.

"I'll get rid of him," I grunt.

Callum's brows shoot up. "Murder's not really your style."

"Not murder, dumbass. I'll scare him off. We don't need

this shit, especially not after what went down this summer with Neena and that crazy fucker she was sleeping with."

"Willa likes him," Callum says, voice neutral, like another man staying in his home isn't a threat.

Interesting.

Callum perceives every man with a working dick between his thighs as someone attempting to steal his *child bride*—Spencer's phrase, not mine. What makes Tate immune to Callum's wrath? I'd gotten a good look at the guy. He was by no means ugly, not to mention, he looked closer to Willa's age than Callum is.

"I don't have to kill him because you will," I grunt, pinning my brother with a probing stare. "The first time he checks out her ass."

Callum's grin is wide and wolfish. "He'll more likely check out mine."

With those confusing as fuck words, Callum squeezes my shoulder and then strides past me. The sound of voices grows louder when he opens the door and leaves it open for me. Pivoting on my heels, I follow after him, eager to get this shitshow on the road. The sooner dinner is over, the sooner I can go back to tucking in with a slice of Violet's heavenly pecan pie and avoiding my family until next Sunday.

Dad's dining room is filled with the usual chaos my family brings, though this time, we're hosting a new person. Therapist Tate. Rather than approach the table where several family members sit, I assess Tate from afar.

Yesterday, he seemed so small.

Lost and afraid.

Today, his fear is erased and his smile is an easy one. His dark brown hair flops to one side and his face is clean-shaven.

Sitting next to Willa as she grins, gesticulating toward her stomach, he listens with rapt attention. He doesn't look my way or even flinch at my arrival, too wrapped up in whatever she's saying to him.

Therapist Tate doesn't look like a therapist at all.

He looks like a little boy playing grown-up games.

What was Dad thinking, not just in hiring a family therapist, but also finding the greenest one he could?

It's not like Dad to half-ass anything or cheap out, especially when his family is involved. So, why this guy? Why him of all the therapists in this town? I'm itching to get back to my office, so I can do a full investigation on this guy. Everyone has secrets and I always find them.

I'm an immovable statue as I take in this enemy, infiltrating our family's most sacred time. Just because I hate attending doesn't change the fact that it's an important time for everyone to connect. Clearly, I keep showing up for them. And while Willa is a new addition to our group, she feels like family.

Therapist Tate?

A splinter piercing our thick exterior, small but no less impactful. His presence will cause infection, spreading and spreading until we're all ruined.

Callum catches my gaze as he takes his seat on the other side of Willa, casually draping an arm over the back of her chair. Amusement causes his lips to curl into a lopsided grin. Asshole. He may not see Tate as a threat, but I do and I'll do whatever I can to protect our family. I always do.

Ignoring his taunting smile, I drop into the chair directly across from Tate. I can sense Dad's penetrating glare, most likely attempting to guilt me for sending Tate away, but I ignore that too. I study Tate intently, waiting for him to notice.

The guy can't be taller than five-nine or ten and probably weighs as much as one of my thighs. That's not saying he's a waif, considering I'm built like your typical linebacker—coincidentally the position I played in high school—thick, tall, and rock-hard. Still, compared to me, he's a little boy.

I smirk at the thought of a little boy coming into the Parks' lair and presuming he can turn us all inside out. The Parks are wolves. Every single one of us men is. Even perfect Hugo—Mr. Attorney General—stares at his stepdaughter, Aubrey, like she's Little Red Riding Hood and he's going to devour her any second. He's a fucking wolf too.

If I didn't have my mask on, I'd take great pleasure in baring my teeth at the threat who sits directly across from me. His soft, pillowy lips and slightly pinked cheeks that give him an air of innocence don't fool me.

He's here to pick us apart.

Worse yet, Dad's paying him to.

Not for long. Soon, I'll pick *him* apart, prove to Dad we're just fine without help, and send this little boy far away with his tail tucked between his legs.

As if suddenly becoming distinctly aware of my presence, Tate's entire body tenses. The easy smile on his lips aimed at Willa melts away into a worried pout. His Adam's apple bobs as he swallows and then slowly, he turns his head my way. Big brown eyes latch onto mine, hope briefly flickering in them. As soon as he feels the intensity roiling off me, aimed directly at him, he flinches as though I've slapped him.

Good.

I'll do a helluva lot more than slap if I must.

My family—even when they're being annoying as

fuck—are the only thing I've got left in this world. They're everything to me, meaning I'd do anything to protect them.

Unlike I could protect her…

I force away thoughts of my beloved mother and grit my teeth as I bore my gaze into Tate. I need him to understand I see him. He may be paid to try and get inside us, but that shit's not happening.

"Easy there, killer," Spencer says, dropping into the chair next to me. "We haven't introduced murder into Rex's diet yet."

Tearing my stare from Tate, I turn to look down at my great-nephew, who's drinking from a bottle Spencer is feeding him. Spencer fucked his stepmom, Aubrey's mother, knocking her up, and little Rex is the byproduct of that crazy-ass shit. And, my brother, Hugo, for a while there thought the kid was his. I imagine he was in for quite the shock when he learned it was his grandson/stepson or something equally screwed up.

Perhaps some of the people in this family do need therapy…

I'm certainly not one of them.

And the need for therapy is less than the need to keep our family's secrets. Because what Hugo and Spencer don't know is that I know they're both sleeping with Aubrey, further complicating things. Those kinds of secrets could destroy all of us, especially my brother and his political career.

"Why does everyone think I'm plotting his death?" I growl, glowering at Spencer.

"Probably because you look like even more of an unhinged psycho than usual." He flashes me a wicked grin. "You should go all in and wear a clown mask, really terrify everyone who has the lovely pleasure of your company."

My skin prickles with awareness. Snapping my attention from my annoying nephew to the outsider in this room, I discover him watching me with interest. Like I'm some puzzle that needs putting together. I'm too broken for that shit. There's no putting me back together. Ever.

Dad clears his throat, interrupting my plan for more intimidating glares, calling everyone's attention to where he sits at the head of the table. I can remember, long ago, having these same dinners with my grandfather. Except instead of being here, it was in the home I share with him now. Grandpa rarely leaves the house since he's wheelchair-bound, but most importantly stubborn as fuck and refuses to indulge Dad.

"I know you've all gotten an opportunity to meet Tate this weekend." Dad's eyes dart my way. "I expect you all to treat him with the utmost respect. He's here to help, not hurt."

I bristle at the attention of everyone pinging off me. It's annoying that they're all looking at me like I'm the problem.

"I want you all to text me your available times this week. Starting Monday," Dad continues, "you'll all get on the schedule to meet with Tate. Everyone, Jamie and myself included, could use a session or two." He chuckles, though it sounds forced. "We're all a little screwed up."

Callum snorts and mutters something under his breath that has Willa frowning over at him. He loves Willa more than anything in this world, but his hurt from Dad's betrayal when he was a teenager is a wound that will forever bleed. It doesn't help that he's spent the better part of two decades watching Dad and Jamie flaunt their love when Jamie was Callum's to begin with.

Therapist Tate can't staunch the bleeding of that cut.

No one can.

"Don't make this an issue," Dad says, attention back on me. "I expect you to make an effort."

I want to sneer at him and tell him to back the fuck off. To remind him I'm a grown-ass man with my own money and means. That I don't have to obey my father if I don't fucking feel like it. Cutting my stare over to Tate, I take in the way he chews on his bottom lip, tense with nerves. He's afraid of me. That much is certain.

What I want is to shrug, put off my father's guilt trip, and move on with this dinner until I can get back home to uncover everything I can about Tate Prince.

But running back home to my cave won't scare him away.

However, running into the flames, directly at him, is the only way to protect my family.

Thoughts of Mom tug at my forever broken heart.

I couldn't save her, but I can save them.

"Tomorrow morning," I say with a grunt.

The dining room falls into silence and Tate blinks at me, shock evident in his saucer-sized brown eyes.

Dad's smile is triumphant, and he waves a hand at Tate. "You have time for Jude tomorrow?"

Tate swallows what I hope is dread, nodding once. "Absolutely."

My family goes back to talking over each other as Jamie brings out a casserole dish. Food becomes the focus of everyone but me and Tate. He visibly trembles as I glower at him.

Good.

We're going to war, you and I, little boy.

Unfortunately for him. This isn't my first war…

CHAPTER THREE

Tate

I can't believe I'm really here—really doing this. A private therapist for such an influential and wealthy family is pretty much a dream come true. Especially now that all my other dreams have been stolen away.

Thinking about Sean always sours my mood.

He took so much from me. My self-worth, my career, my happiness. And because he insists on anonymously sending that horrible video he made to every single employer, he's taken my dignity too. It's humiliating knowing they've seen me at my lowest. Even sadder is they're disgusted by me.

I'm disgusted by myself too.

Unfortunately, people who find themselves in abusive relationships don't always recognize the abuse at first. Further, they may not know how to escape the abuse once they come to terms with what's happening.

Being a therapist, I'm well-trained in helping abuse victims. Hell, I'm even skilled in helping narcissistic or delusional patients.

But me and Sean?

There was no helping either one of us.

I was caught in his web and he didn't want to let me go.

He'll find you eventually…

Ignoring that depressing thought, I give my head a slight

shake before spinning around in Nathan's office chair and surveying the pristine workspace. He'd invited me to breakfast early this morning, where he and Jamie told me a little about each family member and gave me a typed-out schedule for the week. They both agreed Jude would be the most difficult to help.

My first patient, too.

Lovely.

I settle my gaze on a portrait on the wall of Nathan, Jamie, and the twins when they must've been ten or eleven. Their happy, smiling faces warm my heart. They're the family I'd always wished I'd been born into. Instead, I got a single dad who drank away his woes and beat on his only son whenever the alcohol wasn't enough to mask the pain.

I lived that life and still somehow found myself with Sean.

Thankfully, I can help others much easier than I can help myself. I'm determined to get through to Jude, not only to earn the twenty thousand Nathan's promised, but also to truly get him to a place where he feels comfortable removing his mask and leaving the family property again. When Nathan told me Jude never leaves their land, I knew it was definitely something to strive for.

When I swirl around in the chair again, passing the time until my patient gets here, I get an icy chill that runs down my spine. I stop abruptly, startled to find Jude standing in the doorway, filling every inch and looking every bit like a horror movie psychopath.

You never really know how much you use a person's facial expressions to get a read on them until you're unable to do just that.

"Oh, hi," I blurt out, voice unnaturally high. "Please, come in. Have a seat."

Jude doesn't move but continues to silently stare at me through the two eyeholes of his white mask. The sunshine streaming in through the window behind me lights up his intense blue eyes, making them almost glimmer beyond the mask holes.

"Are you even able to legally drink?" Jude grunts out in greeting.

Irritation chases away the awkwardness and slight apprehension I'm feeling. I've always been mocked for my youthful features. Never taken seriously.

Rather than throw a tantrum, huffing and puffing about how I'm actually twenty-seven, I force out a chuckle and gesture at the seat in front of me. "I am. Close the door and sit."

He's still for a moment and then miraculously obeys. The door clicks shut softly and then he prowls my way, sucking the air from the room and filling it with a masculine scent. I can't pinpoint the actual smell, but it's definitely men's soap and something with a hint of cinnamon.

I'm suddenly craving hot, gooey, melt-in-your-mouth cinnamon rolls.

I try not to stare at him, but it's hard. He's huge, much larger than anyone else who showed up for their family dinner last night, and slightly terrifying. It's not just the mask either. There's a feral undertone that permeates the air around him. If I were into reading auras, I'd conclude his would be black.

Not that I even know what black means.

But his definitely gives me dark, twisted, scary vibes.

Slowly, he sits down on the chair, the wood creaking with his weight. Even wearing a black hoodie and black workout pants, it's evident he's not just incredibly fit, but he's bulky with hard-earned muscles.

I must look like a wimp in comparison.

My gut sours again as I think about the gym I can no longer go to. It's Sean's gym—where I met him—and I'm sure as hell never going back.

"How are you feeling today?" I ask, smiling widely. "Having a good day so far?"

Jude snorts and leans back in his chair. His dark hair is tousled and damp like he showered right before coming over. Rather than letting myself get caught up in that visual, I forge on despite his unwillingness to answer.

"Nathan told me a little about you and your family." I resist the urge to nervously fidget in the desk chair that now feels too big for me. "He said you were in a fire at age sixteen, where you lost your mother."

Might as well rip off the Band-Aid.

He stiffens and his breathing grows heavier behind the mask. I can sense his fury in the way his hands tighten around the arms of the chair. Again, he says nothing.

"That had to have been horrible for you."

"No shit," he says finally. "Dad's really paying you for this?"

"I'm beyond qualified to do this job," I bite out, a tad defensive. "I'm here to help, not hurt, Jude. You can talk to me."

"So you can take valuable information about my family and turn it against us?"

What?

This dude has major trust issues.

"Everything you say to me is confidential. Unless you tell

me otherwise, I won't repeat what we discuss to your father or anyone for that matter."

Another snort. He shifts in his seat and then releases the arms of the chair. Lifting one hand, he opens his palm and turns it over to inspect it. I find myself fixated on the thick pink scars marring the flesh there. The back side of his hands is smooth and perfect, but the palms have been heavily damaged in the past.

"Do you have a lot of burns?" I ask softly. "Is that why you wear the mask?"

I try to imagine a younger version of Callum, face scarred over with burns. Despite what the fire did to him, he shouldn't have to hide, especially from his own family.

"Your family loves you, you know," I continue. "You don't have to wear the mask because—"

"Just stop," he bites out, leaning forward and pinning me with a fierce glare. "You're not going to fix me or anyone in this family. We don't need fixing. What we need is privacy. People like you can fuck right off."

I stifle a frustrated sigh. "If that were the case, your father wouldn't have hired me. Clearly, *he's* worried about his family." *Especially you.* Of course I hold that part in. "I'm sorry you see me as a threat."

At this, he chuffs. Was that a laugh?

"Threat? Please, little boy. I could break you without even trying."

His cruel words cause me to tense up. Memories of Sean creep in around me, making it difficult to breathe. He always said he wanted to break me—that it's what gets him off. My lip trembles, but I bite down on it. I refuse to let this man upset me.

"Don't speak to me that way," I choke out, somehow managing to lift my chin with false bravado. "I won't let you scare me off."

He blinks behind the mask, studying me intently. "You want me to talk? Maybe you should talk first. What makes a 'qualified' therapist take a job with a family like ours? Money? Curiosity?"

Desperation.

"Whether you choose to believe it or not, I care about people. Supporting others is a passion of mine. Your father approached me, Jude, not the other way around. He came to me and made a compelling offer." At exactly the right time. "Yes, the money is good. I'm not going to lie to you about that. He's even discussed a bonus for making headway with certain family members. But it's not all about that. Helping people is something I deeply value."

He doesn't answer, so I keep babbling, deciding to give him a nugget of myself even though he doesn't deserve it.

"I do this job because I wish someone had helped me back when I was a child. Helped my dad with his alcoholism." I absently rub at my wrist that used to forever be bruised from when Dad would snatch me up by it. "Let me try and help you. Please."

The room falls silent and my skin prickles with unease. Then, slowly, Jude rises to his feet, towering over me. He's much bigger than my father ever was. It's true what he'd said moments ago. He could break me without trying. I'm no match for the godlike man.

But I can help.

I want to help.

"I'm going to find out who you *really* are, Prince," Jude

murmurs, voice gritty but soft. "And then you'll be out of here. Don't get too comfortable."

With those words, he turns on his heel and stalks out of the room. The chilly atmosphere warms several degrees now that he's no longer here. I glance at the clock and sigh. He lasted a whole ten minutes. Since I won't see Spencer until after lunch, I head back over to my room at Callum's.

Nathan and Jamie are nowhere to be found. Dempsey and Gemma are at school. Rather than hunting Nathan down to say goodbye, I slip out without a word. The air is chilly outside and whips at my face. I squint against the sunshine, looking for any sign of Jude. Even though his house is quite a jaunty walk, he's already disappeared, which means he might've run there.

The thought of big, scary Jude running away from little ol' me is comical. I find myself grinning despite the stressful meeting I just had. Once I make my way into Callum's house, my smile widens to see my cat taking up residence in Willa's lap.

"Oh, hey," Willa chirps with a sheepish smile. "He was whining to be let out of your room. I felt bad." She bites on her bottom lip as her cheeks turn pink. "I hope that was okay."

Willa is different than anyone in this family. She's quiet and sweet. I already like her the best of everyone.

"Nah, it's cool," I say as I plop down on the other end of the couch and scratch behind my sassy feline's ears. "He's good at getting his way."

Funky's tail swishes happily and he purrs as if to agree.

"How did your meeting go with Jude?" Willa asks, features turning sad.

I lean back against the sofa and stare up at the ceiling. "It was fine. I see Spencer later after lunch."

She studies me, intently searching my gaze as if she can find out how it really went, but I keep my features impassive, not giving anything away.

"So you're free until then?" she asks.

"I am. Why? Do you want to talk or need help with something?"

"Actually, I was about to go to a doctor's appointment and wouldn't mind the company. Normally, Callum goes with me, but he's been knee-deep in work. I know he doesn't want me to go by myself, but if you went with me, he could stay and work without feeling guilty."

Leaving the compound and possibly running into Sean is unnerving. If he sees my car, things could get bad.

"We can take Callum's car. He has heated seats." She regards me with widened eyes and a pleading tone. "I'll even buy you a fun coffee drink on the way back."

"How can I say no to heated seats and free coffee?" I joke, grinning back at her. "Yeah, I'll keep you company."

I can do this.

Sean doesn't own this town and he can't be everywhere. The chances of running into him at the doctor's office or a coffee place are slim.

Heavy footsteps thud down the hall and Callum appears, his phone glued to his ear. He frowns heavily, a torn expression on his face.

"Tate's going with me," she whispers. "Stay and work. It'll be fine."

Callum shoots me a quick, grateful look and then bends down to kiss Willa on the mouth. He isn't shy about the dirty kiss he gives her while in my presence. My neck grows hot because their kiss is so intimate and filled with love that I feel weird witnessing it. Finally, he breaks away but not before pinning her with a searing look that promises much more later.

As soon as he's stalked back off to his office, Willa sighs happily as she moves my cat off her lap and gently places him on the sofa.

I wonder if I'll ever get the chance to know that kind of happiness.

Being loved unconditionally, feeling safe, and free of fear would be a foreign concept, but it's one I'd really like to try on for size.

CHAPTER FOUR

Jude

H E'S HIDING SOMETHING.

I knew it before, but after meeting with him this morning, I could feel it. This secret of his was bubbling just below the surface, teasing me to reach down and claw at it. While he threw me a bone about his childhood, I know it was a tactic to distract me.

There's more.

And I will find out what it is.

Just like most days, I hole up in my office, away from Violet and the other house staff, family, and most of all, Grandpa. Grandpa is nosier than Dad. Every night besides Sunday, I have to sit with him at dinner, dodging any and all attempts at him trying to dig into my head.

Sure, Grandpa is old and forgetful, but he remembers every detail about what happened to me, Mom, and the fire that ruined my life. It's his favorite topic to delve into. Secretly, I think Grandpa has made it his sole mission in life to fix me.

I don't need fixing.

I need to be left alone.

My office is my solace—my safe space. I can settle into my comfortable chair and dive into other people's lives, mostly forgetting about my own while on my task.

All too quickly, I zone out, losing myself to the hunt.

Before long, I've located a deserted Facebook profile for Tate. I have programs that allow me to easily hack into social media profiles and I break into his within minutes. The password, FUNKYCAT, may be useful in the future. I save it to a new folder labeled Prince.

The last time he posted on Facebook was two years ago. Interesting. He has exactly thirty-four friends on there, most of which can be linked back to his small-town high school in Iowa. It's all generic posts on his page for his birthday— December 16—when he'll turn twenty-eight.

Okay, so he is legally able to drink.

At least that wasn't a lie.

His messages are all basic "remember me from chemistry class?" type of correspondence. He chats with these various people, but the conversations all die out eventually, leaving Tate on unread.

One thing's for sure. He's evidently lonely. That, I can understand.

Sighing, I abandon his Facebook and do a deeper dive that requires me stepping into the dark web. From there, I search police reports for Tate Prince. He'd hinted about his alcoholic father, and based on the pinched expression, I had the sense it was painful. My intuition proves right when I find several reports of David Prince spending the night in jail for child endangerment by driving with his child while drunk, or physical assault to his son.

I think about how small Tate is. As a child, he must've been a tiny little thing. Imagining a grown-ass man beating on him sours my gut. A surge of anger spears through me, piercing my icy heart.

Moving on, I discover articles on how Tate's mother,

Kathy, died suddenly of a brain aneurysm. The timeline of the police reports shows that the abuse started happening not six months after her unexpected death when Tate was only four.

Four years old?

What a fucking asshole. Who does that to a little kid?

I move away from the sad shit and get back on task. This time, I dig until I find his annual tax returns all the way back to when he worked part time while going to PMU. His employment was steady where he worked at an animal shelter until he graduated college. Then he worked as a low-paid therapist for a local hospital. Everything seems normal until about two years ago.

From there, I can see multiple different employers. This leads me to also find that he's broken his lease on several apartments, even going into collections for unpaid fees resulting from those times. There are also a few hospital bills, including a broken arm that required surgery, that he's been slowly paying on.

The broken arm coincides with the time he let his gym membership lapse. An injury perhaps? Why not talk to the people who own the gym and get out of your contract rather than letting it all go to collections?

I continue my hunt, landing on many mechanic bills. Those were paid, but incredibly frequent, most requiring body work and multiple tire replacements.

Either he's a really shitty driver or someone hates his guts. I'm satisfied knowing I have some dirt on him to dig into later.

In conclusion, I determine he's terrible with money, keeping a job, and committing to one place for very long. The reason behind all this is unclear. Hell, I'm not the therapist here, but it doesn't erase the fact it's who he is.

When I hear a commotion downstairs, I quickly save everything into his file before logging out. I get up from my chair, my muscles aching from sitting in the same position for so long. I stalk out of my office and down the stairs to find Spencer with Rex in his arms, chatting amicably with Grandpa.

"What?" I demand with a surly grunt.

Spencer's lips curl into a devious grin. "Always a bucket of sunshine, Voorhees."

I ignore his barb. If I let all the times Spencer has fucked with me about my mask bother me, I'd be a sobbing, whiny mess who would never leave his bed.

"I'm working. What do you want?"

"Just came to shoot the shit with my two favorite people." He smirks and presses a kiss to his son's forehead. "Want to hold Rex?"

I shudder at the thought. I'm not exactly kid material. "No."

Grandpa holds up his frail arms, gesturing for Spencer to hand him Rex. Spencer, despite his asshole persona, smiles and gently passes the baby to him. Grandpa babbles and coos at him from his motorized wheelchair while Spencer looks on in pride.

"To answer your question," Spencer says, turning to regard me, "I'm killing time before my session with Tate."

This time I don't shudder, but it takes an effort not to. "He's a quack. Don't get too used to him."

Spencer chuckles, eyes glinting with mischief that reminds me of when he was a shithead toddler who used to drive his parents crazy. "I actually like the dude. Plus, you know Grandad has him bound until death by NDAs. We can squeal like little pigs and he can't do anything with that information."

He almost seems excited to unload on Tate with what may be some fucked-up enough shit to make the new guy squirm in his seat. I mean, Spencer's the father of his step-mom's baby. Furthermore, he's fucking his stepsister. If I had to guess, probably while his father, Hugo, fucks her too. I'm not an idiot and can see through their secrets.

"I have nothing to say to him," I grumble, crossing my arms over my chest.

Spencer snorts out a laugh. "Dude, I feel like you have the most to say. You're definitely the most mental around here."

"Hugo, be nice to your little brother," Grandpa chides, confusing Spencer with his dad.

This time, I smirk behind my mask, pleased to see my nephew taken down a few pegs.

Violet appears just in time to break the tension. Long before I moved in with Grandpa, he had staff on hand to help him clean, cook, and handle his affairs. Violet has been with him the longest since Anderson—a man older than dirt who managed all the employees of the home—recently retired and went into assisted living. The few people who take care of Grandpa are also bound by NDAs. Luckily, they're practically family. Violet is an angel when it comes to making pies. There was even a time in my early twenties when I gained a little too much weight between the depression and her need to make me happy with pie. Now, I work my ass off in my gym so I can eat all the goddamn pie I want.

"Let me see my godson," Violet says, stealing Rex from Grandpa. "Oh, Wyatt, he has your eyes."

Grandpa preens like he gave birth to the little thing himself.

"Jude said he wants to babysit Rex," Spencer tosses out.

Violet's eyes widen in shock, but I quickly shut that shit down.

"Pass," I growl. "I'm busy."

"Busy doing what?" Spencer counters. "Polishing your masks? Getting ready for next Halloween? Perfecting your Michael Myers impression? Plotting some unsuspecting victim's demise?"

This earns him the middle finger.

"Jude," Violet scolds. "Not in front of the baby."

Spencer flashes me another triumphant grin. Asshole. Since Mom died, Violet, not Jamie, has stepped into the motherly role in that time. Because I respect this woman for putting up with me at my lowest, I nod at her, letting her know I'll behave.

I leave the three of them for some much-needed space, heading for the kitchen where the scent of apples and cinnamon lures me in. The pie Violet baked today is still steaming as it sits on a rack to cool. I locate the ice cream from the freezer and then set to cutting myself a big piece of pie. After topping it with a generous scoop of ice cream, I leave to seek out more privacy, this time with a slice of heaven.

Rather than facing my family, I slip out the back door and sit on the porch that's leaning to one side. A huge, overgrown bush hides me from my family across the road, but there's a small space I trimmed out of it that gives me a perfect view to watch them without being detected. I settle into a rocking chair and lift my mask enough to allow me to shovel food in. Within seconds, the pie is gone. I pull my mask back down and then peer over at Callum's house, where the garage door is opening.

Callum's car comes into view and then it parks inside the empty garage. I expect to see my brother but am slightly confused when Willa climbs out of the driver's seat. Then Tate exits on the other side, carrying two iced coffees. From this far away, I can't hear them or clearly see their faces, but their body language is easy. Happy even.

For some reason, this irritates me.

Dad, Spencer, Willa—they're all letting Tate in like he's welcome. Like he's not some stranger with dark secrets of his own. What happens when he betrays them all? That's what outsiders do. It's been proven time and time again with our family. Who deals with the messes when that happens?

I do.

I always do.

Dad does his schmoozing to make things right and I clean up digital footprints, sweeping all that I can under the Park Secret Rug.

This time, I won't be caught unaware. They can all succumb to his soft, seemingly non-threatening disposition. I, however, refuse to. I'll be lying in wait, digging and digging and digging. Eventually, I will uncover his dirtiest, darkest secrets and reveal them to Dad. He'll send this dude packing once and for all.

The Parks will be safe.

That's all I care about. Pie and the safety of my family. When those are your only two missions in life, it's easy to hyper-fixate and perfect them.

The chilly wind blows, distracting me from my thoughts. The hummingbird feeder I gave Mom one Mother's Day when

I was a small child dances in the wind. It was the only thing that miraculously survived the fire. Whenever I want to feel close to her, I come sit and remember the day when we saw our first hummingbird. Mom's smile was bright and I was beyond delighted.

If only the hummingbirds would come back.

Maybe they're scared of me and my frightening masks.

Maybe they remember their mother—the one who fed them too—perished in a fire while I did not.

A ball of emotion clogs my throat, burning like acid. I tear my gaze from the stupid hummingbird feeder and rise to my feet with my plate in hand. I should just box the damn thing up and throw it in the attic where it belongs.

I'm sorry I couldn't save you, Mom, but I promise I'll save them.

I'll die trying, just like I should have died saving you.

CHAPTER FIVE

Tate

THIS JOB IS ACTUALLY KIND OF GREAT. SINCE everyone is related or connected in some way, I get to learn valuable pieces about each person, which is incredibly helpful to offer insight into what the others may be thinking or feeling.

Spencer is wild. My mind is still reeling from his theatrical confession. It sure made speaking with Aubrey after a bit awkward. While her story was less dramatic, it confirmed she's indeed sleeping with both Spencer and Hugo. Together at times. Most often, apart. Still, I'm trying to wrap my head around that one. She's also pregnant, unsure of who the actual father is. Because Willa is pregnant and so excited, she thinks telling her secret will in some way ruin Willa's happiness. I encouraged her to tell Hugo and Spencer, but she hasn't worked up the nerve to do it yet.

Most everyone so far just wants to vent their frustrations, unload their secrets, and simply have someone unbiased to listen to them. It's definitely a far cry from the meeting I had with Jude earlier.

My next appointment, Dempsey, is fifteen minutes late. I'm not surprised as Nathan warned me it could be the case. Dempsey is a bit reckless and a bad boy. He's always getting into trouble. Now that I have Nathan's take, I'm curious to see what all Dempsey has to reveal.

"Hi, Tate," Gemma says, waving from the doorway. "If Demps doesn't show, I can take his place."

Gemma is a stunner. It's obvious why Nathan is so protective of her. From what he said, she doesn't need therapy, but she could use a friend. Despite her bright smile, perfect makeup and hair, and flawless outfit, her eyes glimmer with something akin to loneliness. Maybe I can get her alone to talk "as a friend" and see what's bothering her. I make a mental note to make that happen.

"I'm here, I'm here," Dempsey grumbles, playfully shoving past her into the office. "Go dazzle your fans with your skin care routine or whatever it is they salivate over."

Gemma rolls her eyes, the long, thick lashes fluttering. "They don't salivate. They come to me for advice on products to purchase so they don't waste money on crap. It's a very important job, which earns me money, by the way. At least one of us is a contributing member to society."

With those huffed words, she slams the door closed. I lift a brow at Dempsey. He shrugs and saunters over to the desk. Unlike Spencer, who dresses a bit like me—preppy and put together—Dempsey is the stereotypical bad boy. His dark hair is messy and hangs in his eyes, he has plenty of visible tattoos, though I don't think he's even eighteen yet, and his favorite color is clearly black as he's fitted in that color from head to toe.

"She's an 'influencer,' she says," Dempsey reveals with a wolfish grin. "I think she made that up to sound cool."

I can tell he uses ribbing his sister as a security blanket to keep the attention off him. Rather than bite, I dive right in.

"You like having a twin?"

He snorts out a laugh. "She's all right."

"Are you close with your other siblings?"

"Callum not so much," Dempsey offers, "but Willa helps with that. I was going to fuck Willa, but I let him have her since he's so obsessed and shit."

Dempsey, not unlike Gemma with her social media job, likes to put on his own show for outsiders. I'm skilled at pinpointing this behavior, though, and cut straight to the point.

"Do you feel guilty for what happened between Callum, your dad, and your mom that resulted in the birth of you and Gemma?"

Dempsey's eyes glimmer with a fiery emotion, but his easygoing expression gives nothing away. "How is that my fault?"

"I didn't say it was. I asked if you bear guilt for that?"

"Did you get Jude to take off his mask?" he deflects, voice sharp.

Undeterred, I continue on. "It's not your fault. I know you know that. Sometimes people fall in love and it's terrible timing. Hearts get broken. It is what it is." I lean forward in the chair, pinning him with a serious stare. "I know your parents love you. I know Callum loves you too. Despite his beef with your dad, he is protective of his family."

"I guess."

"How are things with you? Life treating you okay?"

He smirks. "I'm a Park. Life was made for us to consume and then shit out. Easy."

Liar.

"Are you seeing anyone?"

His entire body stiffens and his jaw clenches. Good to see there's an actual nerve I can hit with him. Interesting.

"Most girls try to date me because they want to marry a Park one day. I'm easy pickings."

"What about guys?"

"Sorry, bro. I heard you're gay, but I'm not interested."

At this, I grin. "You're not really my type."

"Oh yeah? You like the pissy older guys like Callum?"

"Not going to lie, your brother is extremely attractive. No, my type is actually all wrong for me. It's why I'm not going to date again for a long time."

"All wrong how?" He sits up, brows pinching. "You've piqued my interest."

"I attract toxic men. I guess they see me as someone they can control. I don't like who I am when I date. I'm not me."

"Who's having the therapy session now?" he jokes, grinning.

"I want to help you all," I admit. "I know this is in a professional capacity, but I'd like to earn your trust. If that means revealing parts of myself to help make that happen, I will."

He relaxes and nods. "I only love one woman and she's off-limits."

"I didn't think anyone was off-limits for a Park?" I lift an eyebrow at him to see if he follows my drift. Spencer said Dempsey knows about their little threesome.

"Oh, fuck off, Tate. I don't want my sister."

I snort out a laugh. I didn't expect him to jump to that conclusion.

"I actually wondered if you harbor feelings toward Willa. That could be an off-limits situation that could cause turmoil."

His grin is wicked. "As much as I'd love to see Callum

lose his shit over me stealing his baby momma, I'm really not into Willa like that. It's someone else. No one in our family."

"You want to tell me about it?"

He stares at me for a beat. "I imagine it'll come out in due time. Stick around and you might get to hear that story."

Oh, I'll stick around. Jude may be ready to run me off, but I'm invested now. This entire family and their dynamics interest me. I think I can help them. I really *want* to help them.

"Wanna play a game of pool?" Dempsey asks. "They can't expect you to work twenty-four seven."

I tense up, wondering if Sean would show up at a pool hall. I'd avoided running into him at the doctor's office and the coffee shop. But a pool hall?

"Whatever," Dempsey groans. "I actually thought you were serious about being an actual friend there for a second. I'll be upstairs in the game room if you decide to join."

"Wait!" I call out, relief flooding over me. "Sorry, I thought you meant leave. I, uh, I don't feel like going out in public. A game of pool here sounds great, though. Really. I'm sorry if I made you feel otherwise."

"Cool." He stands and starts for the door, turning around at the last second. "You looked terrified. I thought it was because you didn't want to hang with me. But now I get it. The toxic relationship is still fresh and you were triggered."

I gulp at his summation and nod. "It's a long story."

"Maybe one day if you show me yours, I'll show you mine." Then he cracks up laughing. "Not dicks, Tate. My dick might traumatize your precious eyes."

With that wild remark, I'm left wondering what the hell is up with his dick that would traumatize me.

Yeah, I'm not even going to explore the possibilities of that one.

I like hanging out with Callum and Willa. They're an adorable couple and the love between them is so bright, so infectious, they almost have me believing in it again.

One day, I could find the right man.

A good, honest, kind man.

Someone who wants to protect me, not hurt me.

"Well, you survived your first day," Callum says, stroking his fingers over Willa's small pregnant belly. "You ready to run for the hills yet?"

Willa giggles and playfully smacks his hand. "What's not to love about this family?"

He smirks but doesn't argue.

Funky stirs in my lap, reminding me to pet him. I run my palm over his back, taking comfort in his closeness.

"It was great. Started off a bit rocky, but then Willa swooped in and saved the day with iced coffee."

Callum grins. "My girl has other magical talents—ones you'll never know about."

This earns him another smack from his woman.

"Everyone is really nice." *Except for Jude.* "Me and Dempsey played some pool after our session."

"Did he mop the floor with you?" Callum asks. "I swear he could play professionally. He's a shark. Arrogant about it too."

"We tied," I say with a victorious smile. "There was a

pool table at the bar my dad always went to. I learned to hustle those drunks when I was old enough to see over the top of the table."

"Oh, so like last year?" Callum teases.

We all crack up laughing and it feels good. I don't think he's being cruel or picking on me in a bad way. All the men in this family are tall, solid, and sturdy as hell. In comparison, I'm a waif.

"Keep it up and I'll hustle your ass too, man," I joke back.

"Nah, I only attempt things I know I can excel at."

The therapist in me wants to pick apart that statement, but since we're not in a session—and I don't know that Callum will ever do one—I let the comment blow over. Tonight, it's about making friends and enjoying the company of others without fear of repercussion.

Willa tells him a story about the crazy lady at the coffee shop who took our order while I drift to other thoughts. One that keeps cropping up is that I wonder how Sean is dealing with my sudden absence. He was probably pissed at first, but then went on a rampage trying to hunt me down. Luckily, I left without telling a soul where I was going. On my way here, I took several weird routes until I finally backtracked over to make sure I wasn't being followed.

Which brings me to my next big ask to maintain my safety…

"I was, uh, wondering if I could park my car in your garage." I wince at how shaky my voice sounds. "I know it's a piece of crap next to yours but—"

"Yeah, man. You don't have to ask."

I stare at him, eyes unblinking for several seconds. He

doesn't ask why or challenge me in any way. The relief that rushes through me is dizzying.

I think I'm actually going to like it here.

My bedroom overlooks the dark, imposing home across the road. A few lights shine through the windows downstairs, but other than that, it looks like a tomb. It's hard to believe people actually live there.

Once I finish my nighttime routine and ready myself for bed, I turn off the lights and sit in the chair by the window. The wind howls outside, but it's otherwise quiet. Out here, there aren't noisy neighbors or cars or anything. It's peaceful. Safe. Protected. I can see why Jude wants to preserve that.

I'm about to head for bed when I get the distinct feeling someone is watching me. All the hairs on my arms stand on end as a thrum of nervous energy buzzes through my body.

Sean?

I frantically search the shadows and the dense trees surrounding the homes and road. Nothing stands out or seems out of place. Still, I can't seem to be able to stop my erratically beating heart.

If Sean is here, it's over for me.

He will humiliate me in front of them just like he has all my other employers. If that doesn't work, he'll vandalize their property until they get sick of me being a liability.

Please don't be Sean.

God, please.

A shadow moves and my eyes latch onto it. The outline is massive and bulky, immobilizing me with fear. But then I see the horrible, terrifying white mask.

Not my monster.

Their monster.

It's just Jude.

Somehow, this brings me a tiny kernel of peace. I offer him a small wave to let him know I see him. As I close the curtains, he waits for a brief moment and then disappears into the shadows.

I'm still safe.

Thank God, I'm still safe.

CHAPTER SIX

H E'S AFRAID.

Of someone or something, it's hard to tell.

At first, I thought it might be me since we had a rough first encounter. But last night when I was watching him flit about in Callum's swanky guest room, he'd waved to me from his window.

Hardly scared of the mask-wearing beast of Park Mountain.

That leaves me to think it's some*thing*. A hidden secret I've yet to uncover.

Today, I plan to find out what that is. I woke up early, smashed my gym session, and am already in my office, ready to solve this mystery once and for all. I settle in my chair, pleased to find a steaming hot breakfast sandwich, a cup of fruit, and a fresh mug of coffee waiting for me. Violet is incredibly gifted at attuning herself to my weird schedules, anticipating my needs even before I can.

I lift my mask enough to shovel in food and once I've polished off my meal, I pull it down again, eager to start unraveling Tate's life.

Three hours later, I hit the jackpot.

It's taken some difficult searching, but I've found multiple email accounts with Tate Prince in the name with local IP addresses. I can tie each of them to where he's lived over the past two years and even some from his places of work. Each of these email accounts' creations line up with his abrupt termination of employment as well.

Intriguing, to say the least.

The passwords to get into these aren't easy to hack into as he used a series of random numbers, symbols, and letters. They're all different too. However, I do finally manage to breach the first one.

The inboxes are filled with people matching the clinic of one of the places he's worked at. In the subject of each of these emails is: ***Could we set up a meeting to do this?*** The responses are all ones of outrage, horror, and disgust.

Sicko.

What the hell?

You'll get fired for this.

This is sexual harassment.

Sexual harassment? Tate doesn't seem the type, but people have fooled me before. Each email has a video attached. I click on one and open it.

The sight before me is hard to watch. Tate is on his knees, naked, with a fat dildo between his teeth. He's crying and won't make eye contact with the camera. The camera audio suddenly mutes and then Tate's head snaps up, fear shining in his eyes. The audio returns, and without dropping the slobbery dildo, he whimpers out his words.

"Please fuck me with this. I can be your fuck toy. Please."

He sent this to everyone at his job?

I've seen a lot of weird shit in my lifetime, but this takes the cake.

I'm sure there's a why and possibly even a story behind

this, but that doesn't matter. I've finally discovered his big secret. He's a kinky bastard who shares his videos with his co-workers. That's enough for me.

I forward the email over to Dad and then bolt, abandoning my coffee altogether. Who needs caffeine when you're running on the high of victory? Dad will shit bricks and can him over this. We, *especially me,* can all rest easy once he's gone for good.

The trip over to Dad's goes by in a flash. Bittersweet memories assault my mind, reminding me of the rush of running down the football field, high on the game. If I could turn back time, I'd still skip school that day, but I'd go home instead. I'd save Mom, help her get out of her depression over the divorce, and join the NFL like Coach wanted.

By the time I reach Dad's door, those thoughts fade as more pressing ones enter. I barge into the house and pass by his office door that's closed. I can hear Tate talking to someone, Spencer maybe, muffled through the door. I find Dad sitting on the back patio drinking coffee. His brows lift upon seeing me.

"Morning, Son. Here for a session with Tate?"

I sneer behind my mask. "Fuck no."

Dad frowns and sets his mug down. "What's wrong?"

"Check your email."

He pulls his phone from the table and opens it up. Seconds later, I can hear Tate's voice from the video. I wait for Dad to explode with fury.

Seconds go by.

Nothing.

I clear my throat to gain his attention in case he zoned

out in horror. Finally, he sets his phone down and sighs. "I already knew about this."

He *what*?

"Dad," I growl, anger vibrating through the word.

"I know," he grumbles, waving off my reaction. "It's serious."

Damn right it's serious.

"What was his response?"

"I didn't ask him," Dad admits. "I just realized this was terrible enough he'd be compliant and keep our family's secrets."

Unbelievable.

"You let this man talk to your children and grandchildren? Spencer, and especially Dempsey, are impressionable. Aren't you worried?"

He sighs and pinches the bridge of his nose. "Tate has already proven himself to me."

"Dad, you're fucking blind."

"Watch your tone, Jude."

"I can't," I bark out in exasperation. "You're willingly exposing our family to this bullshit!"

"I'm not firing him."

We have a fierce stare-off to which neither of us backs down. The problem with us Parks is we're all the same. Stubborn assholes.

"We're confronting him then," I tell him in a resolute tone. "I, for one, can't trust someone with this sort of secret. I need to see his expression when he tells us what happened."

Dad nods and stands from his chair. "We'll confront him. I should have from the beginning. You're right about that. But he's already made such an impact. Everyone likes him. They talk to him."

I don't like him.

I certainly don't talk to him.

"Speak for yourself," I grunt. "Come on. Let's get this shit over with."

We end up waiting for a bit while Spencer finishes his session. Dad's idea, not mine. Once Spencer is gone, we both enter Dad's office. Tate smiles in greeting.

"Father and son session?" Tate asks, eyes glittering with hope.

"We need to talk," Dad mutters. The disappointment in his words makes my gut clench and Tate's whole body tense up. "Something's come up."

Tate clenches his eyes shut in resignation—as though he's prepared for what we're going to say. He already knows. Well, he's going to have to hear it anyway.

"You have a kinky sex video that you harass your coworkers with that has gotten you fired in the past," I blurt out, a tad bit gleefully. "Explain."

Tate's eyes pop open, disgust swimming in them. He bites down on his bottom lip and blinks furiously. It takes me a second to realize he's fighting tears. Guilt niggles at me, but I quickly push it away.

"To be clear, I knew about the video," Dad interjects. "One of my country club buddies mentioned it to me, which is why I sought you out."

Tate shudders, mouth gaping. "You tricked me?"

"I saw an opportunity and jumped," Dad explains. "Your reputation is a tool for me."

There's the vicious Park patriarch we all know and love…

"Wow. That's…"

"Deceptive?" I offer. "So is hiding that sick shit from us."

Tate flinches as though my words physically wound him, but he says nothing.

"Well?" I demand. "What do you have to say?"

"I'm sorry," Tate rasps. "I don't understand, though. If you knew about the video and hired me anyway, why are you bringing it up now? To keep me in line?" The tears build on his lids, liquifying his lying eyes. It's almost pretty in a wicked sort of way.

"I think we should fire you," I spit out. "You help minors. Are you showing them this video?"

Tate's defeat morphs into rage and his eyebrows pinch together. "I am offended by such a heinous accusation."

"Just answer the question." I cross my arms over my chest, not giving in to his rollercoaster emotions.

"No." He pins Dad with an earnest stare. "I would never."

Dad relaxes, which doesn't bode well for me.

"But you have harassed people with this damn video," I remind him with a growl. "These things naturally progress—"

"I'm the therapist, not you," Tate snaps, a rogue tear racing down his cheek. "I'm a victim of something private being used against me, if you absolutely must know."

The guilt rears its ugly head again, but I squash it down. "Cyber bullying? Who hates you so bad they'd steal your sex videos and email them to your workplace?"

Tate's lips thin out and a flash of *something* gleams in his eyes. Then he completely shuts down, turning into a fucking robot. "I don't know."

Liar.

"We believe you," Dad says gently.

We do fucking not!

Tate's gaze has found his hands that wring one another in clear agitation. There's more to this story. He may not have sent them, but someone did. People don't go through that sort of effort for random strangers they don't know.

This was personal.

Whether Tate was responsible or not, it doesn't change the fact he harbors secrets that continue to jeopardize our family. Again, if Dad can't see what's clearly staring him in the damn face, then it's my responsibility to take action.

There's only one solution.

One that makes my skin crawl but also gives me great relief.

"You're on probation," I clip out, waving a dismissive hand at him. "This means I'll be watching your every move. After this meeting, you'll be moving into my home where you'll take your meetings."

Tate stiffens and jerks his head up to stare at me in confusion. "What? But I'm staying with Callum—"

"No," I hiss, "you're staying with me now. You want this job, that's the condition."

He turns to look at Dad, giving him a pleading look that might sway my father. Surprisingly, Dad walks over to Tate and squeezes his shoulder in comfort. He leans down and whispers something to him.

I make out the word, "headway."

I'm sure Dad sees this as an opportunity to get inside my mind, but I'm not the fool around here. I can see right through all this and am the only one looking at Tate with any sort of skepticism. It's exactly why Tate belongs with me. Where I can watch his every goddamn move.

"I have a cat," Tate murmurs in a last-ditch effort to plead his case.

"I'll dock your pay for cat boarding," I deadpan. "Go pack your shit."

The glare Tate shoots my way is murderous. Beyond the tears and humiliation is an anger that's lurking. It makes me want to taunt that emotion out of him, bring it to the surface, and tame it into submission.

No one fucks with my family.

No one.

"Jude," Dad says, "he'll meet you outside in a few. I'd like to speak with Tate alone."

I shoot warning daggers at Tate. He's not going to sway my father. I won't allow it to happen. With a clipped nod, I exit the office and stalk out of the house. After a brisk, short walk, I barge into Callum's house. I pass by my brother's office on the way to the stairs. He's hard at work at his desk and Willa sits nearby at a laptop in a cozy armchair. They're in the process of building a finance company now that Callum's no longer a teacher. He's a statistics and econ brainiac, so it suits him well.

Callum waves a hand as I pass but doesn't ask what I'm up to. That's the good thing about this family. We do what needs doing and usually the rest of us will fall in line. Callum trusts me to be in his house.

I make it into Tate's room. Everything is neat and orderly. The only tell that an outsider lives here is the black cat sprawled out on the bed and the pet carrier tucked in the corner. I ignore the cat to hunt down Tate's luggage. In the closet, I find one suitcase and a small amount of clothes. Quickly, I rip them all off the hangers and shove them into the luggage. Then I gather up his meager belongings in the bathroom, check the drawers in the room to remove anything left in there, and drop the suitcase on the bed next to the cat.

"Litter box?" I ask the cat.

He swishes his tail and meows at me. No help at all. Definitely docking Tate's pay for this little freeloader. I eventually find the litter box and extra box of litter stowed in the open carrier.

"Let's go, fucker."

The cat stands and stretches before lazily walking toward the edge of the bed. I pull him into my arms and settle him on my shoulder. Thankfully, he hangs on while I grab the carrier and suitcase.

I nearly knock Willa over as I exit the guest room.

Her features fall and sadness glints in her eyes when she takes in my haul. "Tate's leaving?"

"Moving in with me for the time being," I bite out.

Until we fire him for real.

"What about Funky's food and water bowl?"

"Who?"

She purses her lips. "The cat."

"Bring it over later. Fucky will manage until then."

"Jude, his name is Fun—"

Ignoring her, I sweep through the house in a whirlwind of anger, struggling to get the door open with all the shit I'm loaded down with and then make my way back over to Dad's. Just as I stop in front of the porch, the front door opens.

Tate steps out and winces at seeing me. Another flash of bitter anger washes over his features before he rushes over to me. Reaching up, he grabs his cat and pulls him down into his arms. The cat, who'd been holding on for dear life, claws

the shit out of my shoulder, ripping the fabric of my favorite hoodie.

I'll dock his pay for this too.

"I'm ready," Tate says, lifting his chin. "Let's go."

I'm ready too, little liar.

This is the beginning of the end of your time with the Parks.

CHAPTER SEVEN

Tate

I CAN'T BELIEVE THIS IS HAPPENING.

They know. They know and I'm still here.

Well, not technically *here* since my previous *here* was Callum's place and Nathan's office, but I'm still here with the Parks.

With Jude.

My mask-wearing "bonus" that just increased to a whopping 50k when Nathan spoke to me alone.

Fifty thousand to get through to Jude.

Fifty. Freaking. Thousand.

That's so much money I can't even imagine having it. It'd certainly help pay off all the collection agencies I owe so I can start cleaning up my credit. This really could be the fresh start I desperately needed.

Which is why I'll endure living with the paranoid Park.

"It's going to be okay," I assure my cat, nuzzling his fur with my face. "I promise."

His purring is loud and calms me as we make our trek across the property. Even though Jude is massive and could probably get to his house in three seconds, he walks slowly, checking over his shoulder every once in a while to make sure I'm still following.

It's petty, I know, but I take great pleasure in the fact he has to carry my stuff.

Despite dragging my feet, we eventually make it to his creepy house. It's every bit as intimidating as it was a couple of days ago when I first arrived and he tried to fire me.

This time, I'm going into the belly of the beast.

Jude sets the carrier down to open the door, then he picks it back up and waits for me to enter before him. I swallow down my unease and tentatively step inside.

The inside foyer is exactly as I'd imagined. Dark wood paneling on the walls, black-and-white photos of people from another lifetime adorning an entryway table, and a dim chandelier doing a half-ass job of lighting the space.

Light from outside is sucked away when Jude closes the door behind us. It snicks shut so softly but vibrates with finality through each one of my bones.

I'm really doing this.

"Let's go," Jude grunts. "I'll show you to your room."

Since I'm still shellshocked by what transpired this morning, I numbly follow after him. He turns left and takes the stairs two at a time. I'm given an eyeful of his muscular ass and decide I deserve it for the hell of a day I'm having. Funky meows in agreement. We'll take the small wins where we can.

His figure cuts through the darkness of the hallway, moving with an unsettling determination past several closed doors. Then he abruptly stops and sets the carrier down. "This one's yours. It has a bathroom en suite. Consider your appointments canceled for the day."

I grit my teeth, biting back a snappy remark. I'm not exactly in a position right now to argue. Fifty thousand is on the line here. Quietly, I follow Jude into the room that's a far cry from the one I just vacated.

This room is old. Outdated. Dark.

Everything in this house so far is dark. The shadows cloud around me, clawing at me. It makes me want to open a window or turn on every light.

Jude sets the carrier down and then tosses my suitcase onto the bed. The mattress that covers the queen-sized bed is ancient but at least colorful. When he unzips the suitcase, I stare at him in confusion. Heat floods up my neck and settles on my cheeks when he grabs a handful of my underwear.

"W-What are you doing?" I demand, voice shrill.

"Unpacking."

Funky fidgets, clearly ready to check out our new lodging. With a frustrated sigh, I set my cat down and then rush over to take over unpacking. Jude snaps his head toward me and glowers at me through his creepy mask.

Sometimes he scares the shit out of me.

There's a feral quality in his eyes that screams unpredictable.

Since he's a giant, he could knock me to the floor without breaking a sweat.

Just like Sean.

The oily, terrible feeling Sean causes in me doesn't just slick over me, it downpours. I stumble away from Jude, trying desperately to keep my trembling hidden.

People like Sean and Jude prey on the weak.

They sniff out fear and then feast on it.

I refuse to be another monster's meal.

Since he's dead set on doing all the work, I move out of his way, watching his every move as he stuffs clothing into drawers and then sets to hanging my other clothes. Once I'm settled in there, he moves on to unpacking my toiletries. With an armful, he stalks into the en suite bathroom. I trail after him, wondering if this bathroom has heated floors like Callum's guest bathroom.

I deflate upon seeing a clawfoot tub that's probably been here for a century. Jude sets my shampoo, conditioner, and body wash on the floor by the tub and then dumps the rest of my stuff on the counter beside the sink.

I stare at the wall above the sink, trying to figure out what's missing. The dated wallpaper is brighter in the shape of a large rectangle. It finally hits me.

No mirror.

Of course not.

There goes any and all hope for heated floors.

Before I can stop myself, I blurt out my question. "Where's the mirror?"

Jude slowly turns to face me. His head cocks slightly to the side, eyes burning into me from beyond his mask. All he needs is a butcher knife from the kitchen and he has the whole horror vibe on lock.

Everything in me is yelling, "Run, you idiot! Run as fast as you can!"

My feet remain rooted in place. I hold my ground as he prowls toward me. His towering frame looms over me, our chests nearly touching. I swallow but refuse to retreat.

"Where's the mirror?" I ask again, voice slightly raspy.

"I hate mirrors," he bites out, gesturing at his mask. "Obviously."

Asshole.

He pokes a finger in the center of my chest and easily

pushes me out of the way. As soon as he passes through the doorway, he drops his hand and puts distance between us. Absently, I rub at the spot on my chest, wondering if it'll bruise.

"Dinner is always at six sharp. I'll have Violet bring you your lunch and I'll fetch you for dinner. In the meantime, don't wander. This is a big house with lots of places to get lost. Keep Fucky on a leash."

With those maddening words, he storms out of the bedroom, letting the door slam after him. I jump at the abrupt sound cutting through the otherwise quiet. Seconds later, his words catch up to me.

Keep Fucky on a leash.

Ugh, major asshole!

"His name's *Funky*," I grumble under my breath, "and we don't own a leash."

My cat hops up onto the bed and then settles himself beside the empty suitcase. He watches me with curious eyes.

"I'm sorry," I tell my furry friend. "We went from princes to paupers."

I snigger at my pun. We'll always be Tate and Funky Prince even if we no longer have a taste of the sweet life. *Heated bathroom floors.*

I move the suitcase and then make sure the carrier door is open in case my cat needs to do his business. Since I have nothing else to do, I stretch out on the bed and stare up at the yellow, water-stained ceiling.

How are these people so rich yet they have a house like this in such need of repair?

Jude probably wouldn't let any workers in anyway. I bet he fires them all before they start. Another surge of irritation burns in my gut. At least my worry and fear have subsided. Anger is a good emotion for me. It makes me feel strong and I absolutely need to be at my strongest right now.

I can endure this.

Hell, I endured much worse before.

Both my dad and Sean tested every limit I had. I'm still here. A survivor. An overcomer.

Speaking of Sean, I wonder if he's tried to call me. It feels empowering, though, knowing my phone is shut off and tucked away in the side zipper of the suitcase. Sean can't reach me. I don't have to face his ugly texts or hear his cruel messages.

It's not much, but it gives me enough relief that I'm able to fall asleep.

I wake to someone's voice, jerking upright in a panic.

It takes me a moment to familiarize myself with my surroundings. Guest room at Jude's haunted house. Right. Lovely.

The voice in question, though, isn't Jude.

It's an older woman.

"Knock-knock," she says, slowly opening the door with one hand. "Jude said you'd want lunch in your room."

The old woman with white hair and a friendly smile enters my room carrying a tray. Curiosity gets the best of me and I'm pleased to see a croissant sandwich, a pickle, some orange slices, and a piece of what looks like apple pie. There's also a water carafe, a glass with ice, a coffee mug, and a stainless-steel gooseneck coffee pot.

"I'm Violet," the woman says as she sets the tray down at the desk in the corner. "I cook for the fellas and make sure they're taken care of." Pride shines in her expression. It warms my heart.

"Fellas?"

"Not just Jude here. Wyatt. Jude's grandfather. He's wheelchair-bound but still a firecracker."

My initial fear of Jude and this house fades into the background. At least there are witnesses here. Violet seems nice.

I slide off the bed, rubbing the sleep out of my eyes, and make my way over to the food. "Wow, this looks great. Thank you."

She beams with happiness. "The pie is Jude's favorite. Let me know your favorite and I'll make it for you."

"You will?"

Her pleased expression falls. "Of course. You're Jude's guest."

I snort at that summation. "Hardly a guest."

"But you're in the guest room…" She trails off with a frown.

"I work for Nathan. Therapist. Just helping out, is all. The name's Tate. Tate Prince."

Violet's brows lift. "You're going to help our Jude?"

"I'm going to try."

She shocks me by shuffling my way and throwing her spindly arms around me. I haven't been hugged in, well, forever. I hug my cat. That's all the affection I get. Sudden emotion prickles at my eyes and a lump forms in my throat. I greedily hug this old woman back, inhaling her cinnamon and sugar scent.

"You're a gift from God, Mr. Prince. Truly."

I'm hardly a gift from God and Mr. Prince reminds me of

Dad. Her words make me uncomfortable. I carefully extract myself from the much-needed hug.

"Please call me Tate. And I said I'd try. He's a tough nut to crack."

She nods. "The toughest. But he needs cracking. I'm afraid one day he'll shut himself off from everyone. His mother would have hated seeing him deteriorate like this." She takes hold of my hand, squeezing it in her weathered hands. "Don't give up hope, sweet Tate. He needs someone strong to keep pushing—to not be afraid of the hatred he harbors for himself. You've made it further into Jude's world than any outsider ever has. The man deep inside is worth finding and saving. I have faith you're the one to do it."

With those powerful words, she releases my hand and leaves me alone in my room. As I sit at the desk to eat my meal, I can't help but wonder if she's right.

Maybe I am the right person for this job.

She thinks I'm strong.

That I could save him.

It's a wild concept, but it's one I'd like to get on board with. Not just because the fifty thousand could be incredibly useful in cleaning up my own life, but because this is what I do. What I crave in life. I love helping people.

Even unlikable mask-wearing grumps.

I can do this.

I *will* do this.

For me. For Violet. For Nathan and the rest of the Parks.

And for Jude. *Especially* for Jude.

CHAPTER EIGHT

Jude

AS SOON AS THE PIPES BEGIN WHINING ON THE OTHER side of my office wall, I know it's time to make my move.

He has a phone and he can't bathe with it. Maybe I'll find more information there.

I spring from my office chair and stride purposefully toward the guest room, each step marked by a silent purpose. The door is locked, but every door in this house has a metal instrument sitting on top of the doorframe that can be used as a key. I pluck it down and shove it into the slot on the door handle. It clicks softly, indicating my access. After I place the key back in its spot, I slowly twist the knob and then push open the door.

The cat, from his perch on the bed, watches me as I creepily enter the room. The bath water runs from the other side of the closed bathroom door. For now, I have that sound drowning out my movements, but when it stops, I'll be forced to be extra quiet.

On the desk sit his wallet and car keys. He also seems to have just finished off a cup of coffee. The mug is still warm to the touch. I pick up his wallet, flip it open to look at his license, and then close it, placing it exactly the way it was.

Did he bring his phone to the bathroom with him?

I scan the room and don't see it sitting anywhere. The suitcase I'd unpacked earlier today sits neatly on top of the cat carrier. I walk over to it to see if maybe he has it hidden in there. Sure enough, the side zipper reveals a phone that's been turned off.

The water abruptly shuts off and I freeze. I lock eyes with Fucky, who watches me with rapt interest, tail swishing wildly. Tate doesn't run out like he's heard me, so I take a quiet breath before retrieving my own phone from my pocket. Luckily, his model phone is the same as mine, so I easily hook up the cable I brought with me to transfer any pertinent data.

I just have to hack into his phone first.

While I wait for the phone to turn on, I run through my brain the possible number combinations his passcode could be. Since I've already researched a lot about him, I may have those numbers in my database unless he chose a random, obscure code that doesn't pertain to anything.

The phone eventually powers on. I try his birthday, the last four of his social, and am about to try the numbers of the street he lives on when a thought comes to me. Maybe it has something to do with the cat. I pull up my phone and locate the cat's adoption papers, scanning until I find his birthday.

November 12.

Surely it couldn't be that simple…

1112 opens the phone right up.

He should really think about changing that because anyone could just pick up his phone and get right in. Is that what happened with the kinky sex video? Did someone easily get into his phone just as I did?

If he didn't trouble me so much, I'd almost feel compelled

to have a talk with him about the importance of a secure password.

Almost.

Not bothering to waste any more time, I set to transferring the phone data to my phone. I focus on text messages, photos, and videos for the time being. The program I use is quick but not quick enough to make a copy of the entire thing. I'll do what I can and perhaps come another time to get the rest. Like when he's sleeping.

While the phone copies, I dart my attention over to the bathroom door. He's quiet in there. Doesn't seem like a cleansing bath. Maybe more of a soaking bath.

Is he stressed?

The guilt is back, twisting and tightening my gut. I don't like the heavy feeling—like I'm doing something wrong by trying to protect my family. But Tate's a threat. I have to remember that.

I drag my attention back to his phone, noticing he has a shit ton of selfies with his cat. It's almost cute. Kind of reminds me of Gemma and her selfies. Always smiling and putting on a show for the camera.

Meow.

Glancing at the cat, I cock my head at him as if to ask, "What?"

He continues to stare at me. I can feel his judgment. Why are cats such assholes?

Ignoring him, I flip through the missed calls and texts. All the calls are from the same number, but there're no voicemails and the person didn't text him. I'll definitely do my deep dive later when I'm alone.

At the sound of the tub draining, I nearly drop both

phones. Fuck. Quickly, I yank the cord out of his phone, turn it off, and shove it into the suitcase. I zip it up and stuff my own phone back into my pocket. I'm just starting back for the door when the bathroom door flings open.

He doesn't see me at first and comes sauntering out of the bathroom in nothing but a towel tied around his waist. With all his clothes on, he's thus far seemed kind of small to me. But now? Nearly naked? He's not so tiny. His shoulders and biceps are carved with lean muscle. I skim my gaze down his hard pectorals and tight abs, landing at the bulge under his towel.

"Jude! What the hell are you doing in my room?"

I jerk my stare from his dick and meet his widened eyes. "Nothing."

"Nothing?" His neck burns bright red as he crosses his arms over his chest. "This is not okay."

Shame runs thick through my veins. "I, uh, wanted to see Fucky."

Lies.

Tate's lips purse together as he darts a look over at the cat. "You can't even say his name right and suddenly you're BFFs?"

"Yep," I rasp out, continuing my lie. "I love cats." To further convince him, I sit on the edge of the bed and awkwardly pet the rumbling fur ball. "See?"

For fuck's sake.

I'm a bumbling idiot.

Tate continues to gape at me as if I've lost my mind. "I don't believe you."

I snap my head up to look at him. With just a towel covering his virtually hairless body, he sort of reminds me of the sculptures we studied in school. A Michelangelo work of art. Smooth, made of marble, meant for staring at.

My brain short-circuits as I attempt to make sense of my thoughts. I can hear Tate mumbling things, but I'm still trying to figure out why I think this man's body is so enticing to look at.

And he is enticing.

Distractingly so.

"Why are you really here?" Tate demands. "To order me around some more?"

I fixate on his mouth. Full, pouty lips. The bottom one is slightly bigger and protrudes a little more. His almost black hair is damp and not styled, hanging over his eyebrows messily. I like that he's a bit less put together than usual.

"I, uh, thought I would give you a tour before dinner," I blurt out before I can stop myself.

He unfolds his arms and studies me for a beat. "Why didn't you say that in the first place instead of lying?"

I avoid his probing stare and end up noticing how his pink nipples are pebbled. A ripple of *something* flitters through my body, settling in the pit of my stomach. His nipples are almost as intriguing as his lips.

"I don't know," I rumble. The first truth in this whole conversation. "I know you were upset earlier. I thought I would soften you by pretending to like your cat."

He snorts out a laugh. "Soften me up to my new ice-cold floors and forced captivity?"

Ice-cold floors?

"Is the temperature not suitable for you?" I ask, voice gruff, skimming my eyes down for another quick peek at his nipples. "You're too cold here?"

He rolls his eyes as he makes his way over to the dresser, his back to me. I notice his back is also sculpted to precision like his chest, abs, shoulders, and arms. I wonder what his thighs look like.

"Funky quite liked the heated floors at Callum's. We got spoiled pretty quickly." Tate tosses a pair of black boxers and socks onto the bed. Then he brushes past me toward the closet. I inhale his soapy scent as he walks by.

"Callum has heated floors?"

Tate exits the closet with a pair of sweats and a hoodie. "In the bathroom, yes. It was the most wonderful thing I've ever felt."

I try to imagine how warm bathroom tiles would feel. Yeah, that probably would feel pretty nice.

"You don't leave your bubble often, do you?" he asks, stopping just inches away from me. "You stay up here in your haunted castle, brooding all day and night, eating apple pie with your wonderful cook, too busy to notice what's going on around you."

I smirk behind my mask. So he's met Violet and already loves her. For some reason, this pleases me.

"Turn around, Jude, unless you want to see me get naked."

Another zing travels down my spine. I'm curious to see his thighs…and other stuff, but I do as I'm told. As soon as my back is to him, I hear the towel drop to the floor. We're both quiet as he dresses, the shuffling of his clothes and the cat's purring the only sound between us.

"I'm dressed now."

I whip around quickly—too quickly if I'm being honest—and drink in his appearance. I'm not sure of my sudden fascination with him, but I can ponder over that later with a fat piece of apple pie. Until then, I'm going to continue getting drunk on this strange feeling.

Tate's hoodie engulfs his body, at least two sizes too big. It makes me wonder if one of my own hoodies would fit him this way. The thought is an interesting one. Something else to consider during pie time later.

He stuffs his hands into the pockets of his hoodie and frowns at me. "You're being quiet. And weird. It's unnerving."

I want to tell him he's unnerving. He's confusing too. This guy is young and clearly charming, but behind that is some freaky kinkster who can't pay his bills and has secrets galore. What you see is what you get with me. I'm broken. Completely fucking shattered and unfixable.

He's an enigma.

A box inside a box inside a box.

I can't tear off the layers quick enough.

I want to get down to his very core. To know every detail about him. I want inside of him—his mind—so I can understand who the hell Tate Prince really is.

"When you look at me like that," he continues, voice getting a few octaves higher, "it's downright terrifying."

"Terrifying? How?" I wince when I realize he means the mask. "Oh."

He softens and takes a step closer. His scent is stronger than when he whizzed past me moments earlier. Thankfully, my mask covers the way my nostrils flare to inhale the smell.

"It's the look in your eye," Tate clarifies. "It's intense but guarded. I don't understand you. You give me nothing. I'm here to help you."

Despite his explanation, I still feel shame for some

reason. I'm the big, mean monster. Maybe Tate isn't hiding things to be deceptive or wicked. Maybe there's another reason. If so, does that make me terrifying like he says? A big fucking bully?

"You really want to help my family?" I ask, voice gruff.

"I really do." He pauses and then lets out a huff. "Your father is paying me well to. Especially to help you. I know you're skeptical of me, so I wanted to be upfront about that. Maybe start to build some trust between us."

Sincerity shines in his eyes. It's not going to hurt anything if I stop being a dick for five minutes and maybe hear what he has to say. Hugo always says you get more flies with honey or some shit. Maybe this is what he means.

"I better show you around then." I give him a noncommittal shrug. "We'll see about this whole trust thing."

"We *will*," he says with a huge grin. "That's all I ask for. Just give me a chance, Jude."

Like I said. We'll see.

CHAPTER NINE

Tate

E BROKE INTO MY ROOM.

I'm trying not to freak out about that. It's invasive and a bit frightening. Sure, the money is good, and the bonus is insanely awesome, but at what cost?

My sanity?

My life?

Unease sours the coffee in my gut. Getting inside of Jude's head to help him will be an incredible challenge. I have to make sure I don't lose a part of myself in the process or, worse yet, get caught up romantically with the troubled man.

He was staring at my body. I didn't imagine the interest and low burn of desire in his gaze. If I said I didn't find him attractive, that would be a lie. Despite having no idea what he looks like, his intensity calls to the baser parts of me. And his body? It's hot as fuck.

Focus, man.

I shove up the arms of my hoodie sleeves past my elbows in an effort to cool myself off. I'm flushed from my hot bath and even hotter encounter with Jude. I need to get out of this room and away from this buzzing between us.

"Lead the way," I croak out. "If any ghosts come at me, though, you better save me."

"Nothing will get to you here," Jude says with a confident grunt.

No ghosts of my past? I'm in.

I force a smile and then we leave the room. He walks us to the end of the hall where green lights glow. When I get a peek inside, my eyeballs nearly fall out of my head.

"Holy crap? Did we just enter the Matrix?"

Jude cocks his head to the side as he considers my words. It's really eerie when he does that. I suppress a shiver. "It's my office."

"Obviously." I push past him into the room and admire the many, many monitors. Are there eight of them? "Wow."

"It's just where I work. Nothing special."

I don't think anyone in the Pentagon has anything this intense set up. It's more than special. It's impressive. "What do you do for work?"

He grunts. "I take care of my family."

"Vague much?"

He shrugs, avoiding eye contact. "Everything I do comes back to that. Whether it's keeping them safe from people who want to harm them or making money in whatever ways I can, I do it. Nothing else to say about it."

His answer is frustrating, but at least it's an answer. He's actually talking to me and not acting like he wants to body-slam me to the ground. This is progress. I'm making *headway*.

Once I've seen my fill, he leads me back down the hall-way, pointing out other bedrooms. His room is at the end of the hallway, but he doesn't bother opening the door to show me, much to my disappointment.

So far, I've seen a whole lot of nothing.

"Let's go downstairs." He leads the way, charging down the steps like his ass is on fire.

From my vantage point, above him for once, I can see mottled scarring on the back of his neck. It makes me wonder if that same scarring is what's on his face. How could it be so bad that he would want to hide from everyone?

They're just scars.

Lots of people have them on the outside.

Most of us have them on the inside.

They tell our story whether we like it or not.

Jude shows me the kitchen next. Violet is already in there, chopping away at a myriad of colorful vegetables. When she sees me, she gives me a conspiratorial wink. I respond back with a small wave and a crushing weight of guilt.

She's waiting for me to fix him and I've been lowkey salivating over his muscular body.

Right.

Stay on task.

Get Jude to talk and actually help him.

"Another bathroom," Jude says, gesturing for a powder room off the dining room.

I note there aren't mirrors in here either. Not surprised.

We pass by some French doors. And I stop to see if he'll talk about what's in there. When he realizes I'm not following, he screeches to a halt and darts his gaze back and forth between the doors and me.

"Grandpa. He naps at this time of day. Violet wakes him for dinner. You'll meet him later."

Okay then.

He takes me down another dark hallway past the pristine and severely outdated living room. When we reach another set of French doors, he bursts through them. The light flickers on and I'm met with a room full of gym machines and weights. No mirrors here either. Shocker.

"This is how we stay trim around here. Violet likes to fatten us up."

His tone is softer than usual. Sweet almost. He clearly loves that woman as much as she loves him. This is good. He's not a lost cause.

"Who is we?" I ask.

"Grandpa will do some of the smaller weights in here with me sometimes.

The thought of him and his grandpa working out together softens me even further toward him. He really does love his family. Yes, he's extreme in his efforts to protect him, but it's admirable.

"Am I allowed to use this gym?"

He turns, skimming his gaze over my body as though trying to remember how scrawny I was in just my towel. His Adam's apple bobs and then he nods once.

Sweet.

Free gym membership.

After the gym, he takes me down to the end of the hallway. Beyond that door is the best room in the house. The room is large with windows that take up most of one wall that faces Park Mountain. Beside the gargantuan windows are floor-to-ceiling bookcases filled with books. Toward the tops of the shelves are dustier, older-looking books, but the ones closer to the bottom are colorful and clearly more modern ones. I approach one of the bookshelves and pluck a book out.

A popular thriller.

"Grandpa," Jude says. "He reads a lot. Sometimes I come in here and pretend to read with him."

My heart squeezes at that statement. He pretends to read so he can sit in the quiet with his grandfather. Maybe me moving in here was a great idea. I'm uncovering a lot more about Jude than I ever imagined. Certainly gives me better tools to work with.

"I've read this one. It's really good." I grin at him. "Maybe I can come read one day with you both."

Jude gives me another sharp nod. "The door closes and there is plentiful seating here. You may take your sessions in here with my family."

The library is my new office?

Not going to argue with that one.

I mosey around the office, admiring the titles of many books I've read and loved, and also making a mental note to check out others later to read. Jude stands sentry by the windows, watching my every move but hardly making any movements himself. I'm engrossed in reading the blurb on the back of a thriller from the '80s when I hear a low whining sound.

Whipping around, I face the doorway to learn the sound is coming from that direction. Jude doesn't appear to be startled, so I wait patiently until the sound appears visually in the doorway. A frail, white-haired elderly man with a scowl looks at Jude before turning his attention to me.

"Violet tells me we have a guest and that I must make your acquaintance," the man says grumpily, the oxygen line hooked under his nose wobbling as he speaks. "Wyatt. Who are you?"

I set the book down on the table before approaching him with a smile. "Tate. Tate Prince. I'm—"

"You're what? Jude's friend?"

I glance over at Jude, who gives me a small nod. "I am. I'm here to bring him out of his shell."

To say the least.

Wyatt snorts. "Kid's been in his shell since the fire that killed his momma."

The air chills several degrees. I expect Jude to blow up or storm off. He does neither. Just stands there like a gargoyle made of stone.

"It must have hurt something awful." I give Wyatt a small smile. "Probably for everyone."

My cat, having slipped out of the bedroom, prances into the library and then hops into Wyatt's lap. He startles at first and then chuckles. "Well, hello there."

Funky purrs, rubbing his head against the man's weather hand.

"Funky likes cuddles and he's too nosey for his own good," I say in exasperation. "I'm sorry. I can put him away."

Wyatt scowls at me, hugging the cat to him. "I was just starting to like you, Tate. Don't ruin it."

I smirk at his grumpiness. The old man likes cats. That's a win for me and my furry feline.

"Harlan Coben is one of my favorites," Wyatt says, nodding toward the abandoned book. "Seen a couple of his books adapted for TV. Not great, but when you've seen everything, it's entertainment. I'll always stick with my books over television, though."

"Amen," I say with a grin. "The book is always better."

Jude prowls closer and I shoot him a curious look. Since I can't see his expression, I have to go on his body language. He doesn't seem angry or agitated. If anything, it's as if he wants to get closer to be a part of the conversation. But since he already admitted to pretending to read, I know it has nothing to do with the book. He just wants to be included—desperate to connect.

"I saw a book about a hacker over there who uncovers some shady stuff going on with the government. He gets caught up in a web as he tries to save everyone in harm's way. I think it's a bit of a redemption story," I tell Jude. "Might add that one to your reading list."

He nods more than once. Does that mean he's enthusiastic about the recommendation? Wyatt's bushy white eyebrows pinch together as he studies Jude with narrowed eyes. Then he turns back to me. "After supper, pull the book. We can all enjoy our desserts and read a few chapters of our books before we turn in for the night."

A bell jingles from somewhere else in the house. This alerts Funky and he launches himself out of Wyatt's lap to chase after the sound.

"Dinner?" I ask no one in particular.

Wyatt maneuvers his wheelchair around and races down the hallway, leaving me alone with Jude. I guess that answers my question. Jude slowly approaches until he's towering over me. His dark blue eyes bore into me from behind the openings in his mask. This is the first time his closeness doesn't intimidate me.

It feels…*nice*.

Like he's seeing another side of me than intruder therapist guy.

Like he might see the real me. The hurting me. The terrified me. The lonely me.

I'm not sure I want to allow Jude of all people in to see

those parts I'm not proud of, but I was serious when I told him I wanted to get to know him and earn his trust. If that means revealing those sides of me, then I will.

"I like your home," I tell Jude, smiling. "It's cozy and everyone is nice." I smirk at him. "Well, almost everyone."

He makes a chuffing sound. Was that a laugh? Did big, scary Jude laugh? My heart flutters inside my chest over a stupid laugh.

But it wasn't stupid.

It was a door opening.

A door to him.

I want to open them all, dust out the cobwebs, and let him see it's okay to let someone in.

"Even if you don't have heated floors, I'll stay," I tease. "Callum doesn't have a library and he certainly doesn't eat pie each day."

"We also have ice cream," Jude says as though to convince me further. "This house may be old, but it's got the most soul. And we have Violet. That makes us the winner a thousand times over."

This time, I laugh. "You won't hear any argument from me. Let's go see what she's whipped up tonight."

As I start for the door, Jude gently presses his fingertips to my lower back as though to guide the way for me. The touch is intimate and surprising. Worse, I really like it.

I hate that I like it.

I hate that I want more.

CHAPTER TEN

Jude

GRANDPA LIKES HIM.

I'm not sure why that surprises me, but it does. Everyone likes Tate. Everyone but me, apparently.

And even that one is debatable at times. Like now. Observing him at the dining room table, partaking in a meal with Grandpa, Violet, and myself, warms my heart and eases any lingering tension between us.

Tate is…nice.

His coffee-colored eyes light up in a particularly pleasant way when he sees something exciting. My office, the gym, the library—all of it had a visceral effect on him. He may be hiding more than a need to share his kinky lifestyle, but no one is that good of a liar. His responses are genuine.

I spend dinner with my eyes glued on him, watching him laugh at Grandpa's crass jokes, fixating on how his jawbone visibly moves as he chews, and listening to every small groan of pleasure he lets escape each time he takes a bite of Violet's hearty stew.

Maybe I've been so bored for such a long damn time that anything outside the norm is completely and utterly fascinating to me.

Maybe it's just him.

I'm not one hundred percent sure what to think about

this growing obsession I have with Tate. I've never been so en-thralled by a guy before. If I think way back to my high school days—pre-fire—I can remember feeling a surge of lust when-ever a girl I liked would smile my way or touch my arm. It's kind of like that. Invigorating and all-consuming.

It's all the much stranger knowing he's a guy and has this pull on me.

At least with a female, I can reflect back to what it felt like to get hot and heavy. That first thrust inside of her and the overwhelming feeling that you'll come at any second from extreme bliss.

Pairing that memory, though, with thoughts of Tate is confusing. None of this makes any sense. When I envision myself on top like in my past, fucking, I can't see him beneath me. In fact, I still have Serra's face in mind. We slept together here and there, mostly at parties, but she's the best memory of sex I have.

If I can't imagine a sexual encounter with him, then what the hell are these feelings? It's definitely not platonic. My cock's been at half-mast ever since he stepped out of the bathroom in his towel. There's an attraction to him—one I can't begin to understand.

Not that I'll do anything about it.

Maybe the guy I once was would've been brave enough to explore what it feels like to be with another man.

I'm not that guy anymore.

He died in the fire with Mom.

This guy will be forever alone. No one wants someone they can't even kiss or see. No one wants a fucking freak.

The spoon in my hand bends in my grip. I realize I've been squeezing it. Anger and frustration war inside of me.

I can hear the others happily chatting, getting to know each other, but I'm unable to latch onto the conversation.

I'm in a silent battle of wonder of what could be if I ever opened myself up again and hatred at myself for why I'm in this position in the first place.

I can't be with anyone male or female.

I'm all alone.

"Jude?"

Snapping myself from the tornado of thoughts spinning around inside me, I glance over at Tate, who wears a worried expression. He studies me with those probing eyes of his that slice right through me and cut straight to my core.

Why does he even want to see the real me?

Why does anyone?

Don't they all know by now I have nothing left inside of me?

"What?" I grunt out.

Tate narrows his eyes. He doesn't call me out for being an asshole. However, there's a certain promise lingering there that says we'll discuss this later.

Since. Fucking. When.

Since now apparently.

I have this urge to privately explain that it's not him in this particular instance, it's me.

"Violet asked if you were feeling okay," Tate says softly. "You've barely touched dinner."

Everyone's eyes are on me. Sweat beads form behind my mask, making the ugly skin crawl. I want to rip it off and claw at my flesh. Even with a fucking mask, it's like they see more than I ever care to share.

"Sorry," I grumble, unable to look at Violet. "I'm just tired."

Violet gets up from her seat, flits over to me, and presses the back of her hand to my neck. "You're a bit clammy but not feverish. Maybe you should go lie down, hon."

Guilt swells over me and drags me under, drowning me without remorse. I have people who care about me, like Violet, and I always let them down. Just like Mom.

"I'm fine," I bark out, voice defensive and sharp. "I'll eat. Carry on, please."

Violet slowly withdraws her hand and shuffles away to take her seat again. Uncomfortable silence fills the dining room. No one speaks or clangs a spoon on their bowl. It's completely quiet.

Finally, Grandpa says, "Well, enough of your pity party, Jude. You're embarrassing me in front of my friend."

I snap my gaze up to meet my grandpa's. It shines with amusement and challenge. A snort echoes from Tate next. Then the three of them start cracking up laughing. I feel my own lips that were pressed into a hard line curl with amusement.

"You barely know Tate," I mutter. "How is he already your friend?"

"I'm old," Grandpa says jovially. "Time moves faster at my age. No time to slowly let people in. I'm a good judge of character. Tate's good people in my book. Plus, an old geezer like me can't exactly afford the luxury of wasting time to vet new people out."

Tate shrugs when I meet his gaze. His eyes glitter and his smile remains. He's enjoying the banter and conversation. This, in turn, has me relaxing more.

I finally lift my mask just enough to reveal my mouth and continue eating my stew, which seems to be the catalyst for getting the three of them to hop back into their easy chatter. Thankfully, no one watches me while I eat or stares at the small part of my exposed face. When we finally finish, Violet whisks the three of us out of the dining room, refusing to let us clean up, and says she'll bring our dessert to the library in a bit.

Grandpa stops at his room for his home health nurse to assist him with a bathroom break and to give him his meds, which leaves me and Tate in the library. Alone.

Tate walks over to one of the bookshelves and takes a book from its place. He flips through it briefly, nods, and then makes his way back over to me.

"This is the book we talked about." He lifts his chin, eyes boring into mine. "Is there a reason why you pretend rather than actually reading?"

"I'm not dyslexic or anything."

"And if you were? Who cares? Why do you pretend?"

I shake my head in frustration. He's too intuitive. Latches onto the smallest of words to pick them apart.

"If I want to read, I'll do it before bed in the comfort of my own room," I say to him with a huff. "Spending time with Grandpa feels like a dwindling gift. I'd rather just watch him."

Put that way, I sound like a stalker creep.

Tate pats my chest and then hands me the book. "You're not always terrifying, are you?"

I take the book, my hand brushing over his, and relish in the zinging jolts that rush through my body. He doesn't appear to be as affected as I am because he turns and walks away. My muscles are frozen stiff. Hell, they're not the only thing that's stiff…

Tate settles on the sofa by a lamp, dragging a blanket over his lap. He then starts reading his book while I continue to stare it him, wishing for my dick to calm the fuck down.

After a few minutes, I snap out of it and take a seat in an armchair near the windows where I can observe him without being so obvious. Not long after, Grandpa arrives, his telltale whining wheelchair announcing his arrival. Violet comes in behind him with a tray filled with dessert and coffee mugs.

Grandpa maneuvers his wheelchair to his spot near the end table lamp on the other side of where Tate sits. This pleases me because I can look over the top of my book and watch them both.

"I made Wyatt's favorite," Violet says as she sets down the tray to begin passing out the dessert. "Blackberry cobbler a la mode."

Tate's eyes widen and he shoots me a small, private smile. Ice cream. I told him this house was the best. Pride, over something as stupid as ice cream, surges through me. Who needs heated floors?

I also want to know why it's so damn important to me for him to like my house better. This isn't supposed to be a vacation or a reward. It's so I can watch over him.

Well, I've got the watching over him part covered.

A little too well if I'm being honest.

Violet sets everyone up with their dessert and coffee before leaving. I don't miss the lightness in her step and the perpetual smile. It's evident she loves having another person to dote on. This too pleases me.

Fuck.

I'm not supposed to be getting this much pleasure out of having the enemy in my camp.

He's not the enemy, idiot, and deep down you know that.

The library is quiet, devoid of conversation, and only the clanging of spoons on glass bowls can be heard. After we finish, the quiet becomes comfortable as everyone settles into their books.

Though this book does sound intriguing, and I will read it later in my room, I'm not wasting a second to observe Tate and Grandpa. Grandpa is content to read and sip his coffee, a peacefulness emanating from him that I've always been envious of.

Tate isn't peaceful. He's tense and engrossed in his novel already. With each flip of the pages, he frowns harder, worry lines forming between his eyebrows. I'm sort of impressed with the speed at which he reads. It's as if he's devouring the book like he did his cobbler. Bite after delicious bite, he's a glutton for the story. I feel like him, except *he's* my book. I'm turning each of his pages faster and faster, hoping to learn every single bit about him sooner rather than later.

Time passes, but I'm not sure I even blink. Soon, I notice Tate yawning quite a bit and Grandpa's head is lulled to the side as he's already nodded off. I'm disappointed as I realize our night has come to an end.

I tuck the book into the pocket of my hoodie and then rise, stretching my arms above my head. Tate glances my way and his eyes drag down my front, settling on my exposed stomach. He bites on his bottom lip and quickly looks down at his book.

Like what you see, little boy?

The thought dissipates as quickly as it forms. I can't go there. Ever.

"Grandpa," I grunt. "Time for bed."

Grandpa sits up, droopy eyes hazed over as he looks around. "I suppose it is. Night, kids."

We follow after him. Tate introduces himself to Mary, the home health nurse, when we make it to Grandpa's room, and then we both head upstairs. His cat has already made it back to his room, not at all having gotten lost, and lazily watches us from the bed.

"Tonight was…" Tate trails off, shrugging. "I enjoyed spending time with you and your family."

I fist my hands, wishing I could reach out and touch him, or even return the sentiment of enjoying his company too. All I can manage is a feral, caveman grunt.

"Night, Jude."

He softly shuts the door in my face.

Why, after all these years, do I suddenly feel selfish and want something for myself?

It's dangerous and can't happen.

With a sad sigh, I turn and leave the man who is quickly turning my already fragmented, blackened mind into a kaleidoscope of shattered, colorful thoughts—all of which involve him.

CHAPTER ELEVEN

Tate

Last night was…amazing. Quite frankly, I'm shocked. Yesterday, when I got sent to my "prison," I'd expected to be miserable. At first, I was a bit intimidated. But as the hours went by and I got to meet both Wyatt and Violet, I realized it wasn't so scary after all.

The best part of it all?

Jude.

Getting to see a softer, gentler side of him was nice. It gives me hope for him after all. He's hurting inside, that much is clear, but he loves his family fiercely. That's something I can work with. Maybe just maybe I can help the big oaf so he's not so miserable all the time.

Plus, Violet is a fantastic cook.

And there's a library.

It really is a pretty sweet setup. Minus the non-heated bathroom floors.

Funky meows by my bedroom door, asking to be let out. Over dinner last night, when Jude was spacing out, Violet told me Willa stopped by to drop off Funky's food and water bowls.

"Miss Violet probably added some extra stew meat to your bowl this morning," I say to my cat. "Don't get spoiled, mister."

He stares at me, swishing his tail. Clearly, he's not going to listen.

I open the door and he darts out. I follow him into the kitchen, where Violet has already prepared his breakfast. No stew. Just bacon. Damn cat is going to hate his life whenever we move back out on our own. Back to generic brand cat food for him then.

"Oh, Tate, sweetheart. The grocery delivery person said they're on their way. When they get here, can you bring in the groceries for me? I'll have a breakfast sandwich ready and waiting for you."

Maybe Funky's not the only one who might get spoiled around here.

I give her a quick hug of thanks and can feel my heart swelling when she lingers in holding me, and then bound off to wait for the groceries.

The house is quiet aside from Violet now talking to Funky as she cooks breakfast. I slip out the front door to wait on the porch. As soon as I see my car, I freeze. Panic swells up inside me.

Why is my car here?

It's supposed to be in Callum's garage!

Did Sean steal it to make a statement that he knows where I am?

I can feel my lungs collapsing as all the air leaves them. Dark spots dot my vision. I'm going to pass out. And then what? Wait for Sean to drag me away?

Bile creeps up my throat. I stumble down the rickety porch toward my car. The tires still remain intact and there are no gouges in the paint.

It's a simple message then.

He knows where I am.

How did he get my keys? Did he make a copy one of those times he was with me? God, how could I be so stupid in thinking I was safe?

I stop beside the driver's side door, searching the front seat through the glass for some kind of note, when I hear a door slam.

"Where do you think you're going?" a deep voice growls, low and menacing.

A full-bodied shudder ripples through me. *Run, you dummy!* With tears forming in my eyes, I turn on my heel, feeling very much like a rabbit with a wolf on my tail. I don't make it three feet before a strong hand with a steely grip clamps around my bicep, jerking me to a stop.

I yelp, twisting around to face my attacker.

Mask. Familiar. Jude.

All fight leaves me as relief floods in. He'll protect me. Jude's protective by nature. Even though he doesn't like me yet, I still believe he would stop Sean from hurting me.

"Jude," I croak out in a ragged tremble. "Thank—"

"Running away already?" Jude demands, body vibrating with anger.

What?

"I thought I made it clear the library was your new office. Where you'd take your meetings from here on out," Jude bites out. "And the car was a test. You failed."

Fear. Relief. Confusion.

My emotions are run through the gamut, settling on anger.

"Excuse me?" I say, seething.

"You heard me." Jude releases me like my skin is on fire.

He takes a step back before crossing his muscular arms over his chest. "Explain yourself."

Indignation detonates a bomb inside me. I'm no longer afraid or relieved. I want to punch this big idiot in his Michael Myers face!

"Unbelievable."

"My thoughts exactly," he says dryly. "I knew this was all a game."

Unable to hold back, I take a step toward him, poking him in his rock-hard chest. "You, Jude, are out of line right now."

He makes a chuffing sound of disbelief. "That makes two of us."

"No. It makes one of us. You. I came out here to fetch groceries for Violet. When I saw my car had been moved, it freaked me out considering I have the keys in my bedroom!" My voice turns shrill and I can feel the hysteria clogging my throat. "Excuse me if I was having a moment of panic!"

He doesn't move or say anything. Probably because he knows he's being an idiot.

"I guess I'm just a captive here, huh?" I demand. "Is that what this is? And here I thought an actual human lived underneath that mask!"

I'm being mean and completely unprofessional, but he's pushed me over the edge.

"Captive?" Jude snorts. "With the money my father pays you, you're hardly a captive, Tate. You're a scammer."

A scammer?

"I'm not a scammer," I huff.

"And you're not a captive," he throws back.

"Well, you're still a dick," I growl. "You bring in the

groceries. I need a minute to breathe before I have my first meeting this morning."

He steps aside but doesn't apologize for overreacting. *Not that it's his place to micromanage me anyway.* I know this job is worth a bunch of money, but is it worth losing my own sanity over?

I'm attracted to Jude, yes.

But he also slightly terrifies me and really pisses me off.

I wasn't lying when I told Dempsey I fall for toxic men. I'm seeing similar patterns with how hard I fell into Sean's overbearing grip.

That won't happen again.

It can't.

I refuse to let it.

Battling my warring emotions, I storm inside, ignoring the taunting scent of bacon. I stomp up the stairs like a child to grab my notebook, where I'd written everyone's meetings for the week. By the time I get back downstairs, Jude is carrying in the groceries. I refuse to help him and escape to the library. On the table beside where I sat last night is a steaming mug of coffee and a hot breakfast sandwich. At least Violet is a ray of sunshine in this shit-smeared hellscape I've found myself in.

I wolf down my sandwich, trying and failing to not think about Jude's lack of trust in me. It hurts that he thinks I'm some vile homewrecker. I've always wanted to repair homes, not wreck them. My own home was the worst kind of wreck. For my actions to not seem genuine makes me question my line of work.

What else would I be doing besides helping people through their traumas?

I could work at the animal shelter again. Though that

makes my heart squeeze at the thought of seeing all those sad animals that need rehoming. I know it's not the right place for me. I'm doing the work I've been called to do. This work helps people. It helps me.

Screw Jude.

Screw Sean and Dad and every other asshole who makes me question what kind of man I am.

I'm a good person who just wants to feel safe and loved. That's not a big ask.

After I finish breakfast, I thumb through my notebook and then settle on today's schedule. Willa is first. She had me pencil her in for today while we were out for her appointment. At least with Willa, I can breathe. I love her quiet disposition and the kindness she exudes. I'm looking forward to letting my guard down with her.

Violet slips in to grab my plate and refresh my coffee. Her eyebrows are furrowed as she studies me. Then, in a surprise move, she leans forward and kisses the top of my head.

"You're doing great, sweetie."

I have to bite down on my bottom lip to keep from tearing up. Thankfully, she shuffles out of the room without saying more or seeing the unmasked emotion on my face. Had Mom lived until now, would she have been that way? Offering affection and words of encouragement at every turn?

Pain claws at my heart, but I don't have the time to bathe in the sticky blood of it. I need to get my head screwed back on so I can help these people. Once they're helped and I collect some decent pay for it, I'm out of here. I'll start fresh somewhere far away from Washington.

Heavy footsteps thud down the hall toward the library. I brace myself for another altercation with Jude. This is how it was with Sean. Always waiting for his anger, his accusations, his distrust, and ultimately his physical abuse.

I hate that I fall into these same patterns over and over again, escaping one monster, only to fall into the arms of another.

The scent of expensive masculine cologne precedes my visitor. Instead of Willa or Jude, Callum strides into the room wearing a crisp, well-fitting three-piece suit. His dark hair is tousled and styled to perfection and his piercing blue eyes are fiery with determination.

Crap.

"Oh, hey," I say, choosing to greet him with the calm, casual vibe we had going before I was ripped out of his home. "Where's Willa?"

Callum's nostrils flare and he tears his gaze from me, choosing to look out the window. "Not feeling well. She asked me to take her appointment."

The ticking muscle in his jaw tells me he's not thrilled about this. The therapist in me, however, is a bit eager to get the broody ex-teacher talking. He has beef with his dad and Jamie, but aside from what others have told me, I don't know the whole story.

"Have a seat," I say, settling into professional mode. "I don't bite, Callum."

He smirks and finally looks at me again. "*Right.*"

Callum takes a seat and rests one of his leather shoes on one knee as he leans back in the chair across from me. He's a picture of ease and relaxation. His eyes, though, spark with warning and agitation.

"May as well address the elephant in the room," I tell him

with a small shrug. "You despise your father for stealing your girl nearly twenty years ago."

His lip curls up. "And if I'd rather talk about anything else?"

"We can, but you and I both know Willa didn't play sick in order to force you into that chair." I lift a brow in question. "She's a sweet girl and worries about you."

He relaxes his shoulders and a small, genuine smile peeks out. "I love her."

"Who doesn't? She's a gentle soul."

I wait for him to pick off nonexistent lint from his pant leg, choosing not to speak. He knows what we're here to talk about and clearly needs to work up the nerve.

"He betrayed me," he says, voice sharp like a blade. "The person I trusted most and fucking adored betrayed me."

My heart tightens at his confession. I understand feeling betrayed by your father.

"And Jamie?" He scoffs, shaking his head. "I loved her. I wanted to marry her."

Instead, she slept with his dad, got pregnant, and ended up marrying him.

"Were there problems with you and Jamie or did it come out of the blue?"

"Did I know they were fucking?" he snaps. "No."

These Parks are so damn exasperating sometimes.

"You know what I mean," I say patiently. "Was she behaving strangely?"

He grows quiet for a moment, features darkening as he remembers the past. Then he darts his eyes my way, confusion swimming in them. "I don't know. I was busy with basketball and college admittance applications. We never fought."

"What was she doing while you were so busy all the time?"

"Hell if I know." He shrugs his shoulders, glaring at me like a petulant child. Then the facade melts away and guilt flashes in his eyes. "Her family were assholes to her. In high school, I beat her brother's ass quite a few times for laying hands on her at home."

Now we're getting somewhere…

"Did her mom and dad not protect her from him? Why did this land on your shoulders?"

"Her stepdad was a fucking pervert," Callum growls. "Her mom was always too high to notice or care."

"So she spent a lot of time at your house because it was safe?"

He nods, sadness seeping into his expression. "My house was more like hers than anywhere. She spent the night a lot. Everyone knew she had a fucked-up home life, so no one gave two shits that she stayed with us most of the time."

"How did your dad feel about what was happening to her?"

"Typical Dad, I guess. Wanted to ruin her stepdad in some way. He'd get on one of his rants anytime she'd show up crying about how he was going to destroy them all."

"So he cared and worried over her a lot then, huh?"

He shrugs, not meeting my stare, so I continue.

"When did you notice them getting closer?"

His jaw tightens visibly, and then he sweeps his hand across his face, as if attempting to erase the raw emotions etched there. Unfortunately, he can't. The pain, confusion, and fury are painted clearly and in shades of red and purple.

"It was a lot," he admits. "Trying to get through high

school, prep for college, and also protect your girlfriend from her own family. Dad was just better at it."

"Better how?"

"Hugged her when she needed it. Cheered her up and showed her attention."

"Did she start pulling away from you?"

"If you mean, did we stop sleeping together? Yes." He trembles with anger. "She was closed off and I figured it had something to do with her stepfather. I didn't want to pressure her."

"Did you try asking her if her behavior was because of her stepdad?"

For a brief moment, his hardened face transforms into something more boyish and youthful. I can almost see the teenaged version of Callum sitting before me, trying to figure out his overly complicated relationship that he clearly had no idea how to navigate.

"I just said I didn't want to pressure her."

"Into sex, yes. Got that. What about conversation? Opening up to another person is different."

"That's what she had Dad for," he says with half a shrug. "He was better at having those conversations with her."

I lean forward, pinning him with a questioning stare. "Do you really think they maliciously started sleeping together in an effort to hurt you?"

"They did!" he roars, flinging his arms in the air. "That's exactly what they did!"

"Consider this scenario," I say gently. "Jamie was scared. At your house, she felt safe, cared for, and loved. She had a confidant in your father and someone who viciously wanted to protect her. But she also had a loving boyfriend who was an appropriate match for her. Falling for your father would have been forbidden and wrong. It would have jeopardized everything for her and landed her back on her ass at her house with those horrible people."

I continue with a sigh, "You were a good boyfriend until you weren't."

He glowers at me.

"I'm just saying that when the going got tough, you used life as an excuse to avoid her and her problems. Am I right?"

A one-shouldered shrug is all I get.

"It was easier to let your dad comfort her and deal with the hard stuff. And, in the end, you weren't even interested in pursuing an intimate relationship with her."

"But she cheated on me," he croaks, voice soft and broken. "With my dad."

"Which is terrible, Callum. It's a horrible betrayal. I'm not saying what they did wasn't wrong. I'm just saying things aren't so cut and dry. How did you find out?"

Disgust tugs his lips down into a cruel curve. "I had a feeling something strange was going on, so I stayed up one night to listen."

"I bet what you discovered was heartbreaking."

He closes his eyes and grits his teeth. "She was in her bed in the guest room." He pauses and then lets a rush of breath escape. "But so was Dad. They were…"

"Having sex."

He nods. "It blew up after that."

"How?"

"I told them they were both dead to me, slammed the door shut on them, and spent the night at Grandpa's house." He scowls. "Mom heard all my screaming, I guess, or Dad just decided to confess to her because after that night, he moved out with Jamie and filed for divorce."

"I bet that was stressful for you knowing his marriage was breaking apart too."

"I mean, it was dead already," Callum says with a grunt. "Getting caught with my girlfriend just made it official. Jamie and Dad were staying together no matter what anyone around them thought. They apologized about how it came to be but not for the love between them."

"And you've had to live with their choices ever since."

"I have. Worse is she ended up pregnant. For a moment, I'd hoped it was with my baby. But the math didn't add up. I knew we hadn't had sex in a while. She was having Dad's baby. Dempsey and Gemma are a daily reminder of that shit."

I let silence fill the air as we both digest what all we've discussed. Finally, I speak up. "Do you think you and Jamie would have truly made it past high school?"

His gaze settles on mine, and he gives me a small shake of his head. "Honestly, no. College was…"

"Your escape," I finish for him. "You had no plans on taking her and her problems along with you."

He frowns and studies his shoe for a beat. "I guess that makes me the bad guy then, huh?"

"No," I say softly. "It makes you human. Besides, look what that shitty turn of events led to."

A wide grin spreads over his face. "Willa is the love of my life, Tate. We're having a baby and I…I can't imagine my life any other way. I'm happy now. For the first time, I'm fucking happy."

Callum's shoulders relax. The anger is gone and I can feel his gratitude for Willa shining through. I think I just had a breakthrough with a Park. Wrong Park, but it feels victorious nonetheless.

"You don't have to forgive them," I tell him. "I know it hurts still. But I think working on your anger from the situation while appreciating your current relationship will help you feel a lot better. Carrying all that has to be heavy. It's been a long time."

He nods and then smirks. "I can see why Dad picked you. You're pretty damn good at your job." Then his smile turns evil. "I can't wait to see you unravel my brother."

If only it were as simple as a direct conversation in the library.

If only.

CHAPTER TWELVE

Jude

'M AN ASSHOLE.

I already knew this, but after this morning, I'm surer than ever.

He's a grown-ass man. He can get in his car, drive wherever he wants, and do anything he pleases. So why did I panic when I actually thought he was doing just that?

Because you like him.

You secretly enjoyed your day with him yesterday.

Tate was certainly pissed at my behavior. But before all that anger and vitriol he spewed at me, his eyes shone with abject terror.

Why?

What scares him so terribly that he'd have such a panicked expression and would be ready to bolt? I'd snagged him before he got far and he seemed…relieved to see me.

What are you hiding, Tate?

Who did this to you?

Ever since he left in a fury, I've been mulling over both of our actions. Violet gave me the stink eye, which had me holing up in my office like a coward to avoid her. Even my damn cook knows I'm an asshole.

Guilt has long taken over my curiosity about his behavior.

Now I just want to look him in the eye and apologize. I was out of line and I know it.

Rather than stalking the internet for more clues about Tate, I sit in my chair by the window, watching over our property. Callum eventually leaves my house. He's not storming off but eagerly striding back home.

Tate has a positive effect on this family.

And I'm doing my best to blow it.

Before I can make the decision to seek out Tate, my phone buzzes. I don't recognize the number, but it's local, so I answer it.

"This is Jude," I grunt out in greeting.

A deep, vaguely familiar chuckle greets me on the other end of the line. Though it's older and gruffer, the playful cadence is one I'll never forget.

"Fuckin' Baker," I say before he can speak. "How'd you get my number?"

"Still the same dick from high school, I see," he throws back. "How the hell are you, man?"

"Dandy," I deadpan. "How'd you get my number?"

"Your dad. Saw him in town the other day. Said you might like to reconnect."

Of course. Dad is always meddling, trying to bring me out of the shadow realm and into the human one.

"Nah."

He snorts out another laugh. "Too bad, asswipe. We're reconnecting whether you like it or not."

Chatting with my old buddy is better than facing Tate and acknowledging what a douchebag I was earlier. I suppose I can catch up for a few minutes.

"What are you up to these days?" I ask reluctantly. "Coaching high school ball?"

"Nope," he says, voice growing serious. "After everything that happened to you and, you know…" He trails off. The unspoken words are *your mom* and they make my heart clench painfully. "Well, I thought I'd become a firefighter."

"Really?"

"Hell yeah. Did a little college right after high school and then dropped it. Been a fixture at the PMFD ever since. Just made captain this year, too."

"Congratulations," I say, voice tight.

Dad is usually so forthcoming with all the town news, always trying to pull me out of my cave to reconnect with society. I'm surprised he didn't already reveal this nugget of information to me.

"Lynn, my wife now, is a nurse. We have another baby on the way. It'll make it girl number four." He chuckles again, reminding me of sleepovers when we were school-aged boys. "You remember Lynn?"

"Not ringing any bells."

"Man, you're still a prick. Serra's best friend. You know, the chick you fucked all the time. I'm still surprised you two didn't end up together."

Serra did try to reach out after the fire and what happened to my mother. All my friends did, including Baker. I just ignored everyone. Jude Park, fun-loving, football-playing, life-of-the-party guy died. They didn't know the monster who rose from the ashes, nor did I want to introduce them.

"What are you up to these days?"

Hiding away in my dark-ass house, angry at myself and the world. Alone. Empty. Lost.

"Work."

"Okayyyy," he says with less humor. "You weren't always so vague. Everything okay?"

No.

Nothing is okay.

My mind is a clusterfuck of confusing emotions with Tate right in the center stirring the pot.

"It's fine."

He sighs heavily, frustration seeping into his tone. This is exactly why I didn't keep in contact. I let people down. Every day I let my own family down. But they're blood and have to deal with me. Everyone else got a free pass to not see my surly ass.

"We should meet up for a couple of beers. Maybe watch a game on TV or something. It'll be like old times. Except now I have a full beard and have to be home by eight at night when I'm not at the station to tuck the girls into bed." He chuckles, voice breathy and filled with pride. "Fatherhood. It's fuckin' great, Jude."

Despite the familiar voice and laugh that has me feeling the least bit nostalgic, I have nothing in common with Baker anymore. He's married, enjoying being a father to a mess of girls, and is actually on a career path he enjoys. I have nothing to contribute to the conversation, much less the sad attempt to resurrect an old friendship.

"Listen," I start, but he interrupts.

"You still live in that old dump with your mean-ass gramps or did he kick the bucket? Remember that time he caught us in the woods when we were cutting down trees to make a fort?"

We were like ten and were attempting to take down a

hundred-year-old oak with a chainsaw. Grandpa whipped both our asses that day.

"He's still here. Same with everyone else. It was good talking—"

"I heard through one of the guys at the station Callum got fired at the high school. It's not been confirmed, but people say he's been fucking a teenager."

My hackles rise. Baker was always a gossip, but I draw the line at my family.

"She's legal. I've got to go, man. Talk to you later."

More like never.

He doesn't get another word in before I hang up.

Sometimes I long for the life that could have been. Serra was really cool and I could have settled down with her one day. Maybe. I could have had friends and a different career path. I could have actually gone to the goddamn grocery store without shame.

But that life was taken from me.

Wallowing in what could have been is a waste of energy. I'd rather do what little I can to improve the one I've got. Which, right now, that means making things right with Tate.

I abandon the chair by the window and head out of my office. Tate's cat darts across the hall from an empty room into the cracked door of Tate's room. I peek inside but don't see the man in question anywhere.

I slink down the hallway and take the stairs two at a time, nearly crashing into Grandpa's wheelchair at the bottom. I swear, that man flies out of nowhere sometimes. He's old, but he's not deaf. Any time I get on the phone, which is rare, he's always lurking and eavesdropping.

"Tate's in the library," Grandpa says knowingly, eyes

narrowed. "I figured you'd want to smooth things over with him."

My muscles tighten at his words. "Violet is a tattletale."

"That's why I pay her the big bucks." He grins at me. "Go on now. You're wasting daylight. The kid's been sighing every three minutes. Make it right."

I give my grandpa a nod and then stride down the hall-way, seeking Tate out in the library. When I reach the warm, inviting space, I find him standing by the window, hands on his hips as he stares out. Seconds pass by and he doesn't sense my presence. He sighs heavily—pouty, sad, frustrated. It makes me want to put my arms on his shoulders and squeeze them to assure him everything will be all right.

As if he'd want my monstrous hands on him.

Ignoring the self-loathing, which would make a perfect excuse to back out of this, I stride over to him. As soon as I see my masked reflection in the window, his entire body tenses.

Another sigh.

This one is full of irritation.

"Tate..."

"Jude." Clipped, pissy, challenging. "What can I help you with?"

I can tell my efforts to be friendly will be met with this attitude, so I panic at the last second and try a different tactic.

"You have time for a session?" I ask, voice gravelly. "To talk."

He turns around, eyebrows pinched as he studies me for sincerity. I'm glad he can't see the awkward way my mouth twitches or the way my jaw clenches.

"I do," he says slowly. "I won't see Dempsey until he gets out of school. What's up?"

I'm sorry.

I'm a fucking prick.

Despite your secrets and the way you've embedded yourself under the Park skin like a splinter, being around you captivates me.

"Uh, I had a call from an old friend. Threw me off."

His eyes widen, surprise glimmering in them. I'd meant to say a whole lot of other things, but the safe, easy way came out, which is really saying something, considering I'd rather not talk about my past at all.

"When was the last time you talked to your friend?"

"High school," I admit. "Around the time of the…"

"Fire," he supplies, meeting my stare. "When you were withdrawing from everyone?"

Fuck.

He's just going to dive right into the shit show that's my mind.

Just apologize and change the subject, man.

"Yeah, uh, then."

"And?"

"And, I don't know," I spit out in exasperation, throwing my hands in the air. "It was fucking awkward."

"Awkward how?"

Bitterness rears its ugly head and I blurt out the truth, immediately wishing I could reel it back in the second it's out. "I got a glimpse at what my life could be and it sucked."

His features soften and he takes a step toward me. "Oh, Jude. That's heartbreaking."

I don't want his pity.

"He's got a wife and kids," I grumble, unable to stop the waterfall of confessions. "If I'd stayed with Serra, that might've been me too."

"Do you want kids?"

"No," I snap, anger swelling like a tidal wave. "I mean, not anymore."

He starts to reach for my hand but pulls back at the last second. My own palm twitches with need for him to physically comfort me. I don't deserve it because I've been a rabid animal toward him, but I crave it more than my next breath.

Just grab his hand.

Apologize.

Show him you can be human too.

"He wants to reconnect," I rasp out, choosing my scapegoat once more. "To actually hang out and grab a beer." I gesture at my mask. "Imagine having to explain this shit after nearly two decades. I'm a fucking freak."

Tate's features scrunch at my words as if I've hurt him with them, which is impossible. Those words were aimed at me. I'm the freak, not him.

Well, maybe he's a freak in the sheets according to that video, but that's beside the matter right now.

"You're not a freak," he says firmly. "A grumpy jerk sometimes? Absolutely. A freak? Nope. You can stop thinking of yourself that way right now."

"You think I'm a grumpy jerk?" For some reason, this has my lips curling into a pleased smile. "You're supposed to be the professional here, not admit that shit to your client."

He shrugs, smirking at me. "I just call it like I see it."

Before I can talk myself out of it, I grab onto his hand. It's smaller than mine but fits nicely. He's warm and soft compared to my clammy and scarred. His eyebrow lifts in question.

"I, uh, want to say something to you," I mumble, shifting on my feet. "About this morning."

"Okay." He purses his lips. "I'm listening."

"Not here," I say with a huff. "Let me show you something first."

If he's disappointed by my stalling tactics, he doesn't let on. He squeezes my hand and gives me a nod of encouragement that does wonders to soothe my brittle, aching soul.

"I can't wait to see, Jude." His words feel deeper and laced with more meaning than what's spoken.

See what?

Me?

That can't ever happen.

CHAPTER THIRTEEN

Tate

H E'S TALKING.

He's actually freaking talking.

I'm so mesmerized by this sudden change in him, I nearly forgive him on the spot for this morning. After all, his hand holding mine feels good. Really good. My skin tingles where we touch and I wonder what else would tingle under his ministrations.

Focus, Tate.

Stop thinking with your dick.

I can feel my cock thicken a bit as my thoughts go straight to filthy, wondering what his hand could do to said dick.

Probably a lot.

But that's just me falling into the same old patterns again. Sean was able to pleasure me until it twisted into something cruel and torturous. I fell so easy for his few sweet moments. I can't do this again. I won't.

Hardening my heart, while forcing my dick to soften, I attempt to pull my hand from Jude's to gain my bearings. He simply tightens his hold, refusing to let me go. I can't ignore the way my heart does a little flip.

He tugs me behind him and then leads me out of the library. We pass Wyatt, who lurks nearby like he's been listening in on our conversation. Heat floods my cheeks. I give him an awkward wave and he simply winks at me.

Jude, undeterred by his grandpa seeing him holding another man's hand, continues to stride forward with purpose, towing me along. We pass by the dining room and my stomach grumbles when I catch a whiff of whatever garlicky treat Violet is preparing for lunch. Jude practically drags me up the stairs as I scramble to keep up with his long legs.

At the top of the landing, he pauses and glances over his shoulder. His eyes are electric behind his mask. I'm more curious than ever before about the man who hides beneath.

"It's this way," he says, turning and striding away once more. "Through my office."

He pauses to pull open a desk drawer and then retrieves a bona fide skeleton key. A shiver of anticipation quivers down my spine.

"Not your captive?" I say jokingly. "Right."

He chuffs—a possible laugh from the big guy—and then proceeds to open the closet door in his office all the while keeping his vise-like grip on my hand.

The door swings open. I wait for bats to fly out or dead bodies to thump to the floor. Nothing so sinister awaits. Actually, all that awaits is another set of stairs.

"The attic?"

Rather than answer, he starts his trek up the steep stairs. We reach another landing with a long hallway resembling the floor we were just on. It's kind of creepy to me they have a whole other floor just locked away.

"At the other end is another set of stairs that go all the way down to the kitchen," Jude reveals without looking my way. "It stays locked, though. I'm the only one with the key."

I'm not sure why, but that statement has the hairs on my arms standing on end. Paranoia creeps in. Maybe this is all some great plan to get me alone so he can lock me away forever.

Why, though?

My nosy cat darts past us, having followed us here, and meows in annoyance. This settles my nerves a bit. If I'm going to be trapped, at least Funky will be here to entertain me.

We stop in front of an opening that leads to another dark pocket of this haunted-looking decrepit mansion. Jude pauses before we enter, standing before me, his massive frame towering over mine. There's a window up here at least. I can climb out if he really does lock me up.

"What is this place?" I murmur. "Or, better yet, what is this place to you?"

His head cocks to the side in the eerie way of his that makes me think I'm in a psychological thriller, further sending my nerves buzzing with fight-or-flight energy.

He finally releases my hand. Tension roils off him in waves. I'm rooted in place, waiting for answers to questions I may never get.

Finally, he sighs. "This is where I spent the first few years. After…"

"After your mom died?" I encourage.

He winces and gives me a clipped nod. "It's so isolated and quiet up here. I needed the space and solitude to survive. It was touch and go for a bit."

"Touch and go how?"

"I hardly ate. Was depressed as fuck. Woke up every day wanting to slash my goddamn wrists open and die. It was more than an ideation. I tried a time or two but was too fuck-ing cowardly to finish the job."

His angrily spat out words feel like acid on my heart. Knowing he was hurting so much he attempted suicide wounds deep. He was devastated and his soul ached. The pain he felt must've been overwhelming and immense.

I need to see him.

All of him.

To tell him he's worthy of happiness and love.

That he has a family who cares about him deeply.

I want to do this while touching his cheeks and looking at his lips.

He tenses when I reach up. My hand visibly trembles. I touch the edge of his mask, earning me a hitch of his breath. As my finger slips beneath it, his scruff tickling my flesh, he grabs onto my forearm to stop me.

"Don't." His word is croaked out. Not demanding and fierce. It's a plea, desperate and raw. "Please."

I ache to rip it away and see him—all of him—ugly scars and everything.

My curiosity can wait, though. He's letting me in, despite this morning's tantrum, and I'm not going to jeopardize that.

Funky meows at my feet, having explored enough, and I reluctantly drop my hand. Breaking our stare, I squat to pick up my cat. Jude clears his throat and then walks into the open-ing that leads to a small room. It's cozy with an extremely dated sectional couch with patched and repaired fabric, an old TV from the '80s or '90s, and a record player sitting on top of the TV. There are dusty, built-in shelves in the room lined with old records. The one and only window is small, round, and made of stained glass.

"What is this place?"

"Used to be Grandpa's man cave," Jude says, making his way over to a shelf to peruse the records. "Sit."

I carry Funky over to the sectional and sit on one end. He rubs his head against my neck, his purring the only sound in the room. Jude takes his time before settling on a record. He plucks it from its spot, pulls it from the sleeve, and then places it on the record player. Seconds later, the sound of classic rock plays softly.

"The Doors?"

Jude nods and sets the empty record sleeve down. Then he cautiously makes his way over to me and Funky. He sits down awfully close to me, which has my heart sputtering with awareness.

His scent—manly and intense in this small space.

His nearness, tangible and real.

His touch as he also pets Funky, our fingers brushing against one another.

"It's quiet up here," I tell him, searching his gaze. "A good place to hide out."

"I still come up here often," he admits. "It's peaceful."

"Thank you for showing me your secret place."

Another chuff behind the mask. "Tate Prince, are you flirting with me?"

His playful words stun me stupid. I gape at him, unable to respond.

"Who is this guy and what did you do with my grumpy jerk?"

The teasing glint in his eyes fades and his eyes close. "I was more than a jerk this morning. I was a complete asshole."

"You really were," I mutter, voice raw with honesty. "It wasn't my favorite part of today."

"What was your favorite?" he quickly tosses back. "Seeing Callum?"

I snort out a laugh. "Why? Jealous?"

For fuck's sake. I *am* flirting with him.

Brakes, Tate. Pump the brakes!

"Nah," Jude says with a shrug. "But you can't get out of the question."

Staring down at Funky, I wonder how to explain that *right now* is my favorite part. "I was happy to talk with Callum. I think we made great progress."

His intense stare burns into me, but I refuse to look at him. "Hmph."

I decide to steer the conversation back to this morning. "I'm not here to hurt, Jude. I'm here to help. I thought after yesterday maybe you could see that."

He stiffens and I can't help but finally look at him. Statue-still with his creepy mask, he reminds me of a wax figure in a horror museum. "I could. I mean, I think I'm beginning to understand," he admits, voice rough and gritty. "I just panicked."

This piques my curiosity. "You panicked? Why?"

"I didn't want you to leave…" He trails off and I supply the word he doesn't say. *Me.* I didn't want you to leave *me.*

"Why?" I probe. "Two days ago, you wanted to get rid of me."

He sighs heavily and then meets my eyes. "I, uh, like having you here."

A small grin tugs at my lips despite all the warning bells ringing inside me. Yes, a lot of money is on the line for me making strides with Jude, but it's more than that for me.

Getting to see beneath his mysterious, shrouded exterior feels like a gift.

I open my mouth to encourage him to say more, but then Violet's voice echoes from nearby.

"Sorry to interrupt," she says, slowly entering the room where The Doors croons in the background and my heart does happy, anxious little flips.

Jude jumps to his feet. "What is it?"

She smiles at him and then looks at me. "Aubrey, Hugo, Spencer, and the baby are here. Aubrey asked if she could speak with you for a moment before having a family meeting with all of them."

I shoot Jude an apologetic look. "Talk later?"

He gives me a curt nod.

It's a promise and one I'm going to hold him to.

Aubrey paces the library, wringing her hands in front of her, a worried frown marring her pretty face. She's beautiful and it's no wonder Hugo and Spencer are crazy about her. Seeing her so upset, though, makes my heart hurt for her.

"What's bothering you?" I ask again, voice calm and re-assuring. "Just get it off your chest."

She halts to a stop, bites down on her trembling lip, and gingerly touches her stomach. "I have to tell them about the pregnancy. I'm just…afraid."

I study her, searching for clues and finding none. "Of what?"

"Of everything," she whispers, eyes welling with tears. "For one, I don't even know whose baby it is."

Nodding with understanding, I rise from the sofa and take a step toward her. "Do you care?"

She lets out a sad laugh. "No. I mean, I feel like it'll be loved no matter what. It feels like our baby. Not just Spencer's or Hugo's."

"Are you afraid of their reactions?"

"No," she says quickly. "They'll be happy, I'm sure."

"What is it then? Afraid you're too young to be a mother?"

Again, she shakes her head. "If Willa can be a mom at eighteen, so can I."

"Maybe your fears are something that can be smoothed over by talking to your two men," I say gently. "I think, deep down, you know that since you brought everyone together for this meeting."

Relief shines in her big, glistening eyes. "I think you're right."

"Let's stop torturing them and bring them in here, okay?"

She nods and then continues to nibble on her bottom lip. With her blessing, I walk over to the library door and open it. Hugo takes a step forward, anxiety rippling from him. Spencer lurks behind him, cuddling Rex to his chest, wearing a vicious scowl.

They're both worried.

Whatever she's afraid of, they'll make it better. I feel this deep in my soul.

"She needs you both," I say, inviting them into the library. "Close the door behind you."

The two men walk into the room and crowd the pretty blonde.

"Take a seat," I urge them all, gesturing for the sofa. "Get comfortable."

"Everything spoken in here is confidential," Hugo reminds me. "Right?"

Spencer snorts out a laugh. "I sure as hell hope so because I've been airing all the dirty laundry of this family."

Hugo winces at his son's confession but doesn't appear to be angry, only resigned.

"It never leaves the room," I assure them. "Go on, Aubrey. Tell them why we're here."

Spencer places a possessive hand on her thigh, sitting on one side of her, while Hugo softly tucks her hair behind her ear from her other side. They love her. That's obvious. And she loves them. Whatever her fears are, they'll all get through it together.

"I'm pregnant," she whispers. "I'm sorry."

The silence is brief and then Spencer barks out a laugh. It's almost cruel sounding. I tense up, wondering how she'll react, but then relax when she smacks his hand holding her thigh.

"Don't be a dick."

"What? I think it's funny," Spencer says, unable to keep his chuckles at bay.

"Why?" she demands, glowering at him.

Hugo is eerily silent.

"Because we legit fuck all the damn time—bareback might I add—and you're shocked you got knocked-up. It was only a matter of when, not if."

She shoots him the bird, which only causes more laughter.

Hugo speaks next. "You're sure, Love?"

Ignoring Spencer, she turns to Hugo. "I am. I'm sorry."

He growls, clutching her chin and drawing her close to his face. "For what? What the hell do you have to be sorry for?"

She shrugs. "For being careless like usual. For ruining everyone's lives like usual."

I can tell there's a whole slew of past traumas Aubrey is dealing with and I hope one day she'll trust me enough to confide in. Luckily, Hugo already seems to know about them and is quick to reassure her.

"I'm so happy we're having a baby," Hugo tells her, voice fierce and passionate. "You understand? So. Fucking. Happy."

"Yeah," Spencer chimes in, leaning in to kiss her softly on the neck. "In case you didn't notice, this family makes really beautiful kids. Look at Rex, here. Cute as fuck."

This earns a smile from Aubrey. She tears her stare from Hugo to kiss Rex's fuzzy head as he sleeps in Spencer's arms.

"But what about your dad? Your brothers?" Aubrey asks. "They'll want to know who got me pregnant. They don't know about us—our unconventional relationship. Everything could blow up."

Spencer shrugs at that. "Tell them it's mine. I'm already wearing a scarlet letter for fucking my stepmom and having her baby. Trust me, the family won't be surprised."

Hugo grimaces. "It could be mine. I should accept responsibility—"

"It's ours," Aubrey interjects fiercely as Spencer huffs out, "Dad, don't be a martyr."

"A martyr?" Hugo clips out. "I can't allow you and Aubrey to bear all the weight here. It's not fair. The three of us have tangled ourselves in this beautiful mess. The least I can do is own up to my part in it."

"Do you trust your father and your brothers? The whole Park family?" I ask, darting my gaze to each one of them. "Is it possible you could get support rather than shame?"

Hugo gives me a firm nod. "We Parks stick together. We always have each other's backs."

"It sounds like, to me, this baby is a cause for celebration then," I say with a grin. "Why don't I step away and allow you three a moment of privacy."

As the three of them hug, laugh, and for Aubrey, cry, I feel lighter as I exit the library. This family—the whole lot of them—is a loving family. Sure, they have their fair share of secrets and shame, but they're not without hope.

They may not be my family, but I feel a certain sense of pride at being at the center of helping bring them closer together. I will do my best to get each and every one of them to open up.

Jude may be my biggest challenge yet, but I have growing faith I'll help him too.

CHAPTER FOURTEEN

Jude

'M ANTSY AND EAGER TO TALK TO TATE AGAIN. AFTER our interruption, he's been busy all day. Dempsey's been in the library with him for hours and it's driving me insane.

I just want to drag Tate back upstairs to my special place, listen to records, and pet his cat together. I want to hear him talk and squirm uncomfortably at the way he makes me talk too.

I just want him.

That thought makes my lower belly burn hot. What exactly does that mean? Do I really find him attractive?

When I think about his pouty lips, my dick twitches. Okay, so yeah, I do find him attractive. It's strange as fuck, too, considering I've never once desired another man like this. Sure, I've thought other men looked good. I kind of thought of that as how one would appreciate art. Everyone does that, right?

Or do they?

Have I been bisexual all along and never recognized it?

Perhaps. I never shied away from looking at the other guys in the gym showers when I played football. Mostly, I was curious about what size dicks they had to compare myself to them. Some of the most arrogant dudes on the team had tiny-ass cocks, which I always found amusing. We had this one guy on the team, though, Tim Gallagher, who I found particularly interesting. Gallagher was one of the smaller guys on our team, but he was hung. Biggest dick I'd ever seen in my life. I always wondered how big it actually got like when he was hard and ready to fuck.

Now that I'm actually analyzing things, I'm realizing maybe I wasn't as straight as I originally thought I was. Back then, had Gallagher approached me, stroking his dick, I might've stayed for the show. Hell, I might've even been curious enough to see if I could wrap my large hand around his massive girth.

Right.

So definitely not straight.

My attraction to Tate feels similar to the Gallagher thing. I'm curious, but much more aware. Maybe it's because now I don't have Serra to distract me. She was always pushing for sex and who was I to deny her? I wonder if I'd have realized I was bisexual a lot sooner if she hadn't been there back then.

Not that it matters.

Realizing my sexuality is a moot point. I'm not the guy I was back then. I'm the reclusive freakshow Park who hides away in the shadows, a slave to his past failures. I'm not the kind of guy who pursues anyone—much less a guy—in a romantic way.

Why not?

My brain demands an answer and my heart is quick to lash back.

Because you don't deserve love, remember?

Bitterness rears its ugly head. These new feelings for Tate, like my conversation with Baker, are only a reminder of what

I can't have. It sucks—really sucks—but it's the hand I've been dealt.

My phone buzzes and I break from my melancholic thoughts to see who's texting me.

Dad: Hugo wants everyone over for dinner tonight. He has an announcement. This means you too, Son. Bring Tate. See you in fifteen.

I should be irritated at my dad's bossiness. He always assumes I can drop anything to be there at a moment's notice. But since he wants me to bring Tate, I don't complain. It gives me an excuse to seek him out and spend more time with him, whether I deserve that gift or not.

"Thanks," Dempsey says to Tate as I prowl down the stairs. "See you at dinner."

He slips out the front door without another word. Tate glances my way and gives me a tentative smile. My stomach dips and it's fucking exhilarating despite the self-loathing threatening to drown me.

Unable to stop myself, I take several long strides toward Tate until I'm towering over him. He holds his ground, craning his neck to look up at me. I want to touch him, even if only my fingertips to his pillowy lips. I bet they're soft. I bet they taste sweet too.

I stifle a groan and clear my throat. "Walk with me?"

His eyes twinkle and he grins. "I'd like that."

He would?

My heart stutters to a stop. It's shocking that he keeps giving me chance after chance to be a human when I've been nothing but a raging asshole monster thus far. I'm greedy, though, and don't question how he's able to do such a thing.

Instead, I reach for his hand to see if he'll allow me to take it once more.

He doesn't pull away, squeezing my hand once it's safely nestled inside of mine. "Lead the way."

I itch to thread our fingers together but decide that might be a bit too intimate despite the longing in my gut to keep pushing the envelope with him. Holding his hand just like this will have to be enough.

He lets me guide him out of the house and into the chilly evening air. Neither of us bothered with a jacket and I'm already regretting that decision. But since it cools my throbbing dick some, I continue forward, the porch groaning under my weight.

"It's peaceful out here too," Tate muses aloud. "I like it here."

Pride surges through me. I've always loved our property and home, but knowing he loves it too unlocks something deep inside. It makes me want to share with him more of the things I've found simple joy in.

He steps closer to me. When he releases my hand, I nearly protest, but then his arm hooks around mine. His warmth seeps into me at his close proximity, dizzying my every thought.

"You were in there with Dempsey for a long time. Everything okay?" I ask roughly. "I'm not jealous."

He chuckles, no doubt amused by the last part I quickly spit out. "It's fine. He's just working through some things like everyone else. More than anything, he needs someone to confide in and get things off his chest."

I wonder what Dempsey, the Park bad boy and spoiled baby of the family, could ever be troubled over. He and

Gemma have it better than anyone. They're truly the golden children who can do no wrong.

"Is he crying again because Daddy won't buy him a car?" I say with a sharpness in my tone.

"You're not the only one with trauma and problems," Tate responds tightly. "You're teetering into asshole territory again."

Guilt swallows me whole and I force out a groan. "Sorry."

He shrugs it off, but the magical feeling between us has cooled. As it should. The heat between us is unhealthy and clouding my judgment. My duty is to protect this family, not find pleasure in the one person who is doing his damnedest to help them.

As we approach Dad's house, I feel Tate's grip around my arm loosen. He releases me to walk ahead. I speed up, chasing after his lingering scent and hoping to get high off his magnetism. Unfortunately, he beats me inside and is quickly swept up into the chaos of a typical Park family dinner.

Seconds later, I spot him taking a seat beside Dempsey at the table. I quickly sidestep Gemma and duck into the chair on his other side before she can take it. She frowns at me in confusion. I ignore her, leaning slightly toward Tate to listen in on his conversation with Dempsey.

They're not talking about anything of importance. Dempsey's regaling him with a tale of how he took his mother's car for a joy ride when he was twelve, wrapping it around a telephone pole up the road, barely escaping with nothing but a broken arm and a few stitches on his eyebrow. And yet he wonders why Dad won't buy him a car...

Fucking idiot.

Callum sits directly across from me, his grin wolfish and

knowing. He lets his gaze teeter back and forth from me to Tate. It's irritating. How could he possibly know I'm all twisted up over the family therapist?

He can't know.

Maybe he's just gloating over the fact Tate's here mostly because of me. He probably also knows that it'll only be a matter of time before Tate breaks down all my walls.

Even with my mask, I'm apparently readable.

I fucking hate that.

Discreetly, I flip him the bird. Willa sees the gesture and gapes at me. I simply shrug before turning my attention to Dad and Hugo as they enter the room. Dad wears a pensive expression.

"This is the best I could do on such short notice," Jamie says, entering the dining room with a large pot of spaghetti. "Hold tight while I grab the rest."

Dad's stare follows after her and the smile he reserves just for her is filled with such love my own heart aches with jealousy. Not because I want Jamie. I just secretly crave being able to love someone like Dad loves her—consequences be damned. His love for her nearly irrevocably bombed his family to smithereens and yet he kept on loving her anyway.

Sometimes I wonder if Mom would've ever moved on. Had she seen how much Dad loved Jamie, it might've been enough for her to stop obsessing over the demise of their marriage. She wasn't happy with Dad. Neither of them was. Why she took it so personally when she found out about the affair was a mystery to me.

Thoughts of Mom sour my stomach. The thought of eating spaghetti is almost nauseating. I snag up the water glass in front of me, slightly lift my mask, and then chug the entire thing in just a few gulps. I slam my mask down into place, finding Callum watching me with renewed interest.

Fuck off, brother.

A few more hectic moments pass until dinner is served and everyone is chatting easily as they eat. I sit frozen like a statue, not bothering to pick up my fork or touch the food in front of me. Hugo, who's already wolfed down his meal, clears his throat before rising to his feet. Dad gives him a small nod of encouragement.

"I called you all here today because I have something to say. It's something that not everyone will understand, but it's not for you to try to figure out. The important thing is, *we've* figured it out and we're happy." He smiles at Aubrey. "I spoke to Dad prior to dinner and he's agreed that what I'm about to tell you will remain a secret within our family. I'd still like to hear it from you all, though."

Everyone, including me, nods or agrees out loud that we will.

"Me and Spencer are seeing Aubrey."

No one seems surprised by this news and I already knew. The three of them are always glued together. Spencer, who's now out and proud, draws Audrey to him for a messy kiss. Hugo sighs in exasperation but doesn't chide his son.

"And she's pregnant," Hugo continues. "With our baby."

Willa squeaks out a happy yelp. "Aubrey, you're pregnant? We're going to have babies together!"

Aubrey pushes Spencer away to look at Willa. "You're not mad?"

"Why would I be mad?" Willa asks, confusion making her nose scrunch. "Babies are wonderful."

"You're so excited about being pregnant and everyone is

happy for you," Aubrey says sadly. "I didn't want to take any of the limelight away from you."

Willa shakes her head in vehemence. "No, hon, I'm *really* happy. I'm sure everyone else is too. We can share the lime-light." She smiles in an encouraging way. "This is good news."

"I mean, I knew what you three dirty dogs were up to, but I'm still fuzzy on the actual details. Do you two dick each other down?" Dempsey asks Spencer with a chuckle, clearly amused by his own question. "How does this work exactly?"

Dad stands from his chair, shooting his youngest son a fiery glare. "That's enough, Dempsey. You'll respect their rela-tionship and asking about what goes on behind closed doors is unacceptable."

"Tell me later," Dempsey mouths to Spencer.

Jamie, Gemma, and Willa all get up to go hug Aubrey. I'm lost in their smothering affection over her when I feel some-thing warm slide over my thigh.

Jerking my gaze from the girls to my leg, I find Tate's hand resting there. I snap my head his way to find him smiling at me as he leans closer.

"They're going to be okay," Tate murmurs, eyes twin-kling. "You all will."

I know he's touching me in a friendly, easy way I should be happy about, but all I can think about is how all the blood is rushing toward my cock. It swells and swells until my erec-tion strains against my pants, threatening to rip right through the material.

What would it feel like to have his small hand slide up over my length?

Like fucking heaven.

But all I deserve is hell.

I push away from the table, the legs of the chair scraping over the wood. Several heads snap my way, concern in their features. Fire lashes at my cock and a stinging burn remains in the wake of where his hand was just on my thigh. I stagger to my feet and quickly turn on my heel to hide my blatant hard-on.

"Jude?" Dad calls out. "Just what the hell is wrong with you?"

"Not hungry," I snarl. "Congrats on the baby, though."

There. I wasn't a total asshole.

I just need a second. Alone. With my hand. And then I'll be fine.

Or…I'll just want a helluva lot more.

CHAPTER FIFTEEN

Tate

H E WAS TURNED ON.

Holy shit, he was turned on.

Dinner goes by in a blur, but all I can think about is being face to face with Jude's erection. I'm not sure anyone else saw, which is good. I, however, can't stop thinking about it. All I did was touch his leg.

But the simple touch excited him and he bailed.

I mean, I would bail too if I got hard at a dinner with my family.

I'm such an idiot. Touching him on our walk to Nathan's house felt easy and comfortable. I guess when I leaned over and put my hand on his thigh, I wasn't really thinking about how that would make him feel. Or physically react.

My heart aches at the thought of no one ever touching him intimately. Based on what I've learned so far about Jude, he stays hidden behind his self-made walls, always protecting his broken heart.

I shouldn't have touched his leg like that.

I stifle a heavy sigh as Gemma and Jamie clear the table. Nathan retired to his office once Callum and Hugo left, taking their people with them. Dempsey abandons texting on his phone to shoot me a questioning look.

"Not in a hurry to get back to Freak Mansion?"

I smirk and give him a small shrug. "Guess not."

"Come on. We can shoot the shit outside."

After I tell Gemma and Jamie bye, I follow Dempsey outside to the front porch. He tosses a blanket at me and gestures for me to sit in one of the wicker chairs. I wrap up in the blanket, thankful for his thoughtfulness, and sit. He dons a black leather jacket that doesn't appear to be very warm, yet he doesn't shiver or otherwise indicate he's cold. Once we're settled, he pulls a pack of cigarettes from his jacket pocket and lights up.

A puff of exhaled smoke billows out in front of him and he fidgets with the cigarette between his fingers. It's clear he's on edge too. Even though we spoke earlier at length about his place in this family and how he feels about it, I still feel like we barely scratched the surface with him.

"What was up with Jude?" he asks, canting his head in my direction, eyes pinning me in place.

I flick my gaze to Jude's moonlit house and sigh. "I think he had enough peopling for the day."

And needed to hide his massive erection.

It was totally massive. I'm still reeling from the anaconda that was about to escape its cage.

"That's his usual MO," Dempsey says with an amused huff. "It was something else."

"Like what?"

He smirks. "Like *you.*"

Heat floods my cheeks and I wring my hands together under the blanket. "W-What do you mean *me?*"

Did he see all that transpired at the dinner table?

Oh my God.

"He's just so…I don't know. Obsessed with you." He

shrugs his shoulders before taking another drag. "If I didn't know any better, I'd think he wants to fuck you."

I shift in my seat, growing warmer and warmer despite the evening chill. "He doesn't want to fuck me."

But do I want him to?

Obviously.

I'm too intrigued and attracted to him to keep my distance.

"Whatever," Dempsey says as he leans over to put the cigarette out on the porch floor. "Just giving my opinion."

"Here's my opinion," I say, nodding at the discarded cigarette butt on the ground between us. "Smoking is bad for you. You're not even old enough to legally buy them."

"Since when do I follow any rules?" he counters, voice taunting.

"What does your dad think about you trying to get cancer before adulthood?"

"Honestly, he never really says anything."

"Your mom?"

"She pretends not to notice. As long as I don't blatantly do it in the living room, no one cares."

The last three words are sharp and punctuated.

No. One. Cares.

I feel we're teetering back onto the precipice of something big with Dempsey. In our conversations, he's done a lot of complaining about his family, but I'm beginning to see a theme here. He feels unseen. Lost in the crowd. Forgotten. It makes sense why he's always acting out. It's an obvious cry for attention.

"They care," I assure him. "How do you connect with

your family? Besides riling them up with your words and bad boy behavior."

He snorts out a laugh. "Bad boy behavior. You're such a goodie-goodie, Tate."

Wasn't such a goodie-goodie when I got your brother hard in front of your family…

"Hardly," I grumble, cheeks burning hot once more.

"They're all too busy up each other's asses all the time."

"If they weren't too busy, what would you hope to get from your family?"

He stills aside from the way he spins a silver skull ring around his middle finger. "Maybe a fucking thank you?"

The bitterness in his tone is sharp and prickly.

"Thank you for…"

"For being the goddamn scapegoat. The family fuck-up. Do you know how many times I've taken heat to protect everyone?" He leans forward in his chair, resting his elbows on his knees and staring into the darkness beyond the porch. "No one cares."

There it is again.

No. One. Cares.

"Why do you feel it's your duty to throw yourself on the landmine each time your family runs into problems?"

"That's what we do," he grumbles. "We Parks look out for each other."

"Could they possibly be looking out for you in other ways that you're not aware of?"

"Who the hell knows."

But I do. I know. Jude obsessively watches over his family and tries to protect them. Nathan uses his influence and money to make problems disappear in an instant. Hugo charms people all the time in an effort to keep people from poking at his family. From the stuff Spencer has revealed, I know Callum was always going to bat for his little brother when he worked at the school. And Gemma is his twin. Twins are engrained to help one another.

They do care about him.

How do I make him see this?

"Those times you've gotten in trouble, who got you out?" I ask, turning to study his profile. "Did you do that all by yourself?"

He scoffs and shoots me an annoyed look. "Mostly Dad. Always there to clean up messes so the town doesn't look down upon us."

"Perhaps self-image plays a role," I admit, "but you can't honestly believe that's it. You're the product of an illicit affair with his son's girlfriend. Your dad essentially blew up his life to be with her. Their love must've been pretty intense. You and Gemma are walking reminders of that incredible love story. I think you need to give your dad a little credit for cleaning up messes because he loves you."

Dempsey doesn't say anything, but I know I'm getting through to him. Sometimes people just need pointing out what's right in front of them for them to finally take notice.

"You think they don't care, but they do. Especially your father. I'm here because of him. He wants his children happy and healthy." I reach over and clutch his shoulder. "Try spending some time with your dad. I want you to look past his exterior and truly see his motives when it comes to this family."

We fall into silence, both of us drifting to our own thoughts. Dempsey is a good kid who's hurting for not feeling seen in his own family. Maybe he and Nathan can work on finding common ground so Dempsey doesn't feel so alone.

"Anything else you want to talk about?" I ask gently. "Like the one you want but can't have?"

He rises to his feet, shaking his head. "Nope. I'm tired as fuck."

I grumble out a good night to him as he reenters the house. With a sigh, I stand up and fold up the blanket. The chill quickly seeps its way into my bones as awareness creeps in. When Dempsey was here, I didn't think twice about being outside. I felt safe talking to him. Now that he's gone, the familiar fear crawls down my spine.

Someone's watching me.

Panicked thoughts of Sean prowling about in the darkness have me bolting off the porch like my ass is on fire. The quicker I can get to Jude's house, the quicker I can get my heart rate back to normal. I take off in a sprint, sticking to the moonlit areas rather than the dark, menacing shadows around the trees.

I've barely made it across the road when someone steps out of one of the shadows, blocking my path. I stumble to a halt, chest heaving and head spinning.

Jude.

His lurking ways don't seem so irritating right now. In fact, I nearly jump into his arms with gratefulness. It takes all the will I have not to grab onto him and bury my face in his solid chest.

"Hey," I croak out, stepping closer and closer until I'm in his warm, safe orbit.

He studies me intently through his mask. "Hey."

When he offers me his elbow, I greedily hook my arm

around his. He's warm and smells like cinnamon. I wonder if he got into another one of Violet's pies.

If he's feeling awkward about dinner, he doesn't mention it. Instead, he escorts me slowly back to his house. It's cold and my heart is still hammering in my chest, but I'm not in a hurry to get back either. Being close to him, comforted by his strong, massive presence, is nice.

You once felt comforted by Sean, too.

I try not to think about Sean, but it's hard not to. This time I've spent with the Parks has been a vacation from reality. I'm not stupid, though. Sean's still out there, most likely pissed off to no end, searching for me.

When he finally catches up to me, there'll be hell to pay.

I shiver at the thought of him grabbing me by the elbow and forcefully dragging me into my apartment. At one time, we'd shared a few good times watching movies on the couch and eventually fooling around. Sometimes he was even playful. Sean felt like "the one" for me in the beginning. That is, until I learned he was freaking married with a mess of kids.

I tried breaking it off, but it's like a switch flipped inside him.

He transformed into an abusive, cruel, tortuous monster I can't escape from.

Jude, while domineering, a bit controlling, and completely all up in my business, is not Sean. I even wonder, given the time, would I be able to confide in him about Sean. Would he want to protect me so fiercely like he protects his family?

All too soon, we're stepping inside his warm, dark home. Jude shuts and locks the door behind him. Then he untangles our arms and takes my hand. We're both cold, but his hand around mine quickly creates the heat I crave.

He doesn't stride up the stairs like usual but instead takes his time. It's evident he's not eager to get rid of me. My stomach flops at that because I'm not so ready to leave him yet either. When we reach the stairs, my fuzzy friend greets us.

Meow.

Funky peeks out of my bedroom door that's ajar and meows again. I squat down to pet his soft head and note that Jude hasn't released my other hand. My cat looks up at Jude and then darts away from me, disappearing into Jude's office.

I guess this is it.

Time to say good night.

Jude tugs me back upright and steps into my space. His masculine, cinnamon scent dances in the air around me, making my mouth water for a taste. I tilt my head up to peer into his electric eyes.

"Thanks for walking me," I murmur. "I really appreciate that."

I felt safe and protected because of you.

He takes a step toward me, his body crowding mine. The urge to stand on my toes and lick the side of his neck is so tempting, I find myself staggering away from him until my ass hits the wall. He releases my hand, much to my disappointment, but then stalks closer until we're so close, our chests brush against one another.

What is this?

Why is he so close?

Why does it drive me to delicious insanity?

Both of his hands come up to curl over my shoulders. With impressive strength, he pushes me until my shoulder blades dig into the wall.

I'm trapped.

I'm pinned in his powerful hold, unable to move or get away.

I've been in a situation like this before with Sean and I was useless against him.

Will Jude abuse his power like Sean did?

Or will he prove to me that not all big, intense, grumpy men are cruel?

Only time will tell and it's not like I'm going anywhere.

CHAPTER SIXTEEN

Jude

WHAT AM I DOING?

Honestly, I don't know. All I do know is I like having his small frame trapped in my unyielding grip. Knowing that even if he tried to escape me, he wouldn't be able to. Right now, he's mine.

Mine to do what?

Unable to stop myself, I lean in, grazing my mask along his neck. He smells soapy and addictive. I wish I could bury my nose against his flesh and spend the whole night smelling him skin to skin.

My heart is hammering wildly out of control. I'm afraid to move for fear of doing something I won't be able to take back.

Like what, horndog? Fuck him?

I stifle a groan at the delicious fantasies beginning to take shape in my mind. Since he's not pushing me away, I'd like to think he'd allow me to have my filthy way with him. Maybe he would beg for it.

My cock has been rock-hard since he placed his hand on my thigh at dinner. Even after I lubed up my fist and shot my load in the bathroom sink, it didn't sate me. I wanted his hand on my cock, not mine.

"Jude," Tate murmurs, hot breath tickling the side of my neck. "What are you doing?"

I close my eyes but refuse to move away from him. "Thinking."

"You're thinking awfully hard. I can almost hear your thoughts."

The idea of Tate inside my twisted head makes me shudder. I don't need anyone to ever see the chaotic shitstorm I live with each day. Especially not Tate. He's too sweet for the likes of what he'd uncover and I refuse to be what ruins him.

"Oh yeah?" I ask, wishing like hell I could rip this stupid mask off. "What do you hear?"

He shifts in my grip, but since I'm holding his shoulders so tight, he barely moves. "You're struggling with something. Something to do with me."

I hate that I'm so obvious, but I am pinning him to the wall like he's my prize and I'm deciding on which limb to feast on first.

"You confuse me," I admit, voice raspy. "I thought I hated you, but this feeling is not hate."

I pull back a slight bit to look into his eyes. His pupils are blown and cheeks pink. I'm fixated on his plump lips, especially the bottom one. He tugs at it with his top teeth.

"Do you want to kiss me?" His whispered question sends thrills shooting through every nerve ending.

Kiss him?

Hell yeah, I want to kiss him.

I want to fuse my lips to his and taste his sweetness straight from the source.

"No," I lie. "I-I can't." The second part is the truth.

"Because you don't think you deserve to feel pleasure or because you refuse to take off your mask?"

A dark chuckle barks out of me. "Can the answer be both?"

My hold on his shoulders has loosened. I realize I'm rubbing gentle circles against them with my thumbs. Tate makes me more insane than I already am. I can't think straight or control my physical reactions around him.

"You deserve to be happy," he says softly, sadness making his eyes glimmer. "And you can take your mask off with me. I won't judge you."

His words are a siren's song, tempting me closer and closer to the treacherous shore. I want to believe him. I really, really do.

"I can't do it," I murmur, hating myself more than ever.

Tate reaches along the wall and then flips the light switch. We're bathed in immediate darkness. My frozen spine thaws, relaxing me a bit.

"May I?" he asks, palms skimming up my chest over my hoodie toward my neck. "I can't see."

No.

No. No. No.

Fuck no.

"Y-Yes," I croak out, unable to deny this decadent fantasy that seems so close I can taste it.

He makes a small keening sound of pleasure that wakes my dick right up. I slide my hands down to his hips, gripping my fingers into his lower back as I wait for him to do the inevitable.

His fingertips brush over the bottom of my mask as he seeks it out in the dark. Then, slowly, he begins lifting it. Cool air feathers over my face that's damp with perspiration. He pulls the mask completely off and then it hits the floor with a soft *thwump*.

"You deserve to be happy," Tate says firmly, as though he can drill it into my head.

Rather than hear him talk anymore about my happiness—or lack thereof—I dip down to seek out his mouth with mine. All too easily, I find him in the dark, my lips gently brushing over his.

They're warm.

And softer than I imagined.

He parts his lips and lets out a breathy sound that makes my head spin. Unable to hold back, I crash my mouth against his, desperate for more than a little peck. The second my tongue meets his for a slippery greeting, I'm lost to this insane moment between us.

A feral growl rattles up my chest and it's our only warning before I lose my last shred of control. I devour his sweet mouth, tasting every inch. He whines when I nip at his cute bottom lip and tug it with my teeth.

My cock is aching for relief. I don't think twice about leaning against his body, slowly grinding against him. He gasps at the feel of my erection pressed between us.

His hands are tugging at my shirt as though he can't get enough of me either, which only spurs me on. He trembles and his knees buckle as I consume him with a dirty, desperate kiss. To keep him from collapsing, I nestle my large thigh between his legs and push my knee against the wall. He grips onto my shirt and rocks his body on my thigh.

What if he were naked and doing this?

Would it feel good to rub his balls along my hairy thigh?

Would he let me slip a wet finger into his asshole and finger him while we kiss?

I'm growing dizzy with the need to obliterate him with pleasure. I want so much more than I'll ever deserve or receive.

Neither of us tries to speak. Our bodies have created a new language that's quickly understood. Want. Need. Hunger. Pleasure. We writhe together, taking what we can from one another.

He turns his head to the side, his chest heaving, and whispers, "Jude. This…I'm getting too turned on…"

This makes my lips curl into a satisfied grin. I dip down to his neck and run my tongue along the salty skin. "Is there such a thing as too turned on?"

He moans when I suck his flesh into my mouth. The trembles coursing through him just make me all the more starved for him. I greedily suck and suck on his skin, wishing it were his cock in my mouth instead.

What would his cum taste like?

Despite never having been with a guy, I don't feel grossed out by imagining the taste of him. If anything, my mouth waters with the craving.

"You'll leave a hickey on me," he croaks out, not trying hard to push me away. "Everyone will see."

His worry isn't a worry at all for me. In fact, my dick twitches at the thought of seeing it tomorrow in the daylight. A big, purple bruise on his neck that marks my territory? Fuck yeah.

Except he's not mine.

This frozen moment in time is an illusion. A fever dream. A reprieve from my living nightmare. It can't exist outside of the shadows.

My dick flags at the thought of not ever touching him again. But that's what I need to do. I need to release him and back away before I get too hooked on him.

Happiness is for others, not me.

Tate deserves better than a reclusive, ugly monster.

His fingers tease under the bottom of my hoodie, touching my flesh. It distracts me from my dark thoughts, making me wonder how the skin on his stomach feels. As soft as his lips?

A yelp barks out of him when I untuck his shirt and then slide my palms under the fabric to touch the bare skin of his back. Then I tease them around his sides to the front. He sucks in a sharp breath when my fingers dance circles on his lower belly, feeling the hairs there.

"You're soft," I murmur against his neck. "So fucking soft."

He whimpers and squirms, his ass rubbing along my thigh. "And you're really, really hard."

I know he's talking about my abs because he's running his fingers along the grooves now, but I can't help but think about my cock. My boxers are damp with pre-cum. I'm desperate to rub my stone dick against him to soak him in my release.

"I want things I shouldn't," I admit, voice raw with unfiltered pain. "So. Fucking. Badly."

"You can have them," he assures me breathily. "Whatever you want."

The way he so freely gives himself to me drives me to the brink of sanity. I want to strip him right here and taste every goddamn inch of him. I want him riding my dick, not my thigh. I need inside him like my next breath.

"Are you always so compliant?" I rumble, easing one hand

up toward his nipple. "Always so eager to give in and give your lover what he wants?"

"Are we lovers?" he asks.

I run my thumb over his pebbled nipple. "Do you want to be?"

"Are we answering questions with questions?"

Rather than responding, he moans when I pluck at his nipple. It's tiny and erect. I want it between my fucking teeth. He sighs with pleasure when I twist it slightly.

My mind quiets as I am spellbound by his mewls of enjoyment. I know I need to back away before I do something regrettable, but I can't find the reasoning as to why that's a good idea. All I know is I want to give him pleasure and I ache for him to reciprocate.

"Do you want my cock inside you, little boy?" I rasp out, dragging my teeth along his jaw. "Hmm?"

He shudders and nods. I kiss my way back to his pouty lips, choosing to devour them next.

"Yes, Jude. Fuck me."

Fucking hell.

His filthy mouth is my undoing. I'm unable to back away now. I'm committed, even if only for this dark, wicked night, to our mutual pleasure. Nothing can stop me now.

I slide my palm farther up his chest until it peeks out of the top of his shirt. My hand encircles his throat and I firmly grip it. I like the image of my hand shackling him to me. He whimpers when my thumb presses against his pulsing vein. I love how it dances beneath my touch—wild and out of control. The desire to hold him still, controlling the flow of his blood until he calms, is nearly maddening.

"Jude," he murmurs. "I need—"

I squeeze a little harder, cutting him off as I slide my other hand down toward his cock. I know what he needs. He needs to come. I need to make him come.

His cock is as hard as mine. The outline of it beneath his pants under my palm is a sensation I'll memorize until the day I die. I love it. I love feeling it throb with need, knowing I'm responsible for it.

A wheezing sound jerks me from my frenzied thoughts. I realize my grip on his neck is a little too tight. With how much smaller he is than me, I could easily crush his windpipe if I'm not careful. The thought of hurting him and possibly killing him over something as stupid as my strength when I'm out of control has me freezing.

What am I doing?

I can't do this.

"Jude?"

His voice is hoarse and barely audible. Have I hurt him? Did I break him already?

"Tate," I grunt, inching slightly back. "Fuck."

The disgusted resignation in my voice must alarm him because he reaches up, fingers blindly brushing over my jawline. It's so near to my awful face I panic.

"No," I bark out, dropping my hands from him and yanking my leg away from between his. "D-Don't do that."

"Jude." Again with the tiny, broken, lost voice. "I'm s-sorry I almost touched your face. Can we talk about this?"

I can't.

I can't do this.

I'm the monster and he's…*not.*

We don't belong together like this. It's not fucking right.

"Night," I grunt, stumbling farther away from him. "See you at breakfast."

I don't stop to pick up my mask or to touch him again. No, I run all the way to my room like a fucking coward. It's not until the door is shut and locked behind me that I finally relax. I squeeze my eyes shut and slide down the door until I land hard on my ass, hating how quickly my lashes are turning wet from the pain of leaving him alone in the hallway.

It was beautiful for a moment.

Life was fucking perfect for one stolen moment.

I'll lock it away in my memory to reexamine another day.

But as for happening again?

Never fucking ever.

CHAPTER SEVENTEEN

Tate

*M*EOW.

Funky bats at my face with his paw, his purring rumbling through my chest where he sits.

I get it, cat.

Time to wake up.

I peek open an eye to find him staring at me. "What?"

Meow.

He's probably eager for more of Violet's bacon. Spoiled rotten cat. I flick at his ear until he gets annoyed and bolts off me and onto the floor. Sitting up on one elbow, I try to wake up and make sense of my surroundings.

Still at the creepy mansion that's not so creepy anymore.

In fact, Jude's not so creepy anymore either.

But. He. Choked. You.

My dick perks at the reminder and I stifle a groan. Last night, Jude left me with the bluest balls ever. I hopped right into the bath after he abandoned me and came as soon as I got my soapy hand wrapped around my dick.

He had me so riled.

It was the hottest first kiss I've ever had with anyone.

Why did he bail on me?

Because I nearly touched his face?

I'm still reeling at how ravenous he was. And, like the

naturally submissive man I am, I willingly sacrificed myself for him to feast on.

Why am I this way?

Why do I yield all control when faced with a man like Jude?

Because you trusted him to take care of you.

I did.

I still do.

But I trusted Sean too and look how that turned out.

Maybe it was for the best that we stopped before things could progress any further.

God, but his mouth felt so good on mine. He's an excellent kisser. He doesn't just kiss—he devours and inhales. I loved feeling his desperation for me.

Sicko.

I'm supposed to be helping him get over his past traumas so he can behave in a healthier way, not letting him ravish me in the dark hallways of his haunted house.

Voices can suddenly be heard downstairs. I sit up fully and listen to who it might be. I'm not due for an appointment with anyone since it's Saturday, so I'm curious about who might be bursting into the normally quiet home.

Thunderous footsteps charge up the stairs and down the hallway. Seconds later, the door bursts open and three giggling girls pour in.

"Your first day off," Gemma sings. "You have to hang out with us. We won't take no for an answer."

Willa shoots me an apologetic smile, clearly feeling bad about dropping in on me. She holds up a peace offering, though. "Brought you your fave."

"I love you," I say with a stupid grin on my face, accepting the iced coffee she hands over. "You all are up bright and early today."

Aubrey laughs. "Tate, it's past noon."

I blink at her in shock. "Really? Holy shit. Why did I sleep so late?"

Gemma arches a perfectly sculpted dark eyebrow and wiggles a finger at me. Her nails are long and pointy, painted matte black with sparkly jewels on some of them. They're sharp-looking. Like she could use them for weapons in a pinch if someone tries to abduct her.

"What?" I ask, leaning away from her claws.

She takes a sip of her iced coffee and then flashes me a naughty grin that reminds me of Dempsey a thousand percent. "I know why you slept late. You were up to no good all night."

I frown at her in confusion. "I don't know what you're talking about."

Willa laughs softly and Aubrey snorts.

"Your face is turning red," Aubrey teases. "Also, you have a hickey the size of Texas on your neck."

What. The. Hell.

I slap my hand where Jude had his lips last night. If I was turning red a second ago, I'm probably tomato red at this point.

"It's a bruise," I lie. "Ran into the door."

Gemma rolls her pretty eyes at me. "We're not idiots, Tate. Spill. Tell us what happened…and with whom. Was it Dempsey? I know you were out late with him last night."

Dempsey?!

He's a kid!

All three girls stare at me with matching owlish expressions. I don't know how to lie my way out of this. I don't know that I should. They trust me enough to confide in me during our sessions. The least I can do is offer them the truth.

"Dammit," I grumble in resignation. "You can't say anything to anyone. I'm serious."

Gemma nods. "Duh. Tell me."

"It wasn't Dempsey," I say, a grin tugging at my lips. "It was someone else."

Aubrey frowns. "Who? Do you have a boyfriend?"

"What? No." I suck down more of my liquid caffeine, needing to avoid that second question. Technically, according to Sean, we're still together despite my many requests for him to leave me alone and the whole him already being happily married thing. "I really shouldn't say. It's unprofessional."

"Oh," Willa chokes out. "It's someone in this family. But the only single ones are Dempsey and—"

"Jude!" Gemma and Aubrey both shriek at once.

"Shhh," I hiss, eyeing the open bedroom door. "He'll hear."

The girls crawl onto the bed with me, all of them eager to hear more juicy details. I scrub a palm over my face and sigh.

"He let you see him without the mask?" Gemma asks. "That's just…shocking, to be quite honest."

"Not exactly," I admit. "I turned off the light to make him more comfortable."

"And then what?" Aubrey demands. "He sucked your face off?"

"What else did he suck?" Gemma teases, leaning forward to poke my hickey with one of her finger knives.

Willa averts her gaze and bites down on her bottom lip to keep from smiling.

"Nothing was sucked," I say with a groan. "We just made out and then…"

Aubrey makes a rolling motion with her hand. "And *then*. Come on. Don't stall."

"And then he got…spooked. Left me all hot and bothered."

Despite how unprofessional this confession time is, I can't help but enjoy it. I've never been one to have friends really aside from the guys I've hooked up with or dated here and there. When I was with Sean, he sure as hell didn't allow it. Having people to talk to is nice.

"What spooked him?" Gemma asks.

"I started to reach for his face. He kind of freaked out and left. I don't know. It was really, really good, but something tells me it won't be happening again."

"Why not?" Aubrey demands. "He marked you like a piece of property. I think he'll be back for a double helping of Tate pie."

I crack up laughing. "Tate pie?"

"Mostly sweet but kind of tart too. Especially when you start asking hard questions we don't want to answer in our sessions."

"I wouldn't know," Gemma complains. "Dad doesn't think I need to talk to Tate. So unfair."

"I'm just shocked you broke him down enough to get a kiss," Willa says with wonder in her voice. "He's always so jumpy and gruff. Always ready to bolt when he's had enough."

"He's still jumpy and gruff and ready to bolt when he's had enough," I assure her. "Last night's blue balls can attest to that."

The girls snigger and I join them.

Funky hops back onto the bed and sashays over to Willa. She pulls him into her lap, snuggling him close.

"You have to kiss him again," Gemma says. "He needs this. He needs someone cute and sweet to get him to act like a human. You're obviously the perfect man for the job."

"I really don't think he'll be back for more Tate cake."

"Tate *pie*," Aubrey corrects. "And he totally will. We'll help you."

"I don't need help," I rush out. "Seriously. Please don't bother him."

Gemma laughs. "Too late. Get dressed. Make sure you look hot. We're going to find him so you can tempt him with your sexy ass. Come on. Hop to it."

I gape at her in horror.

She's serious.

She's really freaking serious.

The four of us have trouble containing our laughter. If we're supposed to be sneaking up on Jude, we're doing a terrible job. We pass by Wyatt's room. His home health nurse is inside, rubbing lotion on his old, papery thin-skinned legs.

"Trouble times four," Wyatt calls out, grinning at us.

I give him a goofy wave as we pass. We follow Gemma as she prowls down the hallway, tapping her witch nails on the wooden panels along the way. She reaches the gym door and cracks it open. Then she slowly closes it before whirling around to face us.

"He's in there," she hisses, grinning at me. "You need to go in there and do something flirty."

"Flirty how?" I ask, frowning.

"Bend over in front of him," Gemma says. "Let him see how those jeans hug your adorable ass."

Aubrey groans. "Don't take flirting advice from a virgin who's literally dated no one. Gemma lives in a false reality. Just ask her Instagram following."

Gemma flips her off but doesn't argue. "Whatever."

"Maybe just go in there and talk to him," Willa suggests. "About last night and how he left so abruptly."

"No," Aubrey says, shaking her head as she grabs onto my shoulders and backs me toward the gym door. "Go in there, walk up to him, and say, 'thanks for the blue balls, asshole. Care if I return the favor?' Then grab him by the dick, give him a little squeeze, and walk away. Trust me, he'll be unable to resist."

"Oh God," Gemma groans. "Jude's not Spencer. He's going to require a little more finesse than your horny baby daddy."

"I agree with Gemma," Willa says, wincing. "Tate's not like…"

"Me?" Aubrey asks, lifting an eyebrow in challenge. "Maybe he ought to be. I don't have any issues pleasing a man." She smirks at me. "Or two."

I'm about to argue that we should all just leave, when a cold breeze swirls around me. The scent of cinnamon and manly sweat fills the air. I don't have to look behind me to know who's standing there. Every hair on my arms stands at attention, buzzing with electricity.

"Oh shit," Aubrey mouths to me.

Jude's palms gently grip my hips as he pushes me aside. Fire licks at my body at his touch. All too soon, he pulls his hands away and steps past me. All three girls smother their giggles with their hands while I attempt to reorient myself now that I'm no longer in his orbit but still spinning.

He strides several steps away but abruptly stops. His hoodie is soaked with sweat and clings to his muscular back. I'd give anything to peel it off his body right about now.

Jude looks over his shoulder, locking eyes with me. Heat sears a fiery path straight to my balls when he drops his gaze to my neck.

Where. He. Marked. Me.

His hand curls into a fist and I wonder if he'll pounce on me. Hell, I'll welcome it. He doesn't attack me with his hungry mouth, unfortunately. All I get is a small nod before he pivots on his heel and stalks away.

God.

Why does he affect me this way?

As soon as he disappears, Gemma digs her freaky cat claws into my jaw, jerking my head toward her. Her eyes glitter with mischief and her grin is devilish.

"He is so hot for you," she whisper-yells. "Oh my God. Did you see that barely contained lust?"

Willa and Aubrey both nod fiercely in agreement.

"You could cut the sexual tension with a knife, Tate pie," Aubrey says with a crooked grin. "I got pregnant looking at you two lick at each other with just your eyes."

"Me too," Willa says breathily.

"You two already are pregnant," I say lamely. "It was probably nothing."

Gemma's nails are back, nearly puncturing my cheeks as she turns my focus back on her. "It was not *nothing*, idiot. It was everything. Jude has it so bad for you."

Does he?

My heart does a nosedive, taking my stomach with it. I feel slightly dazed and lightheaded as I allow myself to consider her words.

Jude has it so bad for you.

Well, apparently, I have it bad for him too.

I should do something nice for him. To show my appreciation for…*him*. Yeah, that's all I've got. I'm appreciative for the way he looked at me just now, for the way he kissed me last night, for the way he let me take off his mask and trusted me with such a vulnerable part of him.

"I'm going to woo him," I blurt out. "But I'm going to need wine."

Gemma's grin is downright evil. "I know a guy. Let me track Dempsey down and we'll hook you up. You've got this, Tate."

Do I?

At least the wine will help if I don't…

CHAPTER EIGHTEEN

Jude

Baker: You can't get rid of me that easily, man. It's like you don't remember how annoying I was from high school.

Baker: Dude, I can see you're reading my messages. Don't be a dick.

Baker: Maybe I'll just show up at your house and you'll be forced to hang out with me then.

I groan at his persistence before firing off a response.

Me: Busy.

Baker: Liar. You're avoiding me. Fine, if you don't want a surprise visit, at least tell me how you're doing.

Why the fuck does he care so much?
I'm going to kill Dad for giving him my number.

Me: I'm fine. Seriously. Worry about your wife and kids, not your ex-best friend.

Baker: We'd still be best friends had you not Xed me out of your life.

Me: I don't need any friends.

Except Tate?

Is he a friend? More?

Definitely more. My dick twitches at the reminder of how fucking cute he looked this morning when I came out of the gym. If the girls weren't there, I'd have probably attacked him with my mouth.

Baker: You're so cold, Park. Don't worry. I'm used to hormonal girls. I have a house full of them. I can navigate bitchy behavior. Let's meet next Friday night.

Me: I'll check my schedule and get back to you.

I toss my phone on my desk, refusing to look at it again. If he shows up, I'll have Violet, or better yet, Grandpa, send him away. I'm not up for visitors.

Glancing at the clock on the wall, I note that it's close to dinner time. Violet usually pops in to let me know what we're having, but she hasn't. I also haven't seen Tate all day either ever since our gym run-in.

I've been hiding in my office like a coward.

Well, after the longest, hottest shower where I beat off twice in a row and still didn't feel sated. I don't know what the hell has gotten into me, but I can't get Tate out of my head.

He's an invader.

A foreign object in my fucking life.

Yet, I like him there.

I really, really do.

With a heavy sigh, I stand and stretch my aching muscles. I went pretty hard in the gym this morning, desperately trying to burn off all this frenetic energy buzzing inside me. Obviously, it didn't work. Now I'm just sore, horny, and still fucked in the head.

I stalk out of my office and down the hallway, peeking

into Tate's room along the way. The room smells like him and I inhale, greedily stealing more of him, though I have no right to. After getting my fill, I head downstairs and am met with a new smell.

Something smells good.

I make my way toward the kitchen to see what Violet is cooking up tonight. The second I enter the kitchen, I stop dead in my tracks. It's not Violet cooking, but Tate, instead. He stands at the stove, stirring something in a big pot, swaying to a beat that must run in his head only. In his other hand is a wine glass filled to the brim with red wine.

He doesn't see me as I slowly creep into the kitchen, my gaze dropping to his ass. Those jeans are criminal. They show off his adorable ass, which does nothing to abate my horniness. Fuck, he drives me insane.

I watch with amusement as he chugs the entire wine glass before setting it down on the countertop with a loud clang. He curses under his breath and then checks the glass to make sure he hasn't broken it. Once he's sure he hasn't, he sets to pouring the rest of the bottle into the glass.

Holy shit.

Did he drink the entire bottle all by himself?

His shirt is tucked in and I'm itching to clutch onto it, jerking it out from his pants so I can slide my fingers along his bare skin like I did last night. God, he'd felt so soft and smooth. I'd wanted to do more than touch. I wanted to run my tongue along his ribs, dip it into his belly button, and then tease his nipples.

Staying away from him is impossible.

Tate swirls around and squeaks out in surprise upon seeing me. Then he grins happily, eyes shining with appreciation.

For me?

If only he could see what lies beyond the mask.

A monster who couldn't save his own mother.

A haunted ghost of a man who's afraid to leave the safety of his home.

"Smells really good," I grunt out, voice low and gravelly. "Violet's not cooking?"

He sips his wine and then shakes his head. "Nope. I gave her the night off. She brought Wyatt some leftovers. It's just the two of us tonight."

Just the two of us.

"What are you making?" I inch toward him, thankful for the excuse to get near. "Soup?"

"Zuppa Toscana copycat recipe. A lady at one of my jobs made it and passed on the recipe to everyone. It's the only thing I can cook that I've memorized."

He polishes off the other glass of wine and then goes back to stirring. The magnetism of him has me drifting closer and closer until my body brushes against his from behind. He doesn't stiffen but instead leans back against my chest. Warmth spreads from where our bodies touch. I can feel my dick thickening and I'm helpless to stop it.

"Someone's excited for soup," he teases and then lets out a slightly drunken giggle.

I want to wrap my arms around him and bury my nose in his hair. I'd love nothing more than to let my hands roam all over his tight body, exploring new places that'll make him whimper and moan.

Fuck.

"Very excited," Tate says, pushing his ass against my erection. "Who knew you were such a fan of soup?"

I chuff out a laugh. "It's definitely the soup that does it for me."

He turns off the eye on the stove before turning around to face me. The wine glass in his hand is empty and he blindly attempts to place it on the counter. My fingers wrap around his so he doesn't crash it on the countertop and ruin this moment with broken glass.

I need this moment.

I need him.

I gently guide his hand down to the countertop and urge his fingers loose. Now that we're standing so close and looking at each other, I don't know what to do. What's allowed? I can't kiss him. He'll see my hideous fucking face.

His palms tentatively touch my pectoral muscles over my hoodie. He squeezes them and laughs. I feel my lips curling into a satisfied smirk.

"You're so ripped," he says dreamily. "I bet your ass looks like it was carved from marble."

Actually, it's scarred and grotesque.

"Hmph."

"You do that a lot." He lifts a hand and boops my nose over my mask. Literally makes the booping sound and everything. "You grunt and grumble when you don't like what I have to say or when you don't want to answer a question."

I shrug, my heart rate picking up when his hand dances along the column of my throat. "You see me as something I'm not. You haven't seen all of me, Tate."

Great.

Kill the mood, asshole.

Tate's lip juts out, pouty and adorable. I want to bite it. Of course I fucking can't.

"I've seen enough," he argues, scrunching his nose. "Enough to know I'm really liking the guy hiding beneath the mask."

So he says.

I know better.

I still have nightmares of my reflection after Mom died. No matter how hard I try to forget the person staring back at me, I can't. It forever haunts me.

"I like touching you." He grins beautifully at me. "Do you like touching me?"

Fuck.

Why is he so irresistible?

He makes it insanely impossible to stay away.

"You're drunk," I state, scowling, though he can't see.

His eyes roll and he playfully smacks my stomach. "Tipsy. It's called liquid courage."

"What do you need courage for?" My rough voice is barely audible as my mind zings with possibilities.

"I wanted to do something nice for you, but I didn't want you to hate it."

He cooked for me to do something nice. My chest tightens with an unfamiliar emotion.

"Why?" I growl, hating how grumpy I sound.

His eyes drop to my chest and he shrugs. "I just wanted to show my appreciation."

I'm already missing his adoring gaze, which explains why I reach up and hook a finger under his chin. I tilt his head up so I can admire all the lovely things about him, starting with his unsure expression.

"This is very nice. Thank you."

He beams at me, sending bursts of sunshine slicing

through dark, dusty parts of me. "I know of a way you could thank me." He nibbles on his bottom lip. "It would mean the world to me."

I frown and shake my head. "I-I can't take off my mask."

Please don't make me.

I can't ruin this moment with you seeing the real me.

Fucking please, Tate.

His eyes grow watery and he also shakes his head. "Never, Jude. Not until you're ready to show me."

Relief surges through me and I exhale. "Oh. Okay, what then?"

Despite the relief of not being seen, I can't help but simmer in the disappointment of not getting to kiss him again.

"I want to give you something," he says, voice breathy and fucking sexy as hell. "Something I think you'll like better than Violet's pie."

"Consider me intrigued," I growl.

He slides a hand down my abs to my cock, boldly grabbing onto my thickness with his hand. I grunt out in surprise but sure as hell don't move away from the delicious touch he offers.

"W-What are you doing?"

His grin is mischievous and I want to fucking taste it on his lips. I bet it's decadent like chocolate cake. "I'm going to make you happy."

I want to argue that nothing will ever make me truly happy, but the words die on my lips when he drops down to his knees. I stare down at him through my mask, enraptured over seeing him kneel before me. Then he hooks his fingers into my sweats and drags them down my thighs. My cock is hard and jutting through my black boxers, looking obscene and desperately needy. No hiding my feelings toward him now.

He sticks his tongue out, shoots me a wicked smirk, and then runs it along the underside of my cock over my underwear. A feral growl rips out of my chest and my fingers grasp onto his soft hair.

"Tate," I snarl, unable to say anything else. "Tate."

"I know," he whispers. "I'm going to make this so good for you."

He pulls down my boxers, dragging them down to where my pants sit just above my knees. My cock bounces out eagerly, flinging pre-cum out. Fucking embarrassing. But Tate doesn't seem to be turned off by my eagerness. In fact, he licks his lips hungrily like he's been waiting forever for a taste.

I try to think back to high school when Serra would do this, but my mind is blank. This feels like unknown territory—like being rocketed into the blissful abyss. I sear him with a hot stare, aching to feel his tongue on me.

I know this is a bad idea.

He'll want more and I'm not sure I can ever offer it.

Still, I allow myself this moment.

Just this one.

That's what you thought last night, too, dumbass, yet here we are.

His hand wraps around my cock and then he flicks his tongue over my slit, going straight for the salty seed he's created just by being him. He rumbles out a moan of pleasure before wrapping his juicy lips around the head.

Fuck.

Stars dance around me and I have to release his head

with one hand to grab onto the countertop for support. I'm going to pass out from pleasure and he's barely touched me.

His tongue starts to tease the flesh of my sensitive dick while he begins bobbing up and down along my length. Since my cock is massive compared to his relatively small mouth, he doesn't get far. But his slobber makes for good lube and he uses it resourcefully to stroke the base of my dick. I grunt and groan, unable to keep from slowly thrusting toward him.

"Mmm," he moans around me.

My eyes roll back with pure ecstasy. I've never felt so goddamn good in my entire life. I don't think I can take any more pleasure. Of course, because he's fucking perfect, he inflicts more on me. His other hand gently cups my balls as he sucks my dick.

"Tate," I rasp out. "Fuck, this is going to be embarrassingly short."

He pulls off to grin up at me. "That's a compliment to the chef."

Then he's back to work, sucking and licking and fucking teeth grazing. I can't take it anymore. I'm going to die from bliss.

"This is," I choke out. "Goddamn, you're so good. Such a good fucking boy."

He smiles around my cock, intensifying his efforts. It only takes a few seconds before my nuts are tightening up.

"I'm coming," I warn him. "You need to—"

Whatever argument I had on the tip of my tongue is gone as he forces himself to gag on my cock. I can feel his throat constricting around the top of my dick. The last shred of my control is gone as cum barrels out of me, filling up his perfect throat.

I watch, completely fucking mesmerized, as he swallows the never-ending stream of cum. I can't believe he wants this from me.

My knees begin to quiver and shake. I'm completely satisfied and spent. He pulls off my dick and then sweetly pulls my underwear and pants back into place. I stand there, stupefied, and unsure what to do next.

"We should eat," he says with a sleepy grin.

I'm about to tell him we can do whatever the fuck he wants because I'll be forever grateful for the gift he just gave me, but I don't get the chance.

He curls up on the floor and goes right to sleep.

This guy is going to be the death of me.

The death I never deserved but will gladly take.

CHAPTER NINETEEN

Tate

'M SO…WARM.

And cozy.

If only my throbbing skull wasn't being made worse by Funky's tail whapping me in the back of the head.

Why is my head throbbing?

Why am I so warm?

As awareness trickles in, so do memories from last night. I remember cooking for Jude. I'd been so nervous, I basically chugged an entire bottle of wine. Then I gave him the best blow job known to man.

He'd loved it.

I remember that much.

The rest of the evening is fragmented. I remember being woken up and guided to the table where a bowl of soup awaited. I remember me asking Jude to feed me.

Oh my God.

I cringe at how stupid that must've made me look. But I do remember him complying. And when I stumbled up the stairs, he scooped me into his arms as though I weighed nothing.

I actually said, "Weeee!" like a damn child.

Then what?

Did he put me to bed?

When did we part ways?

Something touches my hand in the dark. Something warm and strong. Not something. Some*one*.

Holy shit.

I'm not in my bed. This one is softer. Plus, it smells like cinnamon and Jude. He put me in his bed. I slept beside Jude.

My heart rate picks up and my head throbs in tune with it. I can't believe I let myself get drunk. Last night was about showing him appreciation, not forcing him to take care of me.

A pitiful whine escapes me.

I realize I'm clinging to Jude's hard body like some sort of koala freak. He probably thinks I'm ridiculous. Slowly, I roll onto my back, trying to make out shapes in the dark. A sliver of gray, early morning light is cast on the wall, but everything else is shadowy. Since I've never been inside his room before, I can't exactly sneak out without stubbing a toe or running into a wall.

And Funky…

I have to sneak him out too.

Ugh.

The bed shifts beside me. Jude's nose presses against my temple. I swear I hear him inhale me. I'm suddenly aware that if I can feel his nose against me, then he's not wearing his mask.

The urge to straddle him, flick on a light, and look at what he hides from me is strong. But I meant what I said. I wouldn't pressure him to show me if he wasn't ready.

Jude's hand finds my belly and he strokes his fingers in lazy circles around my bellybutton. He's definitely awake, so there'll be no sneaking out. Now that he's touching me, I'm quickly forgetting about the humiliating way I behaved last night and falling victim to his touch.

I also realize my shirt is gone.

My pants are too.

Awareness fully settles in, making me aware that I can feel the heat of his skin touching my bare skin all along my body from our heads to our toes. The only things between us are our boxers.

I want to speak—to apologize for last night—but my tongue sticks to the roof of my mouth. Another pathetic whine squeaks out.

Jude's lips brush over my cheek and he murmurs, "Go back to sleep."

Go back to sleep?!

Is he insane?

There's no way I can sleep now that I know we're both practically naked and I made an idiot of myself last night.

His fingers drift lower and he teases the band of my boxers. I suck in a sharp breath of anticipation, praying he'll do more than tease. Blood leaves my brain, making me momentarily forget last night, and settles at my cock, making it plump up. I fidget in the bed, silently asking for him to touch me there, but also not being man enough to actually say the words.

Funky whaps his tail in my face before darting off the bed with an annoyed meow. Jude makes a soft chuffing sound.

We both grow silent aside from our heavy breathing. I shiver each time his fingers tease at the waistband of my boxers. Then he roughly stuffs his hand inside them, clumsily grabbing onto my cock and pinching a few pubic hairs in the process.

"Sorry," he grunts, voice raspy against my face. "I've never done this before to another man."

My dick pulsates happily in his brutish grip. "S-okay," I choke out. "Feels good."

"Like this?" He slowly moves his hand up and down over my cock, gripping it almost too tightly. His scarred skin is rough on my sensitive flesh. Lube would be great, but I also like the rawness of his touch.

"Yes," I whisper. "You don't have to if—"

"I want to. Very much."

His raspy words tickle over my face. I ache to kiss him, but I haven't brushed my teeth. No one wants to kiss wine morning breath. Yuck. I bite down on my bottom lip to keep the whimpering at bay. Despite his rough grip and first time giving another man a hand job, I am quickly overcome with the raw pleasure coursing through me.

Jude's hand is so large, it easily covers most of my cock from top to bottom and certainly wraps around it. I'm not by any means small in the dick department either. He's just that huge.

"Ungh," I croak out. "Holy shit."

His thumb slides over the tip of my cock, teasing the wetness there. He seems fascinated by this because he does it over and over again, driving me insane with need. When he stops to rub at the slit at the top, I nearly come right then.

"I like your cock," he murmurs against my face.

Oh, fuck.

"I like yours too," I hiss. "Jesus, this feels insanely good."

He continues his up and down stroking all the while teasing my slit. It has me trembling with how fantastic it feels. I can't remember the last time I actually enjoyed sex. Sean made sure it always hurt.

Right as I feel like I might come, Jude slows down. My

heart is hammering in my chest and my head feels as though it'll explode. I whimper and beg for him to go faster, harder, quicker. He goes at a teasing pace that drives me wild. The slow build begins again, making me more and more desperate. Then, when I'm close, he lets go completely.

I cry out in protest, clawing at his arm to continue. The bed shifts and moves before he's yanking my underwear down my thighs. A shudder of anticipation ripples through me. Are we going to have penetrative sex now? Does he even know how? I need to prepare to take him. He's too big to just shove it in!

Sean was too big and shoved it in all the time.

You took cock like a pro back then.

Shame coats over me that I'm thinking of sex with Sean. I hated when he'd do that shit. Lube wasn't in his vocabulary. Hot tears form in my eyes, but I don't know how to stop this.

Weak.

You're weak, Tate.

Always have been. Always will be.

Jude crudely shoves my thighs apart, settling his body between them. I can see the dark shadowed outline of his body as he sits on his haunches between my spread legs, towering over me with painful promise.

His massive hands grip my hips, hauling me up the tops of his thighs to meet his dick. I nearly choke with relief to realize his underwear is still on. His cock is hard, straining against the material as he pushes between my ass cheeks.

Pulsing desire shoots its way through my dick, making it bounce up eagerly. I don't know what he's doing, but it's kind of hot. He starts rubbing my balls with both hands like he's admiring the weight of them, the shape, and the fuzzy hair there. One of his thumbs even rubs along my crack, testing the puckered hole. I jolt with a fear of pain, but he doesn't push his thumb inside.

He's not Sean.

This settles me a bit.

Despite being a huge guy like Sean, he's not cruel like him. At least as far as I can tell. I'm further consoled when he starts stroking my cock again with one hand and fondling my balls with the other.

For a guy who's never given a handy to another dude, he's actually quite creative and talented. I find myself relaxing and spreading my legs more, inviting him to rub his fat cock against my asshole that tingles with need. My hands find my knees and I pull them to my chest.

"Tate," he rasps, voice raw and desperate. "I want to make you come."

I cry out as I get closer to my orgasm. "I'm almost there. This feels incredible."

He grunts in approval, continuing his stroking and teasing. His hips flex, pushing his cock against me as though he's actually fucking me. All fear is gone and I suddenly wish he'd rip off his boxers and do just that.

I want him inside of me—stretching me and owning me and filling me with his cum.

My fantasies coupled with the reality of his touch have me coming with a scream. An actual scream. I'm both horrified and shocked that pleasure could make me do that. The scream trails off into more of a long, loud moan as my cum explodes out of me. It splatters everywhere—all over his hand, my stomach, and even a glob landing on my nipple.

He continues stroking me, using my cum as much-needed

lube, until I'm weak, shivering, and no longer crying out in ecstasy.

"I love the sounds you make," Jude rumbles as he releases my dick to slide his palm up my wet lower stomach. "Fucking hot."

I grin in the darkness. "You're fucking hot."

Jude crawls over me, the bed squeaking under his weight. Hot breath tickles over me and I strain in the dark to see him. Nothing but a shadow.

"I don't understand my need for you," he murmurs. "I can't think clearly."

Well, that makes two of us, buddy.

He grabs one of my hands and brings it to his mouth. His lips press to a knuckle and he kisses it. My heart stutters as he repeats the action with every finger.

I want to grab his face and kiss him silly.

As though he can hear my thoughts, he tenses and then pulls away. The air is cold without him touching me. I feel chilled and exposed.

"Go back to sleep, Tate," Jude instructs as he slips off the bed. "I'm going to shower and then get some work done."

I can hear him shuffling about and then a towel is on me as he scrubs away the leftover cum on my stomach. I search for him in the darkness but give up when the door to the bathroom closes with an audible thud and the lock snaps into place.

So much for cuddle time and kisses after.

Sleepiness does clutch at me, though. I yank his covers back over my body, snuggling into his pillow instead. The shower cuts on and I smile when I hear him grunting moments later.

He's jerking off in the shower.

Because of me.

Because *I* turn him on.

Jude is certainly wrong for me in every way that counts. He's definitely in that toxic territory I love so much. There's also something innocent and kind lurking inside him. I'm curious to know all the parts of what make him who he is.

I fall asleep with visions of him stroking his big, beautiful cock.

This better have not all been a torturous dream.

CHAPTER TWENTY

Jude

'M ADDICTED TO TATE.

Fucking addicted.

And I have no idea how to stop it.

Knowing he's been sleeping away the day in my bed, after sleeping with me last night and then letting me get him off this morning, has been trying for my patience. I so badly want to crawl back into bed with him and do so much more.

My soapy hand in the shower this morning paled in comparison to the way his mouth felt in the kitchen last night.

I let out a frustrated sigh and pick up the pie plate Violet brought along with my lunch. She asked if Tate was okay since he never made it down for breakfast or lunch. I told her he was having a much-needed day to sleep in and I'd make sure he was fed when he woke up.

Eventually, he will wake up and I'll be forced to look him in the eye.

Will he regret what we did last night and this morning?

I hate the way my stomach drops at the thought of him feeling badly about what we did. That would fucking gut me.

Why, though?

Because you like him, dumbass.

Really, really like him.

I stab at the pecan pie on my plate as though it's the

reason for my frustration and not my complicated, twisted-up mind. The pie, however, is sweet and decadent, a far cry from my bitter and sour self.

When my phone buzzes, I polish off the rest of my pie and then trade the plate for my phone, eager to take my mind off my exploding feelings for Tate. As soon as I read the name of who texted me, I groan in exasperation.

Baker: Seriously. My birthday is coming up. If you don't want me going to your house, let's go do something. I'll bring the wifey and you can bring a date. I know your sexy ass is seeing someone.

I cringe at the thought of Baker knowing exactly what I've been up to in the romance department. My old football buddy would give me so much shit if he knew I was obsessing over a goddamn guy. He wasn't exactly quiet about his homophobic comments in the past.

Asshole.

Me: Still busy. I'll also be busy for the foreseeable future. Have a nice birthday and life. Lose my number.

There. Maybe the prick will leave me alone.

Baker: You're such a shithead. More than I remember. Don't worry, princess. You can't push me away with a few pissy words. We go waaaaaaay back, man.

A part of me wants to see Baker face to face. Then, he could see what a nightmare of a person I've become. The guy he was friends with in his youth is gone. Maybe I'll creep him out enough he'll ghost me, never to reach out again.

The thought of going into public with my mask drawing

all kinds of attention, though, is nauseating. His wife would probably look at me like I'm some kind of freak. I know Willa about crawled out of her skin the first time she saw me. I'm an embarrassment to the Park name, hence why I stay hidden.

Baker: I already told the wife. Dinner at our place or yours. Either way, it's happening.

At least if they showed up here for dinner, I would make them feel uncomfortable with my mask and they would leave the first chance they get.

Me: Even if you guilt me into saying yes, I'll cancel.

Baker: Do I need to beat some sense into you like old times?

Me: I strictly remember being the one to deliver all the ass whippings when we were kids. You run your mouth and I shut it up.

Baker: There's my bestie! We'll talk soon about the deets.

Me: Oh, fuck off.

I toss my phone back onto my desk, irritated that Baker is getting his way. It really is like when we were kids. He's bull-headed and won't stop until he gets what he wants. If he doesn't, he throws a fucking pissy tantrum. I can't believe he found someone to marry him, much less have four kids with him.

My sour mood dissipates as my mind drifts back to Tate. Last night, he gave me an epic blowjob. I felt like I'd died and gone to heaven. His mouth on my cock was so damn perfect.

This morning was pretty amazing too, returning the favor and drinking in every desperate mewling sound that escaped him.

What happens next?

Is he going to push for more?

Something tells me I'll let him. Tate has this way about getting me to reveal sides of me no one has ever seen. Eventually, though, he's going to literally want to see. As in for me to remove my mask and reveal the monster beneath.

I try to imagine his reaction.

He'd be nice and probably try to smile. But would there be disgust shining in his eyes? Fear?

The idea of Tate being afraid unsettles me. I've seen it several times now, a few times directed at me. He still hangs on to some secrets and they're beginning to paint a picture of an ugly past. If anyone knows ugly, it's me.

The video I discovered when I was researching him doesn't exactly align with the man I know, which leads me to believe there's a lot more going on than I realize. Was the video made under duress? Did someone hurt him? It certainly explains the weary, worried expression whenever he's outside or the jumpiness whenever I startle him.

Knowing that someone could hurt him makes my stomach curdle and anger flash hot through my veins. Who would do such a thing?

One thing's for sure. I'm going to have to get Tate to talk to me. He's been doing his fair share of getting everyone in this family, including me, to reveal their deepest, most intimate secrets, so it's only right he gives me something in return. I want to know more about the video and his firings. I want to know what terrifies him so badly.

Why?

So I can protect him from it?

I don't know how, but I want to try.

"Jude!"

Violet's voice from downstairs draws me out of my head. I grab the dishes on my desk and stride out of my office, stopping to peek inside at Tate along the way. He's still fast asleep, his cat curled up on his chest. I smile, unable to stop it from forming, and then head downstairs. Violet waits for me, a worried frown on her face.

"What's wrong?" I demand. "Grandpa?"

She shakes her head quickly as she takes the dishes from me. "Not him, no. Go have a look outside. Oh, poor Tate. He's going to be so upset."

Poor Tate?

My body thrums with barely contained anxiety. I bolt out the front door, unsure of what I'm going to see. It can't be horrible because he and his cat are upstairs sleeping safely in my bed.

What then?

As soon as I see the red paint, I understand.

His car sits in the driveway, covered in red paint. Someone wrote over his windows through the paint with what looks like their finger. What does it say?

Slut.

It says slut.

What the actual fuck?

My blood turns to ice as I read over the hastily written word over and over again. How the hell does this person know we were together last night? Why are they vandalizing his car for it? Who would do such a horrible thing?

I can't seem to grasp onto any thought very long. Anger

and worry keep zinging through my brain. Could I get this cleaned off before he gets up? Could I spare him from this cruelty?

When I reach the back of the vehicle, there's no paint, but the perp carved words with a key.

Does your new boyfriend know you like a big, hairy fist up your ass?

Someone fucking wrote this on Tate's car!

Fury overwhelms me, making me see much darker shades of red than the paint covering his car. I want to find the person responsible and choke the life out of them. I've never wanted to hurt someone, but whoever did this deserves pain. Lots and lots of pain.

Violet appears and hooks her arm into mine, leaning her head against me. "Why would they do this to our sweetheart?"

Our sweetheart.

That's exactly what he is, too.

Ours.

Mine.

"Someone who doesn't value their life." I snarl, vibrating with rage. "Unbelievable."

She squeezes my arm, shuddering. "He's going to be so upset, Jude. I can't bear to see him heartbroken."

Me neither.

I stare at the carved words on his car. *Does your new boyfriend know you like a big, hairy fist up your ass?* I'd noticed him tense up when I spread his legs but thought it was because it was me touching him. I'm now wondering if he was remembering something bad. Someone hurting him before.

Violet pulls away to walk around one side of the vehicle. She sighs and crouches down. "Got the tires too."

I wince but follow her around to have a look. Sure enough, the tires have been shredded. This wasn't some silly prank. This was personal. Vengeful and evil.

Tate will tell me who did this to him.

I will make them fucking pay.

"What are you going to do?" Violet asks, voice small and sad as she stands back up. "Don't get yourself into trouble, Jude. Maybe you should call your father."

So Daddy can clean up the mess for me since I'm too mentally unstable to do it myself?

Fuck that.

I'm going to handle it.

"I'll take care of it," I bite out, voice sharp like a blade. "Don't you worry about a thing."

She walks over to me and then hugs me tight around my middle. "He needs us. We have to keep him safe."

Keep. Him. Safe.

And she's right. Whoever could do this so shamelessly to his vehicle would have no problems taking it further. They could hurt him. Maybe they already have. It's obvious now why Tate is always so jumpy and afraid.

He knows pain.

He knows suffering.

I feel like an absolute asshole for the way I've treated him now. His secrets were to protect himself and I was so desperate to pry that box open. I thought he was hiding something that could hurt my family when all along it was something far from nefarious.

"No one will touch him," I vow, my voice rattling with fierce intensity. "No one."

"Thank you," she whispers. "I'm going to go update Wyatt. Would you like for me to call the police?"

I shake my head as she pulls away. "I'll get Sloane out here. This is a private matter. We don't need some Joe Schmo meddling in our affairs."

She gives me a small smile before walking away.

I spear my fingers into my hair, tugging until my eyes water. If only I could protect him from what's been done to his car.

There's not enough time.

He'll see and he'll be hurt.

But don't worry, sweet Tate, I'm going to fix this for you.

Someone is responsible for this monstrous act and there will be retribution.

CHAPTER TWENTY-ONE

Tate

'M DOING THE WALK OF SHAME.

Thankfully, the only witness is my cat. He meows behind me as I dash from Jude's room to mine in nothing but my underwear.

Where did my clothes go?

Please tell me I didn't strip or something awful like that on the way up the stairs last night before he scooped me up.

If I did…that means Violet may have seen them scattered everywhere. Oh God. I will die if she had to pick up my discarded clothes.

As soon as I close the door to my room, I scan the space, looking for my clothes. Still nothing. They weren't on Jude's floor either.

She totally had to pick up my clothes!

How will I ever face that woman?

"Stupid, stupid, stupid," I grumble to Funky. "No more wine. Ever."

He ignores me, heading straight for his litter box. I flick my gaze over to the clock on the wall and cringe when I see it's way past noon. Not only did I act like an idiot, probably stripping on the stairs and ending up in Jude's bed only to have to do the walk of shame, I also slept the damn day away.

Violet will definitely be wondering why I wasn't in my room or where the hell I am.

This is so embarrassing!

I wish I had Dempsey's or Willa's number. Not that I can even use my phone or anything, but still, it'd be nice to call in reinforcements to talk me off the ledge here.

Where is Jude?

I throw on some clothes and shoes before quickly brushing my teeth. I can bathe later once I locate some food and assess the shameful situation.

How is Jude feeling about last night and this morning?

I'm dying to talk to him. If I can get a read on him, it'll do wonders for my racing mind. I want to know if he's happy about what we did. If he's not…I may as well just quit and run away.

Once decent, I hurry downstairs. I see Violet peeking out the window by the front door. When she hears the stairs creak, she whips around and stares at me with a guilty expression.

Not disappointed like one would be if she found another man's clothes scattered about…

What does Violet have to be guilty of?

"Morning, er, afternoon," I say, wincing at my error. "I'm a sleepyhead today."

She forces a smile. I don't like that. Not one bit. It puts me on edge.

"It happens, honey. Why don't you come into the kitchen so I can fix you something to eat?"

I hear raised voices outside and pause, craning my neck to listen. It sounds like Jude. He's pissed, too. When I start for the front door, Violet shakes her head.

"Please, sweetie, don't go out there. Let Jude take care of it."

Take care of what?

A chill slides through my veins, turning them straight to ice.

Her behavior, Jude outside, the yelling, him needing to take care of something—it's all adding up to something dreadful. I just know it.

Ignoring her plea, I march straight out the front door. The first thing I see is the bright red blob in the yard. Not just any blob. My car.

As soon as it registers that my car has been vandalized, I completely freeze as suffocating fear cloys the air around me. My lungs seize and I absently claw at my sweater as though it'll help me breathe. I'm rooted to the front porch, unable to move or speak or scream.

It's Sean.

Sean was here.

This is what he does.

A wave of nausea passes over me. I swallow the acidy bile trying to come up my throat. This can't be happening. It can't!

I was safe here.

I made sure of it.

How did he find me?

A cat or wounded animal makes a pained, horrible sound. It takes only a second to realize the sound is coming from me.

I'm the broken one.

I'm the one collapsing under the weight of terror.

Muffled voices are directed at me, but I can't pick out

who they belong to. My eyes are locked on the red blob of my car. It looks like blood.

I gag but thankfully don't puke my guts out.

A white mask comes into view and strong hands grip my shoulders. I blink away the scarring image of my car and fixate on the blue eyes peering through the eyeholes at me. Jude's concern flickers in his eyes as they dart all over me as if to assess where I'm hurting.

It's inside.

It's always deep, deep inside my heart and my head when Sean's not around.

And then it hurts everywhere when he is.

"Tate," Jude barks out, stealing my attention again. "Hey, that's it. Look at me. I think you're having a panic attack."

"His car looks like a murder scene," a voice—Dempsey—counters back in my defense. "I think he's allowed to freak the fuck out."

Jude ignores Dempsey and hauls me against his warm, solid chest. I sink against him, inhaling his cinnamon scent. Memories of last night and this morning dance inside my head. Jude strokes my back and whispers soft assurances. I could get lost in his protective, comforting embrace.

But then my mind jerks me out of his safety and back into panic mode.

Sean couldn't have known I was here. I was so careful. Hell, I didn't even turn on my computer or phone once since I've been here. He's successfully found me plenty of times before and I think it has something to do with his buddy at the police department.

The last time the body shop fixed my car, I had them

look for any kind of tracker, too. I'm almost a hundred percent sure he's tracking me via my phone somehow. I didn't turn it on, though.

I turn statue-still as a thought comes to me.

A memory.

The night I was forced to stay here, I found Jude lurking in my room near my suitcase. Did he…*No.* Surely he didn't turn my phone on and spy on me.

Surely not.

Surely to God not.

He doesn't even know my passcode to get into my phone.

He's a freaking hacker, idiot. You've seen his wall of monitors in his office!

Which means he's a lot more resourceful than Sean.

Being in his arms suddenly doesn't feel so safe. It feels like a prison—his steely arms holding me inside.

I knew, in my gut, he was too much like Sean. I knew it, acknowledged it, and then straight up ignored it. Why? Because this is my pattern. I find the most dangerous, toxic man and entangle myself with him. I crawl right into their claws, let them cut me so fucking deep, and then wonder why I can't escape.

Stupid! Stupid! Stupid!

I need therapy.

Not everyone else.

Me.

I start to push away from Jude's chest, but he tightens his grip. It's so stifling and hot. I just want to get the hell away from him—away from everything and everyone.

"L-Let me go," I croak out, pushing against him again.

"No."

I look up at him and make a grab for his mask. He shoves away from me like *I'm* the monster. Serves him right!

Dempsey watches with a frown, eyes darting between us. "You okay, Tate?"

"No," I snap, stabbing a finger at Jude. "This is all his fault."

Jude grunts in disagreement and Dempsey's eyebrows rise in confusion. I bolt back through the front door, nearly knocking over Violet in the process. She babbles something to me, but I can't listen. I need to get away.

Because not only is Jude a problem—a huge fucking problem—but Sean won't stop at a vandalized car. He'll start messing with everyone here just to get at me. I can't imagine being responsible for him destroying their property, or worse yet, hurting them in some way. No way.

I race up the stairs, making my way straight to my room. Blinking back tears, I snatch my suitcase up and toss it on the bed. Then I begin hastily throwing my clothes and belongings into the suitcase. I don't have much, so it goes rather quickly.

I'm just zipping up the suitcase when the wood creaks in my doorway. From my peripheral, I see Jude standing in the doorway, arms crossed over his chest. Ignoring him, I make a grab for my cat, but he darts out of reach.

"Just where the hell do you think you're going?"

The pure anger in Jude's tone chills me. Is this where he puts his hands on me? Tries to drive my head through the fucking wall? Rape and record me to humiliate me with later? Hot tears spill down my cheeks and a wretched sob escapes.

Why?

Why did he have to be just like him?

"Tate," Jude says, voice much softer. "Don't go, sweet boy."

Sweet boy.

I hate that some part of me still trembles with pleasure at his words. It infuriates me that I'm so drawn to these horrible men who are terrible for me. Harnessing that anger and chasing away the hurt, I whirl around to face him.

"You did this," I hiss as I swipe away my tears. "Why did you have to do this?"

Jude growls behind his mask. "I didn't vandalize your car. I wouldn't."

A disgusted laugh barks out of me. "No. What you did was awful all on its own. You spied on me."

He doesn't respond. Just stares at me through his mask. Ugh.

"My phone?" I spit out, gesturing at my suitcase. "That's why you were in my room that night."

Again, no words leave his mouth. Asshole.

"Well, you fucked up, Jude. You turned it on, hacked into it, and God only knows what else. And you know what? It told him exactly where I was." I sneer at him, stabbing another finger in the air. "You're just like him. A fucking stalker!"

He snaps out of his frozen state and charges for me. I attempt to hold my ground but end up flinching in fear, waiting for the blow. It doesn't come. The weirdo just towers over me, glaring through his mask.

"Who?" he demands.

"My ex!" I cry out, throwing my hands in the air. "You

going to break my arm? Chain me to the bed? Make a fuck-ing snuff tape to send to my next employers? Get a ticket and stand in line!"

"I would never hurt you." His palm cradles my cheek and I almost believe him.

"Yeah, he said that too. That's kind of a pattern for big, scary guys like you and him." I shove at his chest, but the oaf doesn't budge. "Besides, you already did hurt me. You be-trayed my trust and led the monster right to my doorstep."

"I won't let anything happen to you," Jude growls, planting his large hands on my shoulders. "I'll keep you safe."

My lip trembles and another pained sob escapes. I hate that I'm crying. I hate how broken I feel right now. Stupid me let my guard down and allowed people into my heart. Never again.

"It's too late, Jude. What's done is done." I glower up at him. "Now let me go. I'm leaving."

He slowly shakes his head in disagreement. Is he for real right now? Am I about to be in the middle of a damn stalker war?

You brought this on yourself, kid.

I hate that Dad's slurring voice is the one I hear inside my head. Every time he drank and threw me into a wall or rammed his fists into me, it was somehow my fault. I egged Dad on. I provoked him. I pushed and pushed and pushed him until he snapped. It was always the same warning be-fore the pain would come. *You brought this on yourself, kid.*

"Jude," Violet murmurs from the doorway. "The police are here and they want to speak to Tate."

Jude's eyes burn into me, warning me of more to come

later. Joke's on him. I'm going to hightail it the hell out of here the second I get done talking to the cops.

I'll disappear once and for all.

Start over in some Podunk town in the middle of nowhere.

I will have a life I'm in control of. One that doesn't continuously hurt in all the ways. I'm done being a plaything for monsters to toy with.

CHAPTER TWENTY-TWO

Jude

FUCKED UP.

I really, really fucked up.

How the hell was I supposed to know he had some psychopath tracking him? Had I known, I could have avoided turning on his phone. Hell, I could have taken preventative steps to keep him protected in the first place.

He should have told me.

I should have asked.

Tate is kind and sweet, despite my earlier misgivings. I doubted him rather than giving him the chance he deserved at first. Now, he's beyond upset with me. Whatever thing was transpiring between us feels irrevocably snapped.

It's what I wanted, yet…

I fucking don't.

I don't want him to leave me. Not when I finally had my first taste of happiness since high school. If he leaves, that hope and sunshine I was looking forward to basking in each day will be gone. I'll be back to being the recluse of Park Manor, hiding in the shadows and soaking in my pain.

It felt good not to hurt all the time.

Tate was good for me.

By the time I follow him outside to where Sloane waits, my mind is a fucking mess. Tate is shaken and upset, but worse yet, he won't look at me. His walls are slamming into place around him. Is this how everyone else feels when they try to connect with me? Trapped outside with no hope of ever getting in?

Disgust at myself and the situation settles in my gut, souring it. I want to join Tate and Sloane to hear all the details, but I also need to give Tate some space.

He thinks I'm just like him—his ex. Knowing he puts me in the same category as a man who apparently beat and ridiculed him hurts. This ex of his stalks him and vandalizes his property. And I'm just like this fucker?

Dempsey lingers near Tate and Sloane for a bit before meandering over to me. His eyebrows are furled. Is he pissed at me too?

"He's telling her he knows who it is but doesn't want to pursue it or press charges," Dempsey reveals. "Sloane is trying to talk him out of it."

He doesn't want to press charges? Is he insane?

A feral growl rumbles out of me and I crack my neck. Before I can storm over there, Dempsey grabs my arm, stopping me.

"Don't," he warns. "For whatever reason, Tate is fucking mad at you. Going over there and bullying your way through their conversation won't help your case."

I look down at my baby brother and frown. "Help my case?"

Dempsey chuckles lowly. "I'm no idiot. You two clearly have it bad for each other. Are you fucking him?"

My jaw muscles clench and I fist my hands. "None of your business."

"You're dumb as fuck, Jude. It's obvious you two are together."

You two are together.

That small phrase has my heart beating rapidly in my chest. I didn't think I deserved any happiness, especially with Tate, but now that I've tasted it, I'm addicted. I don't want to let go of it.

Tate is mine.

I'm sure your stalker twin, his ex, feels that way too…

"Why won't he press charges?" I ask, changing the subject.

"Says it'll get worse. That's when Sloane gave me the stink eye to leave. Maybe she'll be able to get through to him alone." He stares at her for a long beat before shaking his head and then looking back over at Tate's car. "His ex sounds like a real psychopath. We should fuck him up."

Fucking him up would require leaving my house.

Sometimes I hate how messed up I am in the head. A normal boyfriend—*is that what I am to him or at least want to be?*—would be able to handle this situation for his guy. As it stands, I can't do shit.

I could destroy his ex via online means, but that's not as satisfying as ramming my fist through that violent prick's face.

"I guess it's time to finally put cameras up on your shack," Dempsey says. "Maybe have your porch redone while you're at it. One of these days Grandpa is going to crash through his ramp."

Fuck.

Because of my issues, I'm endangering others. Tate, Violet, Grandpa.

"I'll set something up," I vow, voice fierce.

Dempsey nods, seemingly pleased with my answer. It's pretty sad a seventeen-year-old kid has more sense about the right thing to do than I do. And that's saying something since he's the family fuckup.

Maybe *I'm* the family fuckup.

All of this could have been potentially avoided had I not invaded Tate's personal space, serving him up on a platter for his enemy. At the time, digging into the new stranger in our lives felt warranted. I was protecting my family. But at what cost? Now Tate's important to me and I put a target on his back.

Tate nods at Sloane and then starts back toward the house. Dempsey trots back over to Sloane and whispers something that makes her tense. He can fill me in later on their conversation. Right now, I have to fix me and Tate.

I will fix us.

"Tate," I call after him as he storms into the house. "Wait."

Ignoring me, he stomps up the stairs. I charge after him and then pass him by. He growls something unintelligible to me, but I'm focused on my new mission.

Make. Him. Stay.

I snatch up his suitcase and then the cat carrier once I've made my way into his room. When I whirl around, he's entering the space, face twisting up in anger.

"You're not leaving," I grunt, shouldering past him.

"What the hell, Jude?!"

Funky darts past us, hightailing it back to my bedroom. I follow after him and set his carrier by the window. Then I toss the suitcase on my bed and start unzipping it.

"You can't do this," Tate bellows. "I'm leaving!"

"Not if I can fucking help it."

I start shoving clothes into drawers, pushing my clothes aside to make room for his. He doesn't come near me but continues to argue. It reminds me of a little dog yapping at an intruder. Except he's no dog and I'm no intruder. I'm protecting what's mine. End of fucking story.

I locate his keys in the suitcase and bury them in my closet between my vast array of black hoodies. When I exit the closet, he's standing by the bed, arms crossed over his chest, scowling at me.

Pissed is better than afraid.

I am not like his ex.

"Not pressing charges, eh?" I grunt as I scoop up the empty suitcase. "Sounds like you're letting him get away with hurting you. Again."

Fire blazes in his eyes as he watches me throw his suitcase into my closet. "I don't let him do anything. He takes and takes and takes. Like someone else I know."

Something in me snaps and I decide I'm done with his bullshit. I prowl over to him until I'm crowding his space. Gently, I run my fingers through his hair on the back of his head and then tug until he peers up at me. His nostrils flare and his luscious lips are parted as though he might like my proximity, but the fury in his gaze never recedes.

"I am not like him and you know it." I lean my masked forehead against his, hating for the millionth time I have to hide the ugly from him. "I'm sorry I turned your phone on and spied on you. It was fucked up. I hate that I did it."

His anger cools from an exploding volcano to a simmering pot. I take that as a win and quickly continue forward.

"How can I fix this, Tate? I can't...I can't lose you."

He scrunches his eyebrows together, eyes growing sad. "I'm struggling here."

"Because of me?"

"Not just you." He sighs heavily. "I know you're not like him. I'm sorry I said that."

My heart rate speeds up. I allow my hands to curl around his neck so I can stroke his flesh softly with my thumbs. Does he like it? Is this comforting him?

His eyes flutter closed and he gives me a sad smile. "I'm just scared, okay? No matter what I do, my life just keeps getting ruined because of him."

"Let me help you," I plead. "I can make him pay for this."

He pulls back, shaking his head. "It'll just make it worse. You don't understand. He's been terrorizing me for two years, Jude. Two long years. I've endured more pain and suffering from him than the rest of my life combined. And he's crazy. He doesn't give up or go away."

"Tell me his name," I demand. "I can do something. Anything. Please let me."

"You can't, though. He's ruthless. He can hurt people. You really want to put Gemma in danger? It's what he does."

If he thinks I'm going to stay away now, he's fucking insane. But I'll have to do some digging on my own time. Not now. Now we're on a delicate thread and I need to keep him close.

"I want you in my bed every night," I rasp out, dragging my thumbs along his stubbly jaw. "Every night. Fucky too."

He smirks. "Funky. You're a real dick, Jude."

"You like my dick," I remind him, grinning behind my mask. "Gobbled it up like it was one of Violet's apple pies."

"Funny," he deadpans. "And how do you explain how

much you like my dick? You sure enjoyed playing with it this morning."

Fucking hell.

I loved it more than he'll ever know.

So tell him, asshole.

"I loved how hard you were. The mess you made. The sexy moans that came out of you." I ghost my palms down his front, drifting lower until I can grope said dick. "I've never experienced anything so hot in my goddamn life, sweet boy."

His eyes go all dopey and adorable at the endearment. I lock away that kernel of information to use to my advantage in the future.

"I have an idea," I tell him, stepping back despite wanting to put his dick in my mouth this time.

He groans and gestures at his hard cock pressing against his jeans. "Does it involve doing something about this?"

I chuckle and shake my head. "Later. Right now, you need to relax. Let me take care of you."

"How?" His voice quivers like he doesn't quite believe me. Like this might be a trick. It makes me hate his ex even more for doing this to him.

"I'll run you a bath and feed you pie. After, we can go up to my secret room and listen to music."

He shocks me by hugging me, burying his face against my chest. "I'd like that. It sounds…almost too good to be true."

"Believe it," I growl. "I want good things for you and I'm going to work hard to show you."

"Thank you."

No, thank you, Tate, for barreling into my life and waking me the fuck up from my nightmare.

I pull away from him to start a hot bath. It sucks I don't

have anything fun like bubble bath for him, but I do dump some body wash in that bubbles up nicely. Knowing he'll smell like me is icing on the cake. After the tub fills, I lay out a towel and then exit the bathroom.

Tate stands in front of the bed, looking good enough to eat in just his underwear. His cheeks are pink and he bites on his bottom lip. God, he's going to fucking kill me with how cute he is.

"You better get into that tub before I change my mind," I warn, every muscle tightening with need.

He arches a brow and then boldly pushes down his underwear. His cock eagerly bounces out, making my mouth water. I nearly break my neck as he walks by in an effort to stare at his ass.

A perfect motherfucking ass.

I get another saucy look over his shoulder and then he disappears into the bathroom.

Mine.

He's fucking mine now.

CHAPTER TWENTY-THREE

Tate

J UDE WAS RIGHT.

I did need to relax. Despite all the drama I went through earlier, I'm feeling much calmer. Yes, he made a mistake and shouldn't have spied on me. No, I don't really believe he's just like Sean.

Sean is still the abuser in this situation.

Jude is mentally tormented by his past, but he cares about people, especially those he allows into his world.

Am I part of that world now?

I smile at that thought. Being in Jude's world was terrifying at first. From outward appearances, he's definitely a bit of a freak. Beyond the latex, though, he's human with real needs and emotions.

I close my eyes and sink deeper into Jude's tub. He must've used his body wash for a bubble bath substitute because it smells like him—the manly part, not the cinnamon part. I inhale the scent and lazily run my fingers along the water's hot surface.

"I was going to feed you, but I can come back."

My eyes pop open to discover Jude standing in the doorway, carrying one of the trays Violet uses when bringing us food to our rooms. I perk up, eager for a bite to eat. The grumbling of my stomach makes his decision to stay. He sets the tray down beside the tub on the closed toilet lid and then perches on the edge of the bathtub.

If only I could get him to take his mask off for me.

"Since you made so much soup last night and it was so good, I figured you'd like some of that," he says, gesturing at the tray. "Violet insisted you needed more than just soup, though. There's sweet iced tea, a couple of fresh-baked rolls for dipping, and of course a slice of pie."

"And the flower?" I ask, glancing at the purple carnation resting near the silverware.

He grunts and shrugs. "Violet had a vase of fresh-cut flowers on the table. I snagged one. Thought you might like it."

"I do," I assure him, unable to keep from grinning like a dork. "Thank you."

"Can I feed you again, sweet boy?"

Again?

That's right. Last night when I was drunk and making a fool of myself, I somehow conned him into feeding me. My cheeks burn hot at the reminder. Jude, however, must think it's sexy because he watches me intently like a lion salivating over a gazelle.

"Yes," I whisper.

He scoops up the bowl and one of the rolls. I watch as he balances the soup bowl on his lap and tears off a piece of the bread. After he dunks it in the soup, letting it soak up all the delicious, juicy flavor, he brings it to my lips.

"Open up," he instructs, voice low, as his eyes sear into mine.

I part my lips and accept the bite of soupy bread. It's better than I remember. I'm starving and this is one of my favorite meals. With the suds in the water dissolving, my cock is on full display, the head of it bobbing at the surface. It would be so easy for him to reach over and jerk me off right here.

He doesn't, though, and continues to dutifully feed me. Despite wanting his hands on me, his caring nature is what I need more right now. My heart squeezes, knowing he's doing what's best for me, not what our dicks both want.

He *is* better than Sean.

"Tell me a story," I say after I swallow down another bite. "It doesn't have to be sad. It can be anything."

He ponders my words for a moment before clearing his throat. "I used to play football. Coach thought I was good enough to go pro."

"You certainly have the body for it," I tease, pinching his thick thigh. "I bet you were smokin' hot in the uniform."

"I guess. Looking back, I think that's when I started noticing guys too." He feeds me more soup and continues. "In the showers, I'd compare dicks. I didn't think much of it, but when you and me started…" He trails off and bores his stare into me. "When you and I started our thing, well, I was able to see maybe I haven't been as straight as I always thought."

We have a thing.

Our thing.

I don't know why that makes my heart sing, but it does.

It feels private and precious.

"Did you ever try anything or were you just curious?" I ask, reaching for the tea glass.

He hands it to me and I gulp down the sweet liquid.

"Nah. It didn't even register. Plus, I was with Serra and she was more than I could handle."

I can't believe I'm jealous of some girl he used to sleep

with in high school a million years ago. But I am jealous that she got to have sex with this beautiful man.

"Though, Mom did ask me a day or two before she died if I was gay. Even asked me if I had a boyfriend." He chuckles, a sound that's gritty and rough but lovely nonetheless. "I never knew how she even came to this conclusion. It's not like she didn't see me with Serra all the time and she certainly wasn't there to witness how my eyes strayed in the locker room showers."

"Moms have a sixth sense about things," I say sadly, feeling the familiar pang of losing my own mother.

He goes silent for a few moments, letting me finish up the soup. Then he moves on to the apple pie. I thought maybe I'd feel silly to have him feed me, but I actually like it. This all feels intimate and sweet. It's a new side of Jude that I really like.

"She was a terrible cook." Jude snorts and shakes his head. "Probably the real reason Dad bailed on her. Jamie's a great cook."

We both know the affair was a lot more complicated than food.

"But she could bake well. I never understood how someone could burn chicken but make the best apple pie I'd ever tasted." He steals a bite of my pie for himself, clearly lost in the memory of his mother. "I'll never be able to truly thank Violet enough for giving me a sweet piece of my mother each day."

My heart cracks open at his words.

This pie-loving beast of a man is nothing but a cinnamon roll under all that scary exterior.

"Violet is a great woman. I can see why you adore her." I reach over and touch his arm. "You say you could never thank her enough, but have you tried telling her what you just told me? I bet it would mean the world to hear it."

"I will." He's still for several seconds and then continues. "Every year on Thanksgiving and Christmas, I bring a slice of apple pie to Mom's grave. I'm sure the squirrels and rabbits and birds just love me. The plate is always cleared when I go back to retrieve it." He bows his head. "Sometimes I pretend she's the one who ate it."

Jude was a momma's boy through and through. When she died, she took his heart with her. I'm thankful he's opening up to me. Perhaps his heart is trying to grow again. I'll make sure I take care of it for him.

"Thank you for telling me," I say softly. "I know opening up isn't easy for you. I just want you to know it means a lot to me."

"Thank you for staying." He reaches over to tug at my bottom lip. "Now let's get you dressed so we can go listen to some music."

I keep nodding off despite being a captive in Jude's intense stare. He promised a relaxing day and he's made sure it was just that for me. First the bath and a late lunch, then we spent hours talking and listening to his extensive record collection, and we even ate dinner upstairs.

The man is great at foot massages too.

He's spoiling me with attention and adoration. It almost makes me feel guilty. As though I don't deserve such sweetness. But then I remind myself that's just Dad and Sean picking at me, not the truth.

The truth is, I do deserve to be doted on.

I deserved to be loved.

Is that where we're headed? Love? As much as that intrigues me, I know not to get too far ahead of myself. Rushing into love only gets you hurt. And Jude still has mountains of issues that may crop up for him from time to time that might rain on this little wannabe love parade.

"It's late," Jude says, voice rough. "Ready to go to bed?"

To his bed since that's apparently where I sleep now.

I give him a sleepy smile and nod. Rather than help me to my feet, he scoops me up into his powerful arms. I like how strong he is and that he doesn't try to hurt me. It really does feel safe here with him.

I rest my head on his shoulder as he makes the trek back to his room. I must pass out because when I wake again, I'm in the bed that smells of him. It's completely dark and I'm in just my underwear. Having him undress me for bed is something I could definitely get spoiled with.

The bed dips under his weight and then he slides under the covers with me. I roam my palm up his naked chest on a trajectory toward his face to see if he's wearing his mask. He stops me by gripping my wrist, right before I make it to my destination. A pang of disappointment ripples through me but is chased away by heat when he playfully bites on my fingertips.

"You bit me," I murmur, breathy and shocked.

He sucks on my fingers, making me groan. "Better?"

"Much. Keep sucking and I'll give you something to put your mouth on."

His laughter, soft and adorable, melts my heart. He really should laugh more often. It's a beautiful, happy sound.

"You're supposed to be sleeping," he counters, a smile in his voice.

"I'm thinking about blowjobs now. I definitely can't sleep."

He pulls away from my touch and the bed dips on either side of me as he straddles my legs. I suck in a breath as I try to anticipate what his next move might be. In the dark, he somehow finds my arms and he pushes them down onto the bed on either side of my head. I feel shackled to him, but despite my racing heart, I like the feeling.

It's then I realize I trust him.

He won't hurt me. I believe him not because he's told me, but because I know. Jude is different. A good man with an even better heart.

His hot breath tickles over my chest a second of warning before his tongue flicks out to taste me. I jolt at the sudden burst of pleasure tickling over my skin. He teases his tongue along my flesh, making me writhe and squirm beneath him. When he reaches one of my nipples, he sucks it into his mouth before he starts nibbling on the hard nub.

"Jude," I whimper. "I need you."

On me. Inside of me. Making love to me.

"I know," he rasps out. "I need you too. Can I suck on your gorgeous cock, sweet boy?"

Dizziness washes over me. No one has ever asked. They just do it assuming I'll want it. This feels special—serene even. It makes tears sting in my eyes.

"Yes, but only if you're okay with it."

He grunts out something that sounds affirmative and then he scoots down the bed. I lift my hips when he goes for my underwear. Once my cock is free, he wraps his huge hand around it and gives it a few expert strokes.

I nearly choke when I feel his lips come in contact with my cock. His tongue is tentative as it licks at my crown. It's the most maddening yet delicious feeling I've ever encountered.

"I may be bad at this," he warns, hot breath fanning over the length of my dick. "Tell me how to make it better if I do it wrong."

"Step one, stop talking and start sucking," I tease, a needy whine in my voice. "Please, Jude. Whatever you do will be good."

Emboldened by my command, he slides down over my cock, humming in pleasure. I get lost in the sensation of him bobbing up and down, to the sounds of his slurping and the occasional hungry growl.

How is his mouth so perfect?

How can a man who's never given head before be so damn good at it?

I find my fingers tangled in his hair as I tug and pull, urging him to keep up the good work. I'm spiraling closer and closer to bliss when I feel him rubbing his fingertip around my balls that are soaked with his saliva. As soon as he's coated them, I feel the pressure of his finger against my hole.

"Do it," I croak out, bearing down in preparation.

Slowly, he inches his finger inside of me. I'm no anal sex virgin and have played with many toys over the years, so I easily take his finger with no pain or problems.

"Turn your hand and curl your finger up," I instruct with a ragged voice. "You'll hit my prost—oh fuck!"

Pleasure splinters out and through every nerve ending the second he grazes over the sensitive gland. He's a quick learner and starts massaging the glorious place with firm, slow circles. His mouth finds my cock once more, which is the match that sets off the bomb. The pleasure he's doling out is too much and I detonate, exploding with ecstasy. My back arches and I cry out as cum shoots out of me into his waiting mouth.

I can hear him gulping and it's the sexiest sound I've ever heard.

My whole body goes limp after my orgasm and I feel myself drifting to some relaxing subspace I've never known. The air chills when Jude gets off the bed. Before I can complain, he's back, kissing his way up my stomach until he reaches my lips.

The way he devours my mouth is sinful. It feels dirty and wrong, yet so damn good. I wrap my legs around his strong body, needing him as close to me as he can possibly be. His dick, also naked, rubs against my flaccid one, sending jolts of pleasure through it to make it perk back up.

"I've…" he murmurs against my lips, "never done this. Well, not sex, but sex with you. A guy. Fuck. You know what I mean."

I smile in the dark, wishing like hell I could see all of him. "I know what you mean."

"I'm worried I'll hurt you."

"You won't hurt me. I trust you'll take it slow and stop if I feel any pain."

"Of course," he growls. "Do you, uh, have any condoms?"

"No," I whine, "but I was recently tested after the last time with my ex. I'm negative."

"I haven't had sex since I was a teenager but still get tested every year by one of Grandpa's doctors who comes to see him. I'm negative too."

"Then fuck me raw, Jude. I want to feel you come inside of me."

He does have lube, thank God, and squirts it on something. It's dark, so I have no idea what. A tiny tremor of fear trickles through me.

He's. Not. Sean.

"Is it the, uh, same with guys?" he asks. "Lube it up and stick it in?"

"I've seen what you're packing. Maybe stretch me a bit first so I can accommodate your size."

"With my finger?"

"Plural. Start with one and then work it up to three. Scissor your fingers and rub around the rim. It'll feel good for me, plus make sure I'm nice and stretched out for you."

Jude is an excellent student, doing exactly as I've instructed. It's strange to feel so…in control during sex. He's not tying me up and fucking me how he wants to. He's going slow, asking questions and permission, and making sure it feels good for me too. When he has me taking three of his thick fingers and my dick is so hard I think it might burst, I start begging for his cock.

"Please, Jude," I whimper. "I need you inside of me so fucking badly."

He slowly withdraws his fingers. "Tell me to stop if it hurts."

"I promise."

His fingers are gone and then I feel the slick head of his cock teasing my hole. My greedy body sucks him in as he starts to push inside. The stretch of his incredible thickness burns a bit but nothing I can't handle. He hisses and makes strangled sounds of pleasure, which make me want him all the more.

"Now kiss me," I beg when he's fully seated inside me. "Kiss me and fuck me. I've never wanted anything so badly in my life."

He crashes his lips to mine and begins thrusting in and out at a maddeningly delicious pace. I love how his entire essence consumes me. Minutes or hours go by, I'm not sure, and I lose myself to everything that is him.

When he's near coming, his hand curls around my cock, giving it a few hard strokes in tandem with his thrusting. He moans against my mouth and I bite his lip.

Everything explodes around me until all that's left is just me and him.

I could get used to this, him, *us*.

I'm…happy. I'm starting to think he is too.

CHAPTER TWENTY-FOUR

Jude

THIS IS WHAT I'VE BEEN MISSING MY WHOLE LIFE.

Tate.

It wasn't supposed to happen, but it did. I found this wonderful, sweet, sexy little thing and now that I have him, I don't ever want to let him go.

Night two of having him in my bed has been a gift. He's quite a cuddler and with us both attempting to sleep naked, those innocent cuddles keep turning dirty. If we have another full night like we did last night, my dick might fall off from overuse.

Fuck, being inside his tight little hole was heaven. A bliss I've never known. I vaguely remember sex with Serra when I was a teenager, but I don't remember being so consumed by it. I don't remember feeling like my soul was tangled up in the sexy act like it is with Tate.

Tate is different.

Perfect in every way.

He groans in his sleep and smacks his lips. My chest is wet with his drool where he sleeps. Since he apparently likes to sleep in and I'm an early bird, at least I won't have to worry about him seeing me without my mask.

Guilt pokes holes in my heart, quickly draining it of what little happiness and life was flowing inside.

If there were anyone deserving to see the real me, it'd be him. But what happens when he's terrified of what he sees? I can't let him see that monster. Ever.

As much as I crave to lie in bed with him all morning until the sleepyhead finally wakes, I know I can't. Not because of him seeing me mask-less either. I have a lot of work to do. First order of business will be the porch and cameras. Then I can dig into his ex to see what I can do about it.

I slide out from under Tate's sleeping body and plant a quick kiss on his parted, slobbery lips. Funky, from his perch on Tate's abandoned pillow, meows at me but doesn't move. He likes to lie in bed all morning too.

After a quick shower and getting dressed, I head into my office, now protecting everyone around me with my mask. I remember back when the masks became a "thing." Grandpa initiated it and Dad was pissed.

"Nathan," Grandpa warns. "He needs help and I'm helping him."

Dad, who pats a sleeping Gemma, hisses, "A fucking mask, Dad?"

I'm sitting on the steps at Grandpa's house, listening in on their argument down the hall in the living room. I reach up a bandaged hand and touch the latex that covers my face. It's the first time in fucking months that I've felt…okay.

"He busted every damn mirror in this house," Grandpa bites back. "Had to call Bill out to stitch his hands up. It's because he can't look at his reflection anymore. I did what I thought was best."

Gemma, my newborn little sister I haven't even been able to look at or much less hold, whimpers in her sleep and I wonder if she'll wake. The two men go quiet for a few seconds and then Dad continues.

"He needs a therapist, not a mask."

I wince at Dad's words. A therapist? Hell no. They'll want me to talk about the fire, how much I hate myself, and my dead mother. Fuck. That.

"It's either this or we lose him," Grandpa says with a sad sigh. "He's been living here since the accident, and though I think it's best to have a change of scenery for him, he's not exactly improving. Just the other day Violet found his shaving razor busted apart. I think he's been cutting himself."

The scabbed over lines on my forearm tingle. Why was I so stupid to leave out my evidence?

"Fuck," Dad chokes out. "He needs real help. I'm going to have to hospitalize him."

"No," Grandpa growls. "He needs space and time. We'll make sure he doesn't get a hold of anything sharp and will keep a close eye on him, but you can't take him away. Not now. He's holding on by a fucking thread." Grandpa's cane clacks across the floor. "You go take care of that new wife of yours. The twins too. You're needed over there. I'll make sure Jude is all right."

I can tell their conversation is over, so I hightail it upstairs, through Grandpa's office, and up to his man cave. It's the only place I can truly breathe. I find an Eagles album and turn up "Hotel California" before falling onto the lumpy sofa.

Is Grandpa telling the truth?

Will he make sure I'm all right?

I don't think I'll ever be okay again.

It seems like yesterday that I saw the disgusting guy staring back at me in the bathroom mirror. He killed Mom. I hated him more than anything I've ever hated in my entire life. Rage, unlike anything I ever felt, consumed me. I went on a rampage, punching every mirror in the house. By the time

Grandpa figured out what had happened, my hands, especially my knuckles, were a shredded, bloody mess.

"Morning, hon," Violet says, following me into my office with a plated breakfast sandwich and a cup of coffee. "Sleep okay?"

Her teasing smirk makes my cheeks heat. Thank fuck for my mask right now. Rather than give in, I grunt. Her smile falters as she drops the plate and mug on my desk. As she starts to turn, I remember Tate's words.

"Violet is a great woman. I can see why you adore her. You say you could never thank her enough, but have you tried telling her what you just told me? I bet it would mean the world to hear it."

"Violet, wait," I call out before she exits my office.

I stride over to her and pull her frail frame into my arms. Closing my eyes, I inhale her scent that's always reminded me a little bit of Mom. "Thank you."

She squeezes me back. "Oh, it's just breakfast."

"No," I say, pulling back to look down at her. "Thank you for being you. For being the mother figure I desperately needed. Thank you for the pie and the memories and the love."

Her face crumples as big, fat tears form. I hug her to me again, hoping to convey how much she means to me. She sniffles and is in no hurry to leave my embrace.

"I knew he'd be good for you, sweetie. He's good for the whole family, but he's especially good for you. I'm just so thrilled you're finally finding a little happiness. You deserve it, Jude."

She thinks I deserve it?

Even after knowing I couldn't save my own mother?

I want to argue, but I don't want to hurt her again this morning. I keep my lips sealed. Tate would be proud.

Once she's composed herself, she pulls away, grinning at me. "I'm going to make manicotti tonight with homemade noodles and sauce."

"But it takes forever," I counter because it's one of her least favorite meals to make despite me and Grandpa being huge fans.

"My boys are worth it." She laughs. "Besides, food is my love language. Let me show you how much I love you."

I gape at her as she shuffles out of the office. She loves me? How? Why? And she said her boys are worth it. Does she include Tate in that statement? My heart does a somersault at that thought. I *want* him included.

My phone buzzes with more texts from Baker. I preview them but choose not to respond to his annoying ass.

Baker: Tonight?

Baker: Answer me, dumbass.

Baker: When you get this, let's get together.

Baker: You ignored me all day yesterday. Do I have to show up on your porch to get you to respond to me?

Baker: Bring whoever you're seeing. I don't care. Just need to see you, man.

This guy is fucking relentless. I'm going to block his ass later.

While I wolf down breakfast, I research the best contractors. There's a gay couple here in town who run a home remodeling business. One of the husbands is the interior decorator and the other one is the contractor. I decide they'll be perfect for my projects.

After emailing a request for service, I switch over to the dark web to utilize my hacking programs that'll allow me access to police records. It doesn't take long before I'm in the Park Mountain PD database. I start with a search for Sloane Thurman and then look for reports made yesterday.

I find the one for the victim, Tate Prince, and begin reading her notes.

Victim states past history with ex-boyfriend who has a pattern of vandalizing his vehicles. Mentioned the ex also physically and sexually assaulted him on numerous occasions. After some urging, the victim finally gave up the name of his ex-boyfriend, Sean Baker, but doesn't want to, under any circumstance, have us bring him in for questioning for fear of retaliation.

Sean Baker?

Every cell in my body turns to ice and I remain frozen, staring at the police report. Tate, my sweet, fucking adorable Tate, has been stalked and terrorized by my ex-best friend?

But he's married.

He has fucking kids!

The room spins as I attempt to make sense of this mess. It certainly explains Baker's sudden appearance back in my life. I didn't think the timing was suspect, but now it's obvious. It aligns to around the time I turned on Tate's phone.

I pointed a beacon right at Tate.

But how did Baker get that information? He said he was a firefighter. They don't give you access to phone records or how to locate someone with their phone. Either he's a hacker like me, which is highly doubtful because this shit isn't easy and Baker's not the sharpest tool in the shed, or he knows someone at the PMPD.

Who?

I'm going to need to get Sloane over here so we can figure this out. There's a rat at her station and I'm going to drown them.

First, though, I'm going to beat Baker's motherfucking face in.

How?

Show up to the goddamn fire station and start whipping his ass?

They'd haul my freakshow ass out in cuffs before I could get two swings on him. Plus, I can't leave this house. Not like this. I'm an embarrassment to my family.

Because I'm such a mental wreck, I can't even help my boyfriend.

I can't protect him like he should be protected.

The breakfast sandwich I inhaled sours in my gut. I'm still reeling from how this could be happening. I didn't even know Baker liked men. Plus, he's happily married. How did he end up with Tate?

An overwhelming sense of frustration anchors me, turning every muscle in my body to leaden weights. I don't know what to do. Sure, I can dig and dig into Baker's life, but that won't do shit to stop him. I need proof.

I could invite him here.

Take him up on his offer…

Picking up my phone, I respond to him.

Me: Come over tonight. Alone. We'll do some much needed catching up.

Fiery hatred toward someone I used to care deeply about consumes me. I want to send him some knife emojis, too, but don't.

He responds quickly.

Baker: I'll be there. Tell your little boy toy I said hi.

Fuck. He knows I know it's him.

Me: He's mine. Leave him the fuck alone.

Baker: He was mine first.

I'm vibrating with uncontrolled anger as I text Callum. I may not be able to hunt Baker down and destroy him in a murderous rage, but Callum is smart. He'll help me figure out what to do and how to handle this situation.

One thing's for damn sure.

This ends tonight.

Tate will be safe once and for all.

That's a motherfucking promise.

CHAPTER TWENTY-FIVE

Tate

Oh my God.

Every muscle in my entire body feels achy and used. I haven't had this much of a workout in, well, forever. A smile tugs at my lips as I think about Jude's and my sexfest last night.

It. Was. Amazing.

For someone who's lacking sexual experience, Jude's a quick learner. I've never come so many times in one night.

He's more than great at setting me off like a bomb. He's gentle and kind. Best of all, he respects my boundaries and is clear about getting my consent. I'm uncovering new, wonderful things about him that I love.

We're going to have to work on his escaping in the early hours of the morning, though. I don't care if he wears his mask. I'd like to wake up with him.

My head is in the clouds as I crawl out of bed and start gathering my clothes for a shower. Not only is Jude a sweet lover, but he's great at aftercare. After each romp, he would clean me up as though he enjoyed doing it and then would hold me tight in his arms until I'd fall asleep again.

I could get used to this.

It's almost as if I have nothing to worry about.

Dread makes an appearance as I hurry through my

shower. This thing with Sean is unresolved. I ended up telling the nice policewoman Sean's name, but I definitely did not want her doing anything about it. Sean's vindictive. If the cops showed up at his house or work, not only would he be mortified, but he'd be beyond pissed. I don't even want to imagine what sort of payback I'd receive for that stunt.

At some point, I'm going to have to do something to protect myself from him.

Running away can't always be the answer.

Eventually, Sean won't just try to ruin or hurt me, but something far worse.

So how can I stop him?

Jude's strong, intense presence fills my mind. For once, I don't feel completely alone. He promised to protect me and I believe him. I'd wanted to lump him in the same category as Sean, but he's completely different. Maybe, just maybe, we can figure out a plan together. It would mean revealing my abuser, but if anyone can help, it would be Jude Park.

Once out of the shower, I stop to give Funky a hug.

"I'm going to tell him," I say to my cat. "It's about time we call in reinforcements, huh?"

Funky purrs, leaning into my hand as I stroke his head. That's kitty-speak for, "Duh, dude."

I give him a kiss and then set him back down on the bed, but when I open the bedroom door and the aroma of fresh-cooked bacon makes its way inside, Funky bolts to go see his true love. Violet.

As much as I'd love to follow and see what she might have for me too, I make a detour to Jude's office. I'm going to tell him who Sean is, everything he's done to me, and ask for help. This feels like a huge milestone for me.

It's terrifying to put trust in another man, especially one I haven't known for long, but it also feels right. Peace has settled over me ever since I came to Jude's place to stay. It's felt safe, warm, and homey. The last time I felt that way was when I was a small boy when Mom was still alive. I have a distinct memory of sitting on the counter, helping her bake cookies and feeling so damn loved.

I miss you, Mom.

Since me and Jude both lost our mothers, I feel a certain kinship to him because of it. If anyone understands losing such a huge piece of your heart, it's him. Maybe, with each other, we can both fill up the empty spaces left by our losses. I can't wait to try.

The door to Jude's office stands ajar. When I peek my head in, I discover Callum and Jude both staring at his computer monitors, talking in soft voices. They don't see me, so I sneak away so as not to interrupt them. I'll have to catch Jude after my appointment with Willa then, who'll no doubt be here earlier than expected since Callum is here.

My stomach growls and as much as I want to make a pit-stop for one of Violet's yummy breakfasts, I decide to forgo it to look for Willa in the library.

"Someone's in a hurry," Wyatt says, his wheelchair whining as he exits his room smelling of Old Spice. His hair is slicked over and he's freshly shaven. "You got a date too?"

I stop dead in my tracks. "You have a date?"

He chuckles. "Only one of us knows it."

With a wink, he wheels toward the kitchen. I snigger when I realize he's talking about Violet. It's kind of cute he seems to be sweet on her.

"So sorry," I say as I enter the library. "It was a crazy night and…"

I trail off when I realize she isn't waiting for me. Weird. This whole day is turning out to be strange. Maybe I'm still sleeping.

Confused, I turn on my heel and make my way to the dining room where Violet is plating some food up for Wyatt. Funky meows pitifully from the floor beside Wyatt's wheelchair, watching as the old man shakily picks up a piece of bacon.

"Where's Willa?" I ask, stomach grumbling with hunger. "Callum's here and we have an appointment this morning. I figured she'd be waiting on me."

Violet hands me a piece of bacon. "Oh, those two have been at it for hours, sweetie. I don't think she's coming. Why don't you have a seat and let me get you a plate?"

And ruin Wyatt's date?

Smirking at him, I shake my head. "I'll run over there and see her."

"If you're going to leave, at least bring some muffins with you. Willa loves my chocolate chip pumpkin muffins."

Violet disappears into the kitchen and returns a minute later with a container filled with the treats. She offers me another strip of bacon, which I gladly take, and then I'm off to see my friend.

Outside, my car is no longer there. Jude mentioned something last night between our lovemaking that he'd have my vehicle taken somewhere to be dealt with. I'm shocked that he's already had it towed this morning. Not having to stress over it is a huge relief.

I could get used to this sweet, caring boyfriend stuff.

Though neither of us has said it, it's definitely an unspoken thing. We like each other and enjoy doing nice things for each other. Plus, we're sleeping together both literally and figuratively. Definitely boyfriends.

I scan the property and exhale in relief when I don't see any creeps—specifically Sean—lurking around. Still, I can't help but run as fast as my short legs will carry me all the way to Callum and Willa's. I'm out of breath by the time I reach their porch, but at least I'm in one piece. I hate how Sean always makes me feel on edge.

Banging on the front door, I cast a quick glance over my shoulder to make sure no one is sneaking up on me. A bird squawks at me from a nearby tree, but it's otherwise uneventful.

Willa cracks open the door and winces when she sees me as though I'm the last possible person she wants to see. Ouch. What did I do to upset her?

"Hey," I start, confusion making my voice wobble. "Everything okay?"

She swallows hard and tears well in her eyes. I reach for her, but she jerks back. Or, better yet, *someone* jerks her back. As the door widens, I recognize the burly figure who has a grip on her hair.

No.

"Sean?" I croak out, unable to believe my eyes. "W-What are you doing here?"

A tear rolls down Willa's cheek, her eyes shining with an unspoken apology. I meet her gaze with a firm one of my own. *This is not your fault. This is my mess.*

"Came to see you obviously. You made this a hell of a lot easier by showing up. I thought I might have to go over there and make a huge scene, but no, my little toy came through," Sean says in a jolly tune that makes my skin crawl. "And look, you came bearing gifts."

He reaches forward, snatching the container of muffins out of my hand. I don't know what to do. Do I turn around and run to get Callum and Jude? Run next door to get help there instead? Try to beat Sean up to save Willa? All options might lead to him hurting her.

"Let her go," I say calmly. "You came to talk to me, so talk. Willa doesn't need to be a part of this."

Sean laughs, cold and harsh. "Oh, she's a part of this shit all right. She's fucking a Park. That was her first mistake."

Oh God. This is escalating.

I can't leave her, though.

"Sean, just tell me what you want. Please."

He studies me through narrowed eyes. "I want you, obviously. I've always wanted you."

Fear claws at my throat, but I know I have to be strong right now. I've handled Sean for two years. I can deal with him now. I just need for him to let Willa go and focus on me.

"Okay," I tell him, voice resigned. "You have me. Now what?"

"Keys," he barks at Willa, tightening his grip on her hair and making her cry out. "Where are the keys to your car?"

My heart thuds heavily in my chest. He's going to take me somewhere. Then what? I used to only think he was capable of roughing me up, but now that he's resorting to these bold extremes, there's no telling what he could do next.

Still, it's better me than her.

She's pregnant and I'd never be able to live with myself if he hurt her because of me.

"On the bar," Willa hisses.

Sean backs up through the living room, Willa in his grip. Once he reaches the bar in the kitchen, he pockets the keys.

"Just leave her alone," I instruct. "I'll go with you without argument."

Sean smirks at me. "And leave her to go tattle the second we get in the car?"

I clench my teeth together, hating the antagonistic tone of his voice.

"Clean out the bullshit under the sink," Sean barks to me. "Now. Do it quickly."

Jolting at his harsh words, I rush over to the cabinets. There isn't much underneath aside from a few cleaning bottles and a bucket of dishwashing tabs. Once it's cleaned out, I take a step back.

"Inside," Sean tells Willa. "Go calmly and I won't have to hurt you. You're such a tiny little thing. All it'd take is a good fist to your throat to end your pretty existence."

Bile creeps up my throat at the thought of Sean killing my friend. Over my dead body. I shoot her a look that begs her to do as he says and to not be a hero. She tearfully obeys, crawling into the cabinet.

Sean snatches a dish towel from a drawer after ransacking half the kitchen to find it and then feeds it through the handles. He knots the towel twice before approaching me.

I want to shrink away from him or beg him not to do this. Nothing will help. He'll still hurt me. It's what he does. There's no reasoning with Sean Baker.

"How are the wife and kids?" I choke out, hoping to appeal to his human side before the monster transforms him into something that cannot be reasoned with.

He sneers at me. "Perfect. They're all so fucking perfect. But I don't get to be myself with them. I live a goddamn lie. When I'm with you, though, I can be exactly who I was born to be."

His hand seizes my throat before I can make a move to run away. I'm barely able to hiss out any words.

"J-Just go b-back home to them, Sean. I won't t-tell anyone about t-today."

A loud, booming laugh erupts out of him. I can't believe at one time I found this man attractive. Now, all I see is a psychopath. That's all he is beneath the perfect shell he's created for the outside world.

"I'll go home later, princess," he growls, spittle landing on my face. "After I've fucked my naughty little toy. You know you missed me."

I claw at his hand, aching for air, and he surprisingly releases me. Gasping, I attempt to suck air back into my lungs while still keeping an eye on this lunatic. He grins viciously at me and I know I'm in trouble. With a powerful right hook, he lays me out with just one punch. The last thing I see before blacking out is his horrible, terrifying frame towering over me, and I have a final, fleeting thought.

I won't be coming back from this.

CHAPTER TWENTY-SIX

Jude

A DOOR SLAMS SOMEWHERE DOWNSTAIRS AND I STOP scrolling through Baker's social media feed to cock my head. I glance over at Callum and he frowns. The slamming is soon followed by shouts and pounding up the stairs. Before I can even get to my feet, Callum is racing out of my office.

"Callum!"

Willa flings herself into Callum's arms, sobbing and shaking. I prowl over to them, feeling unnerved and gut churning. The door to my bedroom stands open, which means Tate is awake, which somehow worsens the feeling inside me.

Something is off and I can feel it.

"Sweetheart," Callum rumbles, gripping Willa's tearstained, crimson face and pulling her back so he can look at her. "What's wrong? Is it the baby?"

She shakes her head as more tears spill out. "It's Tate. That man—Sean—took him!"

I freeze at her words, unsure how to process them. He can't have taken Tate. Tate's probably downstairs having breakfast or in the library. We would have heard the commotion. This is all wrong.

"Tell me what happened," Callum instructs, voice low. "Go slow and tell me everything."

She trembles and glances my way. "I'm sorry. I really tried." Her face crumples as the emotion of her perceived failure overtakes her. Then she lifts her chin, braving her way through her story. "Someone knocked at the door. The guy said he was Jude's friend and then suddenly he was pushing inside. He was working out how to use me to get to Tate when Tate showed up."

Black spots dot my vision as I try to imagine what happened next. She puts me out of my misery as she continues.

"Sean trapped me under the kitchen sink—"

"What?" Callum snarls. "He fucking hurt you?"

"No, just barricaded me in there. I kicked and kicked at the doors until the hinges broke off. Then I ran straight here."

"How long were you trapped?" I bark out.

She starts to cry again.

"Willa," I snap. "How long were you stuck in there?"

"Maybe thirty? Forty-five minutes? I don't know for sure."

Baker has had him for at least half an hour. There's a lot he could do in that time frame.

"They took your car," Willa cries out to Callum. "We can track them, right?"

Callum fumbles for his phone in his pocket. He opens the app as we crowd around. Seconds later, it shows the car parked at the end of our property road. The fucker just used it to get to his own vehicle.

"Fuck!" I roar, trembling with a mixture of fear and rage. "Where the hell could he have taken him?"

I rack my brain for possibilities. Baker is a local with a fucking family and a good job. He's not going to just bail and leave town with Tate, right? If he's still trying to keep his double life, he certainly won't bring Tate to his house or the fire station.

A hotel?

Tate's place?

"Call Sloane and get her help," I snap at my brother. "Then we need to look up all the hotels…" I trail off, frustration seeping into my pores.

This will take for-fucking-ever.

We don't have time.

And what am I supposed to do? Sit in my office, tracking and scouring the internet for clues while this goddamn monster takes my sweet boy to do fuck knows what?

No.

I won't sit around and let this happen.

"I'm going to find him." I snarl, gripping the bottom of my mask. "I'll check Tate's apartment first."

Willa and Callum both stare at me as though I've lost my mind. Yes, I'm going to leave the property. No, I don't like it. But Tate is in trouble and he needs me.

I promised to protect him and I've already failed.

When I rip the mask off, Willa's eyes widen. Callum's features turn stony. He knows what lurks beneath. Willa, however, is getting her first taste of the horror show. She blinks so many times I think she might be broken. Then she starts to cry.

"Oh, Jude…"

I shudder, turning away from her, not wanting her to see anymore, and race toward the stairs. When I reach the bottom, Grandpa and Violet are both waiting with worried expressions. Both of them look at my face and gape at me.

"I'm sorry," I choke out, hating that they're seeing me so…lost and out of control. "I have to find Tate."

Rushing past them, I make my way to the door in the kitchen that leads to the garage. Just because I don't drive, and neither does Grandpa, for that matter, it doesn't mean we haven't maintained our vehicles. Dad comes over from time to time to get them serviced and take them for a drive. My old-ass Jeep remains in its spot, ready for its first drive by me in ages.

The engine fires to life and for a second, I remember being a teenager, driving all over this town like I owned it. So much has changed in nearly two decades. So fucking much.

It feels like it takes forever for the garage door to lift. While it does its thing, I hunt down Tate's address in my phone. Once I figure out which apartment complex it is, I back the Jeep out and race down the driveway. I'm shocked that I actually remember how to drive, but it's clearly muscle memory and something you don't forget even after a long-ass time.

My phone starts to blow up with phone calls from Dad and Dempsey. Callum must've already called and told them the news. I don't have time to deal with them right now. I need to get to Tate.

I race through a stop sign and a car blares its horn at me. It then decides to follow me, honking a few more times, gesticulating out the window for me to stop. I stick my hand out the window and flip them off. Out of ingrained habit, I look at my reflection in the rearview mirror and nearly run off the road.

"Monster," I snap, jerking the mirror and twisting it down.

Breathing a sigh of relief that I don't have to look at myself, I continue to barrel down the road. His apartment is on the other side of town, about fifteen minutes away. I feel like time is slipping through my fingers. The longer it takes, the more time Baker has to hurt Tate.

When did Baker turn into this?

I don't remember him being gay or liking men. I certainly don't remember him being abusive in any way. He was always the life of the party. The guy who was always down to have a good time. And he never stopped fucking grinning. As a teen, that kind of person was fun to be around.

Going back further, when we were kids, he was rambunctious and adventurous. We'd get into a lot of trouble together for tearing shit up with one of our shenanigans.

Never once did I think him to be violent or cruel, though.

If anything, he was the exact opposite.

Some people hide their ugly deep inside.

My ugly is on my face for all to see.

I swerve around an old person driving twenty below the speed limit and race past them. If a cop sees me, they can follow my ass all the way to the apartment building and provide reinforcement.

Of course I don't have such luck.

When I was sixteen, I got plenty of tickets. Where's a cop when you're actually trying to get caught?

As I get closer to my destination, fear curdles my stomach, making me nauseous. Baker has been leading two very distinct lives—like Dr. Jekyll and Mr. Hyde—so the very fact he's letting those two lives intersect right now is terrifying.

He's losing control.

If he's losing control, that means he'll be reckless and might do something he can't take back.

Please, for the love of God, don't hurt my sweet boy.

Pain lances at me from all directions until my heart feels

like it has thousands of stab wounds. I can't lose another person I care so deeply about. It'll destroy me completely this time.

My phone rings again and it's Dad. I answer just to get my mind off terrible thoughts of Tate dying.

"Where are you going?" Dad demands through the line.

"Tate's apartment. Baker has him."

"Baker? The kid you used to run around with until…" Until Mom's death.

"Yup. And I'm guessing he just bullshitted me when he said you gave him my number?"

"Jude, I haven't spoken to the kid since you were in high school. Why?"

"He's no kid anymore and apparently he's Tate's ex. The one who's been vandalizing his car and sending the sex videos to his employers."

"No shit?"

"Tate was so fucking scared of his ex. And now that I know Baker has him, Tate must be terrified."

"Isn't Baker a firefighter? Why would he ruin his life by abducting Tate?"

"Because he's fucking crazy? I don't know, Dad, but he has my boyfriend and I can't let him hurt him!"

He's silent for a moment. "Boyfriend?"

Cat's out of the bag. Not that I give a shit.

"He's mine. I'm his. We're a thing. I'm fucking happy. I can't lose him."

"You won't, Son," Dad assures me. "Everything is going to be okay. We're going to get our boy back."

Our boy.

I clench my teeth together hard, fighting emotion. "I'm going to kill him."

"You can't kill Baker," Dad says with a grunt. "Just get Tate away from him. Let the cops do the rest. Don't do anything stupid."

"Can't make any promises."

I hang up before Dad can argue. I'm not going to vow not to do something stupid. If I have to beat Baker's face to a bloody pulp just to make Tate feel safe again, I will. Old friend or not, Baker is not the guy I knew. He's fucked in the head and messing with *my* man.

My heart rate starts to race when I pull into the apartment complex. I drive around the back of the building and discover a Suburban that's been wrapped in Park Mountain Fire Department vinyl.

They're here.

Relief vies for attention, but fear is still the star of the show.

Time to rescue Tate.

I *will* have him safely in my arms no matter what.

CHAPTER TWENTY-SEVEN

Tate

"I S MY LITTLE TOY FINALLY AWAKE?"

I blink away the lingering darkness and try to make sense of my surroundings. Is this a nightmare? A firm smack on my bare ass sends awareness jolting through me.

Not sleeping.

This is definitely real.

As my eyes come into focus, I recognize the furniture in my living room. It's been destroyed. Someone—obviously Sean—must've taken an ax to it as it's punctured in a million places, white, cottony stuffing pulled and discarded all over.

I'm sure that was a result of one of his tantrums when he realized I'd ghosted him.

I attempt to move and come to the conclusion I've been bound. Based on the cold, hard surface I'm on and location, it must be my dinner table. I've been placed naked and face down on the surface. Rope binds my wrists and it stretches down over the other side, no doubt attached to two of the legs.

My ass is on full display as my bottom half is folded over the other end of the table. When I can't move either leg, I realize they've been bound as well. Each leg is spread apart, leaving my whole backside vulnerable and exposed. Even though my cock is smashed against the edge of the table, I'm not worried.

Sean doesn't want my dick.

He's always been more of an ass man.

A full-bodied tremble ripples through me. Dizziness from the blow to the head keeps passing over in waves and my skull is throbbing.

What's he going to do?

I test my restraints and am not surprised to discover I'm not going to escape them anytime soon.

"Sean," I croak out. "Please. Just let me go."

His chuckle, something I once thought warm and infectious, chills me to my bones. "Never, Tate. I thought I made that abundantly clear. You're mine. My necessary outlet for my mundane life. Most men have a man cave to retreat to. I have you. My secret little fuck toy."

I shudder when he squeezes my ass cheek and grit out, "I'm not yours anymore."

"Why? Because you're fucking Jude?" He scoffs from behind me. "How did you manage that anyway? Turning Jude gay?"

He speaks of him as if he knows him. "What are you talking about?"

Sean rounds the table until he comes into view. He dips down to meet my gaze. Normally, that penetrating stare of his would make me shrivel up inside. For some reason, today, I'm angry. So angry that if I could get my hands free, I might actually be able to hurt him for once.

"Oh," Sean says gleefully. "Believe me, when I found out my little fuck toy was playing house with my ex-best friend, I was shocked stupid."

"Your what?"

He leans forward to stroke the hair out of my eyes and

smirks. "Small world, right? Me and Jude go way back, all the way to when he was fucking normal and spent all his time with me."

I yank at my restraints, but all I end up doing is rubbing the skin raw where the rope digs into me. Finally, I let out a frustrated huff and glower at Sean. I'm in no position to taunt him, but my pleading tactics don't work. He's clearly bitter about Jude. I can play into that.

"Jude's in love with me," I tell him in a cool tone. He may not be in love with me yet, but we're on the fast track of getting there. "He has money and means. It's only a matter of time before he shows up and makes a fool out of you. The cops, along with your wife and everyone in this town, will know what a sadistic freak you are." That I do believe a hundred percent.

He barks out a cruel laugh. "Jude won't leave the house. I've done my homework. The fire fucked him up and he's afraid for the world to see him. He's not coming."

Last time I was in a position like this with Sean, I went along with his sadism, begging for the terrible things he wanted to do to me in an effort to get it over with quicker. He'd filmed me and used that footage against me to keep me unemployed. Sean had his thumb over me because I was afraid of him.

So why am I not so afraid now?

Because you're changing and growing, Tate. People value your advice, your friendship, and your companionship. You're a friend and a giving lover. There's a life with the Park family you're destined to be a part of. This nightmare with Sean ends now.

"He'll come," I tell him with confidence. "And if it's not him, it'll be the police or his dad or brothers. No matter what, he's not going to let you just steal me away. Your days of ruining my life are over. It's time to ruin yours."

His body tenses and then he walks out of my line of vision. My heart rate is thundering in my chest as I prepare for pain. What he won't get from me—not anymore—is fear and defeat.

I'm not giving up.

Not on me or Jude.

"You can't ruin my life," Sean grits out. "No one will believe you."

"You've fucked with the wrong family, man," I toss back, voice even and steady. "You trespassed, terrorized Callum's woman, and have kidnapped Jude's boyfriend. You know Jude and that family. Are they really going to sit back and let you do this to them? To me? I'm one of them now."

I believe that.

Every single one of the people in that family has welcomed me. They care about me more than just an outsider to confide in and seek therapy with. I'm a bright spot in their world just as they've done the same for me.

I belong.

I never knew what a found family meant, but now I get it.

Jude made it abundantly clear that he protects his family at all costs. It's his number one mission in life. Sean won't get away with his cruelties this time.

"You've really made a mess of your life," I continue, venom dripping from my words. "You're letting down your wife and children. For what? To have the chance to humiliate me? To get your rocks off by raping the small guy you picked up at the gym? You're pathetic, Sean. Truly fucking pathetic."

"Shut up!" he roars, ramming his fist through the drywall. "Shut up or I'll stuff your mouth so you can't speak!"

Angering him is dangerous, but it's my only move at this point. I'm trapped and at his mercy either way. Lying here and taking it won't do anything but further traumatize me for years to come. Fighting back, even if just with my words, I feel as though I'm doing something.

I'm stronger than I was the last time I was with him.

Knowing I've been doing some growing too while with the Parks fills my heart despite being in such a harrowing predicament. At least if I'm going down by Sean's hand, I'll do so with dignity.

"Make your videos, Sean," I continue to taunt, squirming against the restraints. "But rest assured, I'll make sure everyone in this town knows you're a rapist. These fear tactics won't work anymore!"

He makes a hideous growling sound before storming into the living room. I crane my neck to keep him in my sight. When he picks up an ax from the floor, all the blood drains from my body.

Okay, so maybe provoking him was a terrible idea.

With long, purposeful strides, he storms over to me, raising his ax in the air. I scream when he slams it down into the end of the table just inches from my face. The wood splits beneath me but doesn't fully collapse.

Was he aiming for my head?

Did he miss?

Tears of horror blur my vision. So much for being brave. He's not going to rape me. He's going to murder me. Chop me up into pieces like he did my couch.

Please, God, let it go quickly.

I don't want to lose limbs, feel every bit of the excruciating pain until I bleed out and die slowly.

"Y-You'll kill me, but t-this won't go away," I croak out, teeth chattering with fear. "They'll all know w-what a monster y-you are!"

The blunt end of something wooden—probably the other end of the ax—probes at my ass. I clench my cheeks together because I do not want whatever he plans to do with that thing. He digs his brutal, fat fingers into my crack, clawing one cheek aside. The press of the wood handle against my hole makes me howl, my whole body writhing as much as I can in an effort to escape.

That thing is too big!

It'll rip me in two!

"Stay away from me you psychopath!"

Something crashes from the living room. I want to look at what it is, but not with Sean trying to sodomize me with an ax handle. Thankfully, he pulls it away and snarls at the intruder.

The intruder?

My heart skyrockets into my throat as I focus my teary eyes on the person stalking into the room like an avenging angel. The man is huge—like Sean—but rippling with an unearthly power that makes me cry out with hope. His face is familiar. Same dark hair. Same blue eyes.

Callum?

No, wait, Hugo?

It's not Callum or Hugo. It's an angel. The most beautiful creature I've ever seen. This man's face is perfect, unmarred, and stunning. I'm mesmerized by the sight. All he's missing are the wings and a giant, fiery sword.

The electric blue eyes land on me and they practically glow with relief.

He's come to save me.

Jude. *My* Jude.

My shockingly and confusingly handsome *Jude.*

"So you *do* have time for that beer—" Sean taunts but is cut off when Jude launches himself at him.

The two of them crash into the table and then disappear out of sight onto the floor. Cracking and splattering can be heard as fists meet tender flesh.

Please don't hurt Jude!

But then Jude rises from the other side of the table. Blood dots his breathtaking face but he's otherwise uninjured.

"Sweet boy," he rasps out. "Fuck, what has he done to you?"

"You're here." A sob catches in my throat as more tears well and fall. "You came for me."

"You knew I would."

He's right.

I absolutely knew it.

Jude promised to protect me and he's made good on that promise.

"I didn't give in," I tell him as he leans over to kiss my head. "He said all these terrible things and I fought him. Even like this. I was trying to be brave and stand up for myself."

He runs his fingers through my hair before he starts untying one of the ropes. "Of course you did. You're Tate fucking Prince. You saved me. I had no doubt you'd save yourself."

I saved him?

My beautiful, tortured Jude?

As my left hand comes free, I let out a cry of relief. He

moves on to the next one. Once he's untied my hands, he disappears out of sight to work on my legs. Now that my arms are free and I can draw them to me, my muscles begin to quiver out of control.

Soon I'll be out of here.

The cops can haul that bastard away and this will all be over.

It's then I begin to smell something. Something bad and sinister considering our situation. *Gas.*

"Jude," I croak out.

My warning is too late. Jude may have got a few hits on Sean, but he clearly didn't incapacitate him. And while Jude was focused on me, Sean took his own opportunity.

Sean staggers out of the kitchen into my view and backs himself toward the front door. "Saved?" he sneers, gesturing wildly at us with an unlit match in his hand. "Nothing can save you now."

CHAPTER TWENTY-EIGHT

Jude

’M VIBRATING WITH ANGER AND THE DESIRE TO RIP Baker's head clear off his shoulders, but helping Tate is the main priority. Then I can fuck Baker up.

As I help Tate slide off the table, I keep an eye on the motherfucker who hurt my man. He's standing in the doorway of the apartment, an evil sneer on his face.

Two things happen at once. I smell gas and then I see Baker strike a match. The flame is small and insignificant, but I know the second he tosses it, we could be in real trouble.

Baker's eyes meet mine as he flicks it into the living room. It lands on the sofa and goes out. Tate is throwing on his clothes as I take a step toward Baker.

"Don't," he warns, striking another match, this time threatening to toss it into the kitchen. "I really don't want to have to do this to you again, Jude."

Again?

Tate, who's now dressed, clutches onto my arm and squeezes. "Just leave, Sean. Go back home to your family."

The match goes out and burns Baker's finger. He curses and quickly strikes another one.

"You know," Baker says, eyes searing into me. "You're a real piece of work. Your mom's death could have been avoided had you"—he points a finger at us and waggles it between me and Tate—"figured this out in high school."

This time, he tosses the match into the living room. It doesn't go out and ignites a puff of cotton stuffing that's been torn from the couch.

"What the fuck are you talking about?" I demand, voice shaking. "Mom died because I couldn't get to her quickly enough."

The familiar pain sears my heart. I was too late. I'll never in a million years forgive myself for that.

"You weren't even supposed to be there." He tosses another match into the living room. "I fucking bawled my eyes out when I learned you'd skipped school and almost died with that meddling bitch."

I shudder at his words. I'm unable to speak as my mind whirls at his confession. Tate takes a step out in front of me as though he can shield me from this motherfucker. I hate that I allow him to do just that.

Baker lights another match and flings it onto the carpet in front of him. It quickly catches fire and spreads over the cheap material. Although the flames are small, I'm being transported to the worst night of my life.

I can't move.

I can barely breathe.

"W-What are you saying?" I manage to croak out.

Baker shakes his head and barks out a sinister laugh. "You always looked at my dick, Jude. I didn't fucking imagine it. You're the whole reason I found out I like guys too. That night..." He claws at his hair before angrily striking another match. "That night, I got the balls to finally act on the mutual feeling. You were asleep, but I was trying to wake you up."

What in the ever-loving fuck is he talking about?

"Just let us leave, Sean. It's not too late." Tate starts toward the kitchen, but Baker stops him by tossing the match toward the stove.

A hot blast of heat sends Tate hurtling into me. The two of us land in a heap. I gape in horror at the flames that are now billowing out of the kitchen and spreading all too quickly up walls and across the carpet. The smoke alarm shrieks from nearby.

"She walked in on me," Baker yells, pain and fury dripping from his tone. "Said I fucking 'sexually assaulted you' since you were asleep. Told me to leave and that she would be pressing charges."

I remember the weekend before the fire. Baker stayed over. We got into Mom's liquor, got drunk, and I passed out. He was gone by morning.

That next day, Mom asked if I was gay and was acting strangely.

With the flames and smoke burning through the small apartment, I can barely make out Baker's form in the doorway. His voice is loud and clear. Tate is tugging at me and speaking inaudible words. I'm unable to move or respond.

I'm a captive to Baker's horror story.

"I fucking went mental, man," Baker growls. "I had a girlfriend and my dad would have lost his shit if he found out I'd been sucking off Jude Park, a fucking guy."

I really was drunk because I didn't wake up.

Mom saw him?

Fuck.

"I only had one option," Baker says with a growl. "Set that bitch's house on fire with her in it."

No.

This can't be real.

Tate's fingers claw at me, tugging and tugging, but I'm stuck, unable to comprehend the terrible things Baker is confessing to me.

The fire wasn't an accident.

And Mom didn't start it like Callum always thought.

She was murdered.

By my best friend.

"It's too bad you have to die the same way she did," Baker says sadly, voice trembling with unshed tears. "But it's for the best. My life was almost ruined back then, but I stopped it. Just like how I'll stop it now."

Another explosion happens, making the entire apartment feel as though it's detonating like a bomb.

Everything turns black, but then heat licking at my flesh jerks me to the here and now. Tate shakes me, sobbing for me to wake up. I sit up and try to make sense of my surroundings.

Fire.

Nothing but hot, punishing flames.

I deserve to die, but not Tate.

You do not deserve to die either. You deserve life and love.

"Mom?"

Tate lightly smacks my cheek. "Focus. Look at me. You're not giving up and dying," he says. "We have to get out of here."

I blink in confusion but quickly realize I said those words aloud and it was Tate who responded, not Mom.

Mom's dead.

But it wasn't an accident.

Tate grunts as he pulls me. I stumble to my feet but succumb to a coughing fit as the smoke chokes my lungs. The smoke dazes me and I might've just sat back down had he not yanked on my arm.

The flames singe my clothes and hair, a couple times actually getting my skin and hurting like hell. I roar in pain—both physically and the ache inside my chest—wishing to just die a quick death.

But. He. Won't. Let. Me.

We stumble along until we collapse into the hallway of the apartment building. It's much cooler here and my mind starts to clear.

"We have to get out of here," I rasp. "We have to get you safe."

If I couldn't save Mom, I can at least save Tate.

"We will," he assures me, stopping to kiss me hard on the mouth. "But first we need to get everyone out of the building."

With the smoke pouring into the hallway and now more smoke alarms going off, the warning shrieks are all too much, rattling my brain inside its cage. I keep flopping back and forth between memories and reality. Between Mom and Tate.

Tate drags me to his neighbor's apartment and starts banging on the door. An elderly woman peeks out and then coughs when smoke rushes into her apartment.

"Ethel, we have to go," Tate says. "There's a fire and it's spreading."

"Oh dear," the old woman says. "Oh dear, oh dear, oh dear."

He finally coaxes her out of the apartment and then practically shoves me over to her. I snap into action and scoop up the frail woman in my arms. Tate rushes across the hall and bangs on that door next. The fire seems to chase after us as we collect any stragglers in the building.

The sound of sirens approaching fills the air, which gives me hope this could all be over soon.

Tate guides everyone to the stairwell, where we're nearly knocked over by several firemen dressed in their gear. It's a blur as we're all herded to safety outside where more firemen are already making attempts to put out the blaze.

I set Ethel down in the grass and then fall onto my ass, my mind still spinning with Baker's confession.

Mom walked in on him and he freaked out.

Baker murdered my mother because she caught him sucking me off.

Tears burn at my eyes, but they're not from the smoke. I'm attacked by emotions, lashing at me much like the flames in the apartment were. It hurts. It fucking hurts. Mom just wanted to protect me. When she yelled at me for not being at school the day she ended up dying, it was because she thought I would get hurt and she was angry.

I wonder if she knew it was Baker who started the fire.

Oh, Mom, I'm so fucking sorry.

A ragged, pained moan rips out of my chest before full-on sobs overtake me. I cried when Mom died and have many times over the years, but this feels like a lot more than a normal cry.

This feels like a release.

Like someone opened a valve and let out all the pressure—pain, guilt, sorrow. It all rushes out at once and I'm unable to stop the flood.

Small hands cup my face, swiping at my tears, and I lock eyes with Tate. He's crying too, but he looks so strong and fierce with the fire behind him. Mom would have loved Tate.

She'd have accepted him into our lives with loving arms. I just know it.

He kisses my lips and then hugs me tight. I cling to him, sobbing like a baby. Tate straddles my lap to get closer, holding me as though he has the power to keep me held together.

And he does.

But things are shifting and changing already inside me. I'm releasing so much hatred for myself to make room for love. Love for Tate. Love for my protective mother. Love for my family.

I can't continue to punish myself any longer.

I can't if I plan to take care of Tate and the rest of my people.

An EMT crouches beside us. "Everything okay? Are you injured?"

Tate shakes his head. "We're fine. Help the others."

As soon as the EMT is gone, Tate leans his forehead to mine. "I'm sorry."

The pain bleeds away as anger burns hot. "For what?"

"For Sean. It's because of me that this is happening."

I want to scoff and tell Tate to fuck off for taking the blame for something that was out of his control.

Wait…

Is that what I've been doing all these years? Taking the blame for something that was out of my control?

"This isn't your fault," I say to him, but needing to hear the words as well. "None of this is your fault."

His smile is gentle and he nods. "Okay. You're right."

I kiss him deeply this time. He tastes like smoke and love and mine. The small moan of surprise that rasps out of him melts my heart.

I want to hear all his sounds.

I want to see him smile and laugh.

I want to touch every part of him, worshipping him with the gentleness he deserves.

"You kids okay?"

We break from our kiss to find Dad striding over to us. He kneels beside us, brows furled as he inspects us for bodily harm. Once he realizes we're okay, he squeezes Tate's shoulder and then kisses my forehead.

"Thank fuck you're all right," Dad says, voice tight. "When I saw the fire, I thought I'd lost you."

He rises to his feet and then stalks away to meet Sloane, who's speaking with some of the people we helped escape the fire.

I hug Tate to my chest, stroking my fingers up and down his back. "You think you can pencil me in for a session when we get home."

Tate laughs, snuggling closer. "Yeah, big man, I think I can. Only if you promise pie, though."

"Deal." I inhale his smoky hair. "I'm done hiding, sweet boy. I think I'm ready for you to see me—all of me—especially the ugly. I just hope you'll stick around after."

He pulls back and threads his fingers into my hair. "I already see you, Jude. I've seen your heart and it's beautiful. This face is a pleasant surprise. There's not one single ugly thing about you inside or out."

"He killed my mom."

Tate is silent for a beat and then nods. "I am so sorry he did that to you."

"I couldn't save her..." I trail off, searching for that

never-ending self-loathing that's always crawling at my skin and finding nothing.

"You did your best, Jude. I'm proud of you for trying. You're a hero to me."

His words play out over and over in my head until I can almost imagine Mom saying them. Is that how she would have felt too? Proud of me for trying? Would she have seen me as a hero?

Yeah.

Yeah, I think she would have.

CHAPTER TWENTY-NINE

CINNAMON.

Gah.

My favorite Jude smell usually comes from his bed, where his scent lingers the strongest. This time, it's coming from the air. Someone is baking at the crack of dawn and I'm forced to get out of bed early to follow my nose.

Of course my traitor cat is already gone.

I pull on one of Jude's hoodies because I like how it swallows me and then grab my sweatpants from the floor to dress in before leaving the bedroom. Outside of the room, the heavenly aroma teases of something sweet and decadent for breakfast. I cannot wait. I continue to follow my nose all the way to the dining room.

Wyatt sits in his wheelchair, an amused grin on his wrinkly lips. "Food always lures you out of bed, huh, Tate?"

"Every time," I say with a dramatic sigh. "If only the people in this house were normal and had cereal for breakfast, maybe a guy could get some sleep around here." I squeeze his shoulder and he pats my hand. "How are you feeling, Wyatt?"

"I'll feel better when I get my hands on one of those cinnamon rolls."

"Let me see if I can scrounge you one up."

I leave Wyatt to peek in the kitchen. Jude, hoodie sleeves pushed up to his elbows and his hood covering his profile, is hard at work drizzling creamy icing all over a batch of fresh-baked cinnamon rolls.

These people are going to make me gain twenty pounds!

Violet, busy at the stove flipping bacon and scrambling eggs, winks at me when I enter. I walk over to her and give her a quick hug. It's a thing now. If I forget, she gets onto me for breaking her heart. And I can't have that on my watch.

"Morning, sweetie."

"Morning."

I break away from her to hug Jude from behind. He's stiff at first but relaxes in my hold. This past week has been stressful, to say the least. Dealing with the aftermath of Sean, both me and Jude have been spending our fair share of time at the police station and with our lawyers, hand-selected and approved by Hugo.

Yes, I, Tate Prince, have an attorney—the best of the best—who is helping me with my case against Sean. It's surreal to think he's actually going to be punished for the monster he is.

When he was arrested later on the day of the fire, I cried like a baby. It was mostly relief and happiness for myself that I could finally breathe easy. But I also cried for his family. I'm sure his wife was shocked and humiliated by what Sean had done. Their girls are probably confused and miss their daddy. The whole situation sucks.

"You're thinking loud," Jude murmurs, his body rumbling from the vibration of his deep voice. "You okay?"

I pull away and step beside him to watch him with his

task of icing the cinnamon rolls. "I'm fine. Just thinking about the girls."

He glances my way, blue eyes tender and probing as he studies me. God, I still can't get used to seeing his handsome face without the mask. Sure, he still hides in his hoodie, but at least he's facing everyone with no mask to hide behind.

"They'll be fine," Jude assures me. "It's not for you to worry about."

I lean my head against his shoulder, smiling so wide it hurts. He's such a sweet, caring man—something I failed to see at first. Now that we've opened up all our wounds and shared with each other, I can see who he is to his very core.

A good, gentle man.

My man.

"I'm the one who's worried," he grumbles, gesturing at the cinnamon rolls. "Violet made me do these all by myself. I probably messed them up."

Violet laughs from her place at the stove. "You did them perfectly, hon. They're made with love. I told you that's the secret ingredient in everything I make."

I tilt my head up to look at Jude, who grins at me. A couple of days ago, he asked Violet if she would show him how to make his favorite apple pie. Then he wanted to know how to make Wyatt's beloved blackberry cobbler. Now it's cinnamon rolls, which happen to be my favorites. Seeing him in the kitchen, truly enjoying himself as he learns to bake things near and dear to his heart, is such a wonderful thing to witness.

"Bring those delicious cinnamon rolls to the table before your grandpa has a conniption fit," Violet orders to Jude. "Tate, sweetie, grab the orange juice from the fridge. It's time to eat."

As soon as she leaves for the dining room, I take a

moment to steal a deep, filthy kiss that's only for Jude's and my eyes. By the time we finish, his eyes aren't so sweet anymore. He watches me intently, the electric blue crackling with heat and desire.

"Later," I promise, shooting him a saucy look. "We'll pick this back up soon."

His palms cup my ass and he dips down to nip at my ear. "Not soon enough, sweet boy."

◎

"Look at me," Jude commands, his strong hand around my throat as he pins me to his bed. "I want you to see how horny you make me."

I'd thought sex was hot the first time we did it, but being able to see him has been a whole other level of awesome. His expressions are so vivid. He also smiles and smirks a whole heck of a lot more than I realized when he was hiding behind his mask.

"You're beautiful, Jude," I murmur. "So beautiful."

He shudders at my praise but doesn't look away. Since the day Sean kidnapped me and we ultimately made it out of that harrowing situation, I've been making sure to give Jude more praise. Not just about how handsome I think he looks, but also how kind and gentle and smart and compassionate he is. Now I can add fantastic baker to the list of compliments too because those cinnamon rolls were nearly orgasmic.

Jude's powerful hand presses against my throat. I find myself hissing as my breath grows more labored. Whenever he does this, and I relinquish control knowing he isn't going to truly hurt me like my ex, I come hard. Like really, really hard.

It feels kinky in a safe way because I know all I need to do is tap on Jude's arm when I've had enough and he'll back off.

Who knew this sort of thing could be so sexy?

I tap at his arm, not really needing air, but needing him. He releases my neck to spear his fingers into my hair. We both moan as he starts recklessly driving his dick deep inside of my ass over and over, hitting my prostate just so perfectly that—

"Ahhh!" I cry out, ecstasy obliterating my every nerve ending. "Jude! Oh God!"

Cum jets out of me, soaking my belly between us. My ass clenches around his cock as I orgasm, which in turn has him groaning with pleasure. When Jude comes, I swear it feels like his dick grows three times as fat right before he fills me up with his never-ending rush of cum.

Thank fuck I'm not a woman or this man and his super seed would have me pregnant in the blink of an eye.

When he finishes coming, he pecks my lips and then gently pulls out. We make yet another mess all over the bed and I'm glad Jude washes his own bedding. I'm not sure I could look Violet in the eye if she had to wash our messy sheets several times a day.

"Stay there," Jude orders as he slides off the bed and heads toward the bathroom for a towel. "I'm going to take care of you."

I smile and lie there like the Prince I am, waiting for my man to spoil and dote on me. He comes back and sets to cleaning me up with a warm rag until I'm feeling less like a puddle of cum and more like a human being again.

"Get dressed," he says after stealing another kiss. "Dad'll be here shortly."

Frowning, I sit up and gape at him. "What?"

"He texted before we came up here and said he was on his way."

"Y-You fucked me all slow and sweet knowing he was on his way?" I scramble off the bed and snag up my clothes from the floor. "What if he's down there right now and we've kept him waiting?"

Jude laughs—warm, rich, and wonderful. "He probably is. Violet will shove cinnamon rolls down his throat until we get there. Don't worry your pretty little head, sweet boy."

I throw on my clothes and then walk over to him, craning my neck up to look at him. "You think I'm pretty?"

His eyes twinkle with amusement before growing serious. "Tate Prince, I think you're pretty, handsome, hot, sexy as fuck. All of it."

I preen at his words, grinning stupidly at him. "Is that all? Tell me more."

He rests his forehead on mine and sweetly strokes my cheek. "I think you're way more. In fact, you're everything."

I'm everything.

A month ago, a statement like that from my boyfriend might terrify me considering my past with Sean. But with Jude? I'm safe, cared for, protected.

"You're everything too, big guy."

My cheeks blaze with heat as me and Jude walk into the living room where Nathan waits. Jude squeezes my hand, encouraging me not to freak out, but it's too late. This is super awkward.

"Hello," Nathan says, an empty dessert plate sitting on the arm of his chair. "What took you two so long to come downstairs?"

I choke on my words and Jude just laughs. Nathan jolts at the sound, clearly surprised, but quickly recovers to grin at his son.

"What do you want, Dad?" Jude asks, ignoring his father's ribbing. "I already told you we'd be at family dinner tonight."

Nathan nods. "Good. Jamie made taco soup and it'll feed an army."

Jude tugs me over to the sofa, sits down, and then pulls me into his lap. I groan at him and he chuckles, letting me slide off and onto my own cushion.

"What's up?" I ask, voice shaky with embarrassment. "Did you want to have a session?"

That's right, Tate. You're still their family therapist. Behave.

"Actually," Nathan says, eyebrows furling. "That's exactly what I wanted to discuss with you."

The room goes silent aside from the ticking of the clock on the wall. Unease trickles through me, making me fidget nervously.

"Oh, yeah? Everything okay?" I croak out.

Jude's arm around me tightens and he pulls me closer. I force myself to breathe through whatever this is. This family likes me and they know about my past—about everything. I'm not being fired.

I'm not.

This isn't like all the times before.

I know my worth and I help people. I'm damn good at it too.

Nathan pulls a check from his pocket and then leans forward to hand it to me. I take it from him, glance at the amount, and then nearly stop breathing.

Okay, so maybe not *that* good at helping people.

Damn.

"Nathan," I rasp out. "This is too much. I haven't even been working here that long."

"Your bonus is included," he says, eyes darting to Jude. "As agreed upon."

I shake my head. "Actually, I can't accept that bonus. I've fallen for your son and it wouldn't be right or ethical. I'm sorry, but I can't take that money."

Nathan's smile is wolfish and slightly terrifying. "You're a good man, Tate. I had a feeling you'd say that."

Okaaaaay.

"Um, yeah, here," I mutter, thrusting the check back at him.

Nathan chuckles and shakes his head. "Nah, I'm not taking it back. Call it overtime or whatever makes it 'ethical' in your mind, but it's yours."

"Nathan," I start, but Jude gently clasps the back of my neck, which settles me from arguing more.

"You'll need it to start your own practice," Jude says, leaning over to kiss my cheek. "You helped all of us crazy motherfuckers. Just imagine who else you can help."

"You want to start your own practice?" Nathan asks, perking up. "This is the first I've heard of it."

Ugh. Because that was pillow talk late last night when me and Jude were dreaming out loud, whispering things we'd love to do one day. I didn't think he'd literally try to make that happen for me the very next day. I don't deserve this man.

Or maybe I do.

"It's just an idea I was throwing around," I admit with a sigh. "Something I might like to do one day."

"I like it. I'm sure us Parks will be your number one clients, too," Nathan says with a genuine smile that makes his eyes light up, reminding me of Jude. "And if you need an investor, you know where to find me."

He stands, grabs his dessert plate, and then saunters off without another word.

Turning, I straddle Jude's lap and cup his gorgeous face in my hands. "You think I could do it? Really?"

Jude closes his eyes and covers my hands with his. A serene smile ghosts over his lips. "Tate, sweet boy, I think you can do anything."

My heart patters in my chest and I feel full.

Full of happiness and belonging and *love*.

EPILOGUE

Jude

TATE FITS PERFECTLY IN MY LAP. I'M LEARNING I LIKE having him there. It's one of those moments I am completely serene and at peace.

Like when I bake…

It's hard to obsess over past mistakes and heartache when you're worrying about folding in flour instead of stirring or adding just the right level of "warm" water to yeast. There's a lot more than just the "love" ingredient as Violet claims. Baking is challenging.

It's also rewarding.

Who knew I could enjoy it so much? I can afford for someone to cook for me, but getting in the kitchen and doing some things myself to surprise Tate, Wyatt, and Violet with what they actually like is incredibly gratifying.

Tate sits up in my lap to greet Violet as she shuffles toward us on the porch. It's a bright, sunny day, though cool, and I'm enjoying my blissful Sunday afternoon with my man doing absolutely nothing.

"A little treat to hold you two lovebirds over until you have supper over at your daddy's," Violet says, passing a plated piece of pecan pie, a scoop of ice cream, and two forks.

"Are you sure you don't want to come over?" Tate asks as he accepts the pie. "I know the family would like having you."

She smiles at him but waves him off. "Someone has to keep Wyatt company. I'll be fine here with him."

Tate shrugs, satisfied with her answer, and thanks her before she leaves. Then he stabs at the pie with one of the forks before offering me a bite. Our eyes meet and like usual, heat burns hot between us. We still have a couple of hours to burn before going over to Dad's…

"Jude!" Tate exclaims, eyes wide in mock horror at the feel of my growing erection beneath him. "Do you have a pecan pie kink?"

I bite the delicious dessert off the fork and smirk as I chew. "Maybe if I can eat it off of you."

He snorts with laughter. "Gross. That would be so sticky."

"Don't worry, sweet boy, I'll make sure I clean you up good with my tongue."

Despite being eager to play in bed with Tate and sticky pie, I ignore my cock to live in this moment. The crisp air bites at my nose, ears, and fingertips, but the warmth between us is quite nice.

Soon, contractors will be here to redo our porch. By spring, it'll be like new and much more inviting. I can't wait to spend many days just like this one eating pie on the porch with Tate.

"Look, Jude!"

I peer past him to look at where he's pointing. When I see a blue-and-green hummingbird hovering near the feeder, I blink several times to make sure I'm not imagining it.

"It's…a hummingbird."

"I've never seen one this close," Tate says, voice breathy and filled with awe. "How beautiful."

A ball of emotion clogs my throat and my eyes prickle.

I'm learning not to bottle up my feelings or direct the bad ones toward myself, but instead talk it out. Tate is a great listener.

"Jude?" He sits the plate down on his legs and nuzzles his head against mine. "Oh, honey. What's wrong?"

I sniffle, embarrassed that I'm getting upset over a damn bird. "I bought that feeder for my mom. The birds loved it. It was one of the very few things that survived the fire."

He uses his thumb to swipe away a rogue tear on my cheek, his own bottom lip trembling.

"This is the first time I've seen any birds since Mom died," I choke out, sounding much like a sad little boy and not the grown-ass man I am. "I thought maybe they hated me."

His lips curl into a sweet smile and he kisses my lips. "Birds can't hate, silly man."

I guess it is kind of silly to think the birds were holding some sort of grudge against me.

"Maybe they've been here all along, but you're just now seeing them." He rests his forehead on mine. "You're finally seeing past that cloying cloud of smoke your heart was suffocating in. There's love and beauty all around you."

He's got that right.

Tate is both of those things.

We return to lazily eating pie and watching the hummingbird. I feel like I've missed so much of my life for nearly twenty years. I'm finally awake and experiencing the world for the first time in forever.

It's nice.

It's really fucking nice.

Dad's house is the usual chaos, except I have a squirming

baby in my arms. I stare at Rex and he stares right back at me. Whose harebrained idea was it to hand me the baby?

"Don't look so freaked out," Tate says from beside me. "He doesn't bite."

"Yet," Spencer chimes in from my other side. "Only because he doesn't have teeth yet."

My nephew makes a playful chomping sound with his teeth that makes me shudder. His baby continues to stare at me, drooling a little while kicking his little legs.

I'm hit with a sudden longing deep inside my chest. I felt like after Mom died, my life was gone. I never allowed myself to dream of things like a family or children one day. But now I wonder. Is that possible for me?

Visions of Tate cuddling a little one while he reads him a bedtime story floods my mind. Then I see small children helping me knead dough in the kitchen, making one hell of a mess. Fuck, why does that make my chest want to explode?

"You're smiling," Tate teases, nudging my knee with his under the table. "What are you thinking about?"

You. Us. A future together. A family.

"Stuff," I say with a smirk. "I'll tell you another day. Maybe in a year from now."

Tate narrows his eyes at me. "Tell me now."

"Nah. I like watching you get all flustered."

"That's just mean."

I lean in and peck him on the cheek. "I'll make it up to you later."

Gemma shrieks from across the table. "Oh my God. Could you two be any cuter?"

Glancing up at her, I arch an eyebrow. "We're not doing anything."

"Except being adorable," Willa adds from next to Gemma. "I'm with your sister on this one. You guys are precious."

Rex starts to fuss, so I hand him back to his dad. Spencer, with a bottle ready, starts feeding him. Sure, he's a young father, but he's definitely a natural at it. With Aubrey pregnant now, I know the new baby will fit right in with their strange family dynamics.

I used to take these family dinners for granted. Sitting around, counting the seconds until I could bolt and get back to my own house, away from everyone. I'm done hiding, though.

Callum is in an intense conversation with Hugo and Dad. Jamie is laughing as she and Aubrey chatter nearby. Everyone around me is happy.

Well, aside from Dempsey.

Ever since all the drama with Sean unfolded, he's been different. Distant and more broody than usual. The shadows under his eyes seem darker too. He absently spins his skull ring around and around on his finger, lost in deep thought.

What's going on with my baby brother?

Tate squeezes my thigh and shoots me an understanding smile before leaning in. "I'm going to grab him after dinner and see if he wants to talk."

"Good idea. Thank you, sweet boy."

Tate loves helping people because he's a good, kind, compassionate soul, not because of a paycheck. Knowing he cares so deeply for me and my family is a priceless thing I certainly don't take for granted. Sure, in the beginning, I was skeptical about him, but now I know it's just the way he is.

Mom would have adored him.

Hell, everyone else does, especially me.

"I don't deserve you," I blurt out, eyes locking onto his perfect, pouty lips. "But I'm not letting you go anytime soon."

Even though I don't deserve someone so pure and sweet like Tate, I can certainly appreciate him for all he is and all he does. He's the gift I've been given and I won't ever stop cherishing him.

"Not letting me go anytime *soon*?" he scoffs. "How about *never*?"

I smile at him, heart filling with so many emotions, I doubt I'll ever get a hold of them. "Never sounds really, really good."

*Or, if you're dying to read about Spencer, Hugo, and Aubrey,
check out The Tangle of Awful!*

ABOUT THE AUTHOR

K Webster is a *USA Today* Bestselling author. Her titles have claimed many bestseller tags in numerous categories, are translated in multiple languages, and have been adapted into audiobooks. She lives in "Tornado Alley" with her husband, two children, and her baby dog named Blue. When she's not writing, she's reading, drinking copious amounts of coffee, and researching aliens.

Download at books.bookfunnel.com/k_webster_short_story_bundle

JOIN MY NEWSLETTER
at authorkwebster.com/newsletter

JOIN MY PRIVATE GROUP
at reamstories.com/authorkwebster

Follow K Webster here!

Facebook: www.facebook.com/authorkwebster

Readers Group:
www.facebook.com/groups/krazyforkwebstersbooks

Patreon: patreon.com/authorkwebster

Twitter: twitter.com/KristiWebster

Goodreads:
www.goodreads.com/author/show/7741564.K_Webster

Instagram: www.instagram.com/authorkwebster

BookBub: www.bookbub.com/authors/k-webster

Wattpad: www.wattpad.com/user/kwebster-wildromance

TikTok: www.tiktok.com/@authorkwebster

Pinterest: www.pinterest.com/kwebsterwildromance

LinkedIn: www.linkedin.com/in/k-webster-396b7021

EXCERPT FROM

THE LAW OF DECEIT

Dempsey
Graduation Night

ALL HAIL QUEEN GEMMA.

While I barely made it to this night considering my shitty grades, my twin sister gracefully arrived with perfect attendance and straight As, earning the adoration and praise of every single person in this auditorium.

They all cheer proudly as she takes her turn across the stage I just dragged myself across.

I just want to go home, dammit.

"Can you believe we finally did it?" she whispers once she's seated again beside me in our chairs, diploma in her dainty hand. "PMU, here we come."

Nudging her with my shoulder, I smirk at her. "You're going alone, sis. I told you, I can't do college."

Her bottom lip juts out despite us having this same conversation over and over again. No matter what I do, I'll never be as smart as my sister…or good.

Gemma is just good.

The angel to my devil.

A twin who stole all the decent genes and left me with all the genetic garbage.

"You can't live with Mom and Dad forever," she says with a frown. "And why would you want to? They suffocate us."

Her.

They suffocate her.

If she thinks they'll allow her to live on campus like she wants, she's out of her mind. Dad is overly protective of her.

"I'll figure something out," I say with a shrug.

The last person walks across the stage and then the principal is back at the microphone, speaking about following our dreams and living life to the fullest. Gemma and every other fool around me grins at him, eating up all his empowering words.

Not me.

I just want to get the hell out of here.

"Cool tattoo," Brandy, a girl sitting on my left, whispers. She points a finger at my newest tattoo on the back of my hand.

"Graduation gift to myself," I tell her. "Designed it myself."

Gemma elbows me. "Mom is going to freak when she sees you got another tattoo."

We're eighteen now. It's not like she or Dad can actually do anything about it.

"I'm so scared," I deadpan.

The rest of our conversation is drowned out by the principal congratulating our class and the auditorium subsequently exploding with cheers and applause. All the girls around me with their fancy hair and caps pinned neatly on clap happily. The guys, however, all try to see who can toss their caps highest into the air. I decide to use mine as a frisbee to try and nail my annoying-ass English teacher in his bald head.

My cap disappears and unfortunately misses. Not that I give a shit. I'm ready to get out of here and go home, hiding away in my room until I'm forced to socialize with family for the graduation party Mom has planned.

The next hour is a blur as we shuffle through the crowd, looking for our parents to hitch a ride back home with because we still don't have cars of our own. Finally, we load up in Dad's SUV and make the trek back to our property.

As Mom and Gemma chatter with way too much enthusiasm, I stare out the window, wondering what happens from here. I can't go to college. No way. I'd die from boredom. But I'm also not cut out for working with Dad or my brothers. The military can fuck off because I'm not about to be some meat shield.

It won't matter that I don't exactly have it all figured out, though. Dad will expect a plan bright and early tomorrow morning. I'll have nothing but smart-ass remarks and general disrespect. It'll end in frustration and slammed doors. I know the drill.

There's a car waiting in our driveway when we arrive. I practically fling myself out of the SUV, eager to make my escape until the party starts. In the darkness, I can't make out whose car it is, but when the person steps out, I know.

Golden blond hair flutters in the late May evening breeze, sending a hint of lavender my way. I inhale the scent, knowing it without ever having to see who it belongs to because I've memorized it—obsessed over it.

She's a gorgeous, long-legged beauty with lips that beg to be kissed.

Local cop and pillar of the community.

Twice as old as me and my mom's best friend in the whole world.

Sloane Thurman.

I'm obsessed with her, but she's completely off-limits. She was in the room when we were born, babysat us twins on occasion when my parents needed a break, and has been a part of our lives for eighteen years.

Because she's *Mom's best friend.*

I can look all I want, but I can never touch no matter how much I want to.

And, goddammit, I really, *really* want to…

Read Dempsey and Sloane's story in *The Law of Deceit* up next!